PLUT

A new sound alerted Denning. This time it was the faint but unmistakeable growl of a heavy truck. Powerful headlights swept around the bend of the access road leading to the storage plant. Denning snatched the glasses.

'Time?' he snapped.

'Eight forty-two.'

'Write that down.'

The truck's rear lights illuminated two lines of large red letters on the tailgate. Through the glasses Denning was able to make out the words:

DANGER
PLUTONIUM

Vic Mayhew

PLUTONIUM

arrow books

Arrow Books Ltd
3 Fitzroy Square, London W1P 6JD

An imprint of the Hutchinson Publishing Group

London Melbourne Sydney Auckland
Wellington Johannesburg and agencies
throughout the world

First published in Great Britain by Arrow Books Ltd. 1979

Set in IBM Press Roman by Tek-Art Ltd. S.E.20.

Made and printed in Great Britain by The Anchor Press Ltd Tiptree, Essex

ISBN 0 09 919310 8

All the information in this book on the assembly of nuclear weapons has been obtained from publications available to the public.

I wish they were not. I wish this disaster story were not so feasible. I wish it were not possible to steal weapons-grade nuclear materials. I wish it were not possible for one man, given these materials and an elementary knowledge of physics, to construct a nuclear bomb.

Alas, a growing number of officials in the nuclear industry believe that not only is such a disaster as this book describes feasible, but inevitable.

Vic Mayhew

'The world has dealt with nuclear weapons as if restraint were automatic. Their very awesomeness has chained these weapons for almost three decades; their sophistication and expense have helped to keep constant for a decade the number of states who possess them. Now, as was quite foreseeable, political inhibitions are in danger of crumbling. Nuclear catastrophe looms more plausible, whether through design or miscalculation, accident, theft or blackmail.'

Henry Kissinger

'Let me tell you about a nightmare I have. The Mayor of Boston sends for me for an urgent consultation. He has received a note from a terrorist group, telling him that they have planted a nuclear bomb somewhere in central Boston. The Mayor has confirmed that twenty pounds of plutonium is missing. He shows me the crude diagram and a set of outrageous demands. I know that the device would work. Not efficiently, but nevertheless with devastating effect. What should I advise? Surrender to blackmail or risk destroying my home town? I would have to advise surrender.'

Dr Bernard Feld, head of department of nuclear and high energy physics, Massachusetts Institute of Technology, and vice-president of the American Academy

I

Earl Denning's pocket-sized walkie-talkie crackled.

'Earl? Are you there?'

'Yes.'

'The mailman's on the way.'

'Roger.'

'Roger and out.'

Denning and a blonde woman companion had lain hidden in a ditch at the side of the winding country road for more than an hour. He grabbed the girl's wrists and hauled her to her feet.

'This is it. Now play dead.'

The girl began to massage her stiffened leg muscles.

'I've got pins and needles.'

'Dammit, you'll have holes in the head if you don't hit the deck fast. The bike'll be here in less than a minute.'

The faint whine of a motorcycle could now be heard. The girl lay on the crown of the road.

'Show your legs, for Christ's sake.'

Denning ran to where she lay and tugged her skirt up to her waist. He repositioned her legs.

'Your head on one side . . . right. That's it. And throw one arm out. Good. I want him to see you're a girl, you dumb broad. He'll be more likely to stop. Now play dead or, God help me, you will be.'

Denning ran back to the roadside and scrambled down the ditch. The engine note was louder. Soon the bike's headlight swept around the nearby bend and flickered on the girl's naked legs. The bike skidded to a halt. The rider, in the uniform of a US mailman, kicked down the bike's rest stand and switched off the ignition. He hurried to the girl's side, knelt and placed a hand below her left breast. He recoiled in surprise from the warm flesh and rapid heartbeat.

In that instant Denning looped a length of wire around the man's throat and tugged slowly. The girl sat up and her hands leapt in horror to her mouth. Stifling a scream, she watched spellbound as the wire sank into the mailman's neck like a tree trunk thrown into quicksand. Blood oozed from the wound, then spurted in a pulsing stream from the jugular vein. Denning dragged the corpse into the ditch and began to remove the uniform.

'Get to the van. Fast. And stay there.'

'You've killed him. You . . . '

The girl's voice rose hysterically. Denning climbed hurriedly from the ditch and viciously slapped her face.

'We killed him, stupid.' He emphasized the 'we'. 'Now shut up and get to the bloody van.'

The girl, sobbing, fled down the lane in the direction the bike had been travelling.

Denning put on the mailman's hat, undid the jacket buttons, then turned the corpse onto its front. Shaking the body like a bird with a worm, he pulled the jacket free, slipped it over his T-shirt and cursed as he struggled to fasten the buttons. He slid the trousers from the corpse and pulled them on over his jeans. The trousers were a reasonable fit. Delving into the mailman's satchel, he found the telegram; Denning had dictated it less than two hours earlier, then set the trap for the mailman. It was addressed to 'Mr G. Holland Packer, Woodland Cottage, Syosset, Long Island, New York, New York'. Denning grunted with satisfaction, returned the telegram to the satchel and swung it over his shoulder. From around the mailman's throat he detached the wire, wiped it clean on a handkerchief and put the wire and handkerchief in his hip pocket. He dusted the lapels of the jacket and flinched as his fingers slithered on the still-warm blood of his victim. Denning sponged the blood from the lapels with his handkerchief, this time tossing it into the ditch when the task was completed. From the ditch he pulled branches of fern and laid them over the stripped body. He paused briefly to ensure that it was well hidden, mounted the motorcycle and sped down the lane. He ignored his fleeing companion as he overtook her and swung through a wide gateway and down a maple-lined gravel path. An illuminated wooden plaque, staked in the front lawn, showed the words, 'Woodland Cottage'.

He parked the bike, mounted the white stone steps to the cottage's oak doors and pressed the bell push.

A portly middle-aged woman in a yellow housecoat opened the door and smiled.

'Telegram, ma'am. Mr G. Holland Packer. Personal delivery.'

'Oh, thank you.'

She held out a hand.

'Sorry, ma'am. I have to deliver it personally. I need a signature.'

'Oh, very well.'

She returned down the hallway and entered a room at the rear. Seconds later, a tall distinguished figure emerged.

'Good evening. You've something for me?'

'Mr G. Holland Packer?'

'Yes, that's me.'

'I have a telegram, sir.'

Denning held forward the telegram and coaxed the elderly man into the full glare of the light over the doorway. As the man reached for the envelope, Denning flung himself to the ground.

From a clump of rhododendron bushes in a shrub bed on the front lawn spluttered the zap-zap-zap of a burst of fire from a silenced automatic rifle. Bullets splintered the door frame and ornamental side windows and traced a line of neat, tiny holes across the old man's pale blue shirt as he stood in the doorway. He staggered backwards for three steps and tumbled onto his back. His eyes, wide open, gazed unseeingly at the oak-panelled ceiling.

'George . . . oh, my God . . . George.'

The woman who had answered the door bell returned to the hallway and crouched beside the dead man. She cradled his face in her hands.

'No . . . George . . . oh, please God, no.'

Denning, drawing the wire from his pocket, heaved himself from his prone position. He leapt on the woman's back and looped the wire around her throat in one movement. He grasped each end of the wire tightly. The white of his knuckles showed as he gave a single, sharp tug. Again, he returned the wire to his pocket.

He stood and shouted, 'Anyone home?'

There was no reply.

He quickly opened the five doors leading from the hallway and glanced inside the downstairs rooms. Satisfied that no one else was in the house, he ran back to the bike.

The engine of a waiting green two-door van was running when he pulled up alongside. At the wheel was the gunman who had fired from the bushes. In a rear seat was the girl who had lain in the roadway. She was still sobbing.

'Shut up, you snivelling bitch,' Denning growled.

He dumped the motorcycle in the ditch and struggled out of the mailman's uniform.

To the driver he said, 'See anyone, Wayne?'

'Not a soul. We're home free, buddy.'

Denning dropped the mailman's uniform near the motorcycle and pulled himself into the passenger seat.

The van lurched forward, its tyres squealing. It passed the spot where the murdered mailman lay and Denning smiled on noting that the corpse was completely hidden from the view of passing motorists.

'This will show the bastards we mean business.' Denning whooped and clapped his hands. 'Now those bastards will sit up and take notice.'

The van halted briefly two miles down the road. A tall, thin man ran from behind a tree. Denning flung open the passenger door and leaned forward as the man climbed into the rear seat.

Denning handed the man a receiver-transmitter which

matched the one he already held.

'Thanks for the message, Sean,' Denning said. 'The timing was perfect.'

'A pleasure.'

'We got three of the bastards – the ambassador, his wife and the mailman. Oh boy, are we in business.'

'Three . . . ?' The girl almost shrieked the word. 'You can't mean . . . three . . . dead?'

Denning turned in his seat and silenced her with a glare.

Forty minutes later the van coasted to a halt outside a shabby clapboard house in Queens. Only the peeling paint seemed to hold the warped wooden strips in place. Denning rented the attic of the house.

He swivelled on his seat to face the other three.

'Now look. We're clean. The mailman isn't talking, the ambassador isn't talking and neither is his wife. If anyone talked it would have to be one of us. Right? And we're not talking, neither.'

He glared directly at the girl.

'Understood, Wanda honey?'

The lights of a passing car lit up her tear-blotched cheeks. She nodded passively at Denning.

To all three he continued, 'This is going to put us in big with the KGB. That means backup. And money. We're going to get the chance to be something, and that's what we all want. Right?'

Denning clapped the driver on the shoulder.

'OK. We'll get together tomorrow. For tonight, Wanda stays with me. OK, honey?'

'No, damn you. I won't.'

Denning made no reply. He stepped from the van, pushed forward the passenger seat, snatched the girl's arms and pulled her to the sidewalk.

'I'm not going to touch you, sweetheart. Believe me, it's not your body I'm after.'

He waved his free arm to the driver and the youth in the back of the van.

'So long, till tomorrow. Keep off the streets.'

The carpet of fallen autumn leaves rustled as Denning trudged to the doorway. The moonlight, partly shielded by roadside trees, speckled his wide, muscular back as he put his key in the lock. The girl followed submissively. He closed the door silently and led the way up the narrow staircase.

On entering the attic he flicked a wall switch and a single naked bulb, hanging from the apex of the uncovered wooden roof framing, lit the dingy sitting room. The only furniture in the room was a threadbare sofa, a chair and a small table. A television set stood in a corner on the bare wooden floor. Shelves jammed with books lined three walls. On the fourth wall was pinned a large poster of Che Guevara, on which had been painted in red, 'Murdered by the CIA'.

'Welcome to the penthouse,' Denning said. 'You'll sleep on the sofa, but first we'll talk.'

Denning had never previously admitted a woman to his apartment. Though physically attractive and capable of showing a superficial charm, he exuded an aura of barely suppressed anger and frustration. His few amorous adventures had not been successful. With each rejection his manner had become rougher and more graceless. He was annoyed by his sexual needs and preferred to gratify them dispassionately with prostitutes. He never solicited the same hooker twice, shunning any possibility of emotional involvement.

His adrenolin was stimulated by the strange thrill of the killings and he considered making a pass at the girl. She was petite and small breasted but had slinky, supple hips. Her blonde, straight hair was worn in an urchin crop. She was clearly frightened. Her thin lips were pressed tightly together and her smooth, pale skin was smudged by tears. Denning dismissed the idea of trying to seduce her. He realized that if she refused him he would probably rape her. And that could undermine his authority over the group.

'It had to be done, Wanda. Surely you can see that. The system has to go. And so do the bastards who stand in the way.'

She raised her head to look into his cold, hazel eyes. Denning stood menacingly. His heavy biceps bulged below the sleeves of his T-shirt and his broad chest heaved as he breathed deeply. His tightly fitting jeans hugged his slim hips and showed the contours of his muscular legs. The gently waved dark hair and the pink, glowing sheen of the skin would have given him a boyish look but for the thick, heavy eyebrows and stubbled, square jaw. Denning continued to hold the girl's stare.

'You don't feel anything, do you?' she accused, anger overcoming her fear. 'All those people . . . dead. And you don't feel a thing.'

Denning had told the girl only that someone had to be 'fixed'. Some unnamed victim would be beaten up, but not too severely.

'Sure I feel something. I feel good, sweetheart. Really good. Now listen. The ambassador was a stinking capitalist. Well, he mouthed off just once too often. And the KGB are going to just love us, sugar. They'll just love us. With them behind us we can really get things done. Now get me a beer from the kitchen. Help yourself.'

Denning flopped into the chair as the girl opened the kitchen door. It was true, he thought; he felt no remorse. So three people had died. A few statistics had been transferred from one column to another. So what? They had been trash. He clenched both fists and relished in the strength that flowed from his back muscles, through his powerful shoulders and down the heavy arms to his thick, stubby fingers. Millions could die and the world wouldn't give a damn. Three people could be wiped out and he was supposed to feel sorry. Well, he didn't. He felt great.

The girl returned, handed him a beer can and sat on the sofa. He flipped off the ring top and guzzled the cool liquid. The girl poured her beer into a glass.

Wanda Pniewski and Denning shared the same courses – political science and economics – at New York's Columbia University. Domineering with other women, she had become a staunch supporter of Women's Lib. Then, indoctrinated by Denning's forceful arguments, she had graduated to a wider school of revolution. During the summer vacation she had learned just how committed he was. The realization was frightening, but exciting. She began to envisage the fulfilment of her idealogical dream – an end to poverty. It would take time, but it really could be brought about.

'You're in this up to your pretty little neck, Wanda.'

Denning crushed the empty beer can with one hand, flexing his biceps.

'You're an accessory. That means you're with us. All along the line.'

Denning noted the time and switched on the TV to catch a newscast. The set had long since ceased to produce a picture, though the sound still functioned. There was no mention of the killings.

'But why did you do it? Why?'

Wanda had begun to regain her composure and cringed less noticeably from Denning.

'Why three people?' she persisted. 'The ambassador's death . . . well, I really can't say I'm sorry. But the others . . . '

'We had to waste them, you dumb broad. Now there are no witnesses. Nobody knows a thing, except us. And we're all guilty, Wanda. All of us.'

'I know . . .'

Denning pulled a cigarette pack from his back pocket.

'Let's smoke. Have faith, baby. Keep your cool. What do a few people more or less matter? The bastards we're after kill thousands every day.'

He lit a hand-rolled cigarette, inhaled deeply and handed it to the girl. She swallowed a lungful of smoke. The titles of the books surrounding her began to zoom repeatedly into focus, then become blurred. She noticed that many were biographies . . . 'Stalin' . . . 'Hitler' . . . 'Guevara' . . . The room suddenly whirled around crazily. She giggled and submitted to a dizzy euphoria as the marijuana seeped into her bloodstream.

The van dropped Sean Gallagher four blocks north of Denning's flat. Gallagher shared an equally shabby house with his widowed mother. He put his walkie-talkie on a shelf of a hallway cupboard.

'Mum? Are you home?'

'Yes, Sean. Don't come in. I'll only be a minute.'

Gallagher moved stealthily toward the bedroom door. He heard muffled voices. As usual, a boyfriend was staying the night.

'It's all right, mum. Don't bother. I'm going straight to bed.'

'OK. Goodnight, son.'

'Goodnight.'

There was silence now. He imagined his mother smiling at the man who was with her.

Since his father's death, Gallagher's mother had launched herself into a succession of affairs. Any agreeable companion was likely to be favoured. Gallagher feined ignorance of his mother's activities. He wrongly supposed that she would be embarrassed if she knew the extent of his knowledge. Some of her more bizarre episodes he had overheard being recounted in the bar where he worked.

He took a half-empty bottle of white wine from the fridge and wandered into his bedroom. He slipped a Chopin tape into the stereo player and turned down the volume. The music was quiet, but loud enough to drown the noise of the sexual acrobatics being performed in the next room. He gazed at his face in the mirror as he brushed his long, thinning sandy hair over the growing bald spot on the crown of his head. The sunken blue eyes, large beak-like nose and bony cheeks gave him a haggard appearance. It wasn't helped by his floppy loose lips and protruding ears.

He lowered his tall, gaunt frame onto the bed and contemplated his role during the evening. He was astonished at his coolness. His task had not been a major one – he had simply had to send the radio message that the mailman was on the way, then wait to be picked up by the van. He realized with satisfaction that the chances of him being implicated were remote, unless someone else was caught and talked. Yet he had the thrill of having been involved. After tonight he would enjoy new status with the rest of the group. There would be no turning back.

Wayne Henrick, student of physics, higher mathematics and revolution, drove the van into the garage of a modest three-bedroomed townhouse in the same area of Queens. He winced at the pain from the stump to which his artificial foot was fitted. The air was heavy and damp, and at such times the throbbing always seemed more acute. The foot had been amputated after a head-on car crash. It had been crushed under the caved-in bulkhead above the control pedals. The emotional impact of the accident had been even more damaging. Henrick felt a perverse urge to hurt, punish and even destroy. Suffering inflicted on others seemed to make his own pain more tolerable.

He removed a blue suitcase from the van, limped to the door and knocked. A young blonde woman opened the door a couple of inches. She left the safety chain attached.

'Wayne! It's nearly midnight.'

She released the chain and opened the door fully. At first glance Sarah Jane Kaye was outstandingly attractive. When she smiled she was breathtakingly beautiful. She had the rare sensual combination of blonde hair and rich brown eyes. The straight hair was swept back from her forehead and nestled on her softly rounded shoulders. Her full lips parted as she smiled at Henrick and revealed her gleaming, perfectly formed teeth. A full-length cream robe hung loosely over her voluptuous figure. Henrick limped through the doorway.

'I want to leave this suitcase here. Hide it.'

She took the suitcase, walked into an adjacent room and placed it on top of a wardrobe. When she returned to the living room she playfully swayed her hips. She walked with the controlled poise of a fashion model, firmly placing one foot directly in front of the other.

'Very mysterious, aren't we? What's this all about?'

Henrick slipped his arms inside the robe. She wore no clothing underneath and he luxuriated in the sensation of his growing longing as he stroked the warm flesh. She crushed her large breasts against him as he kissed her.

'First, help me get this blasted thing off.'

He sat on the sofa and she kneeled to tug off his left boot. Henrick sighed with relief as she released the straps securing the metal artificial foot to the bandaged stump. He moved his legs onto the sofa. She sat beside him and the robe fell open as she leaned forward to kiss him. He tried to kiss her breasts, but she pulled herself away.

'Later,' she said. 'Right now I want to know what's been happening.'

Henrick ran a hand through his tightly curled ginger hair. His freckled face creased in a frown.

'Sarah, tonight has been a beginning. You are with me, aren't you? We can change things, Sarah, but we might have to change the rules first.'

He looked intently at her.

'What sort of beginning, Wayne?'

'Things have started to get rough.'

She had known that violence was inevitable. So it had begun already. Retaining the same elegant poise, she moved to a cabinet and poured two gin and tonics.

Sarah Jane had reluctantly abandoned hopes of being an actress. As a young girl she had become an expert dancer and had taken elocution lessons. But despite her looks, she was given only minor parts at drama school. Her performances always seemed to be over-rehearsed and stilted. She compensated for her failures by continuing her training in private life. She spoke slowly, carefully considering in advance the impact her words would produce. Now she immersed herself in the tense atmosphere of mounting drama. She felt strangely as if this was happening to another person.

'How rough, Wayne?'

She handed him a drink and remained standing.

'We blotted out the ambassador.'

Sarah Jane drifted to a chair and gracefully lowered herself.

'Who's "we", Wayne? Who did the killing?'

'I did. I hit the ambassador. The gun's in the suitcase.

Earl got a couple of people who got in the way. Sean and Wanda were in on it, too. She's spending the night at Earl's pad.'

'Oh, Wayne . . . '

Sarah Jane placed an arm on the side of her chair and theatrically raised a hand to her forehead.

'Darling, listen.' Henrick sat up hurriedly. He sucked in deeply through clenched teeth and held his breath in an attempt to relax his taut muscles. 'No one saw us. We're clean. We're just a bunch of all-American boys. There's nothing to connect us with the killings. Nothing. And if we hadn't hit him, someone else would have done. Now Earl reckons we're going to get backing from the KGB. We're going to be big, Sarah. Big.'

The pained heroine was already mentally reverting to her role as hardened revolutionary.

'I love you, Wayne. I believe in you. Of course I'm with you.'

She glided to the sofa, flung her arms around him and kissed his eyes, face and lips. She allowed the tears to start.

'I love you.'

Sarah Jane was not overburdened with intelligence. Her life until recently had been unutterably dull. The daughter of an attorney and a local do-gooder, she had been eased into marriage at eighteen to the son of old family friends. Acting out the bride had been great fun, but after the honeymoon her husband returned to his job at a local bank and she was cast as a suburban housewife. He was a creature of frustratingly regular habits. Even their love-life was played out to a timetable – sex every Monday, Wednesday and Saturday. It was on a Saturday that she walked out and threw herself at the mercy of Wanda, an old high school friend. The girls now shared the townhouse. Through Wanda she met Henrick. He was energetic, restless and competitive, and his accident had made it easy for her to place him in a heroic role. She was excited by his talk of revolution. Life with him would be one of great drama, she persuaded herself.

She stood, removed her robe and returned once more to

the sofa.

It was time for the heroine to reward the warrior hero.

2

Delegates to the International Atomic Energy Agency were assembled at the agency's headquarters at 11-13, Karntnerring, Vienna. Desks, facing inward, were arranged on three sides of the room; on each desk rested a red folder, a microphone and a mounted wooden plaque identifying one of the agency's thirty-five member nations. At the rear of the room sat secretaries and translators. All the delegates had headphones, over which translations could be received.

'The situation, gentlemen, is potentially disastrous. Our conclusion is that a determined group of terrorists could readily secure nuclear materials.'

The British delegate remained impassive as he measured the impact of his bombshell. First there was shocked silence. The words lingered in the air. They were inescapable, insidiously enveloping all present.

Many delegates uneasily avoided the anxious glances of others across the room. Some stared blankly at the red folders. Each folder contained a report, translated into the appropriate language, entitled, 'Security of Nuclear Materials'. It made horrifying reading.

The director-general was the first to react. He coughed and shifted uncomfortably, then leaned toward his microphone.

'But surely . . . ' He despairingly held forward his open palms. 'Surely our security is not totally ineffective. God knows, we've spent millions . . . '

Transparent plastic tags on a console in front of the director-general began to light up. Each delegate was able to operate one of the lights by pressing a button on the stem of his microphone. The illuminated tags on the console identified those delegates who wished to speak.

'Our report indicates that those millions have not been spent wisely,' Ken Sheehan continued, enunciating each syllable carefully. As ever, he spoke in a low, controlled voice. He often irritated colleagues with his tendency for understatement. Now his sombre manner heightened the alarm the others felt. 'We'll have to spend much, much more to remedy this situation.'

Sheehan had headed an investigation into security at nuclear plants in member countries. He had personally visited more than fifty plants throughout the United States, Canada, Britain and India – in most cases, ostensibly as a casual tourist. It was a role he was able to assume easily. Of medium height and build, he was remarkable only for his ordinariness. The beginnings of a paunch testified to a liking for good food and wine. His straight, brown hair was neatly trimmed and greying at the temples.

Other members of Sheehan's group, using tactics identical to his, had visited another two hundred nuclear plants. Officials at the plants had been questioned in detail. Many of the answers had been revealing, and startling.

Sheehan flipped open his red folder.

'Page twenty-two, gentlemen. That details my visit to the nuclear fuel fabricating plant in Apollo, Pennsylvania. It seemed a good place to start. Some time ago they were unable to account for sixty kilograms of uranium-235 – the stuff, you will remember, that we used to wipe out Hiroshima. The loss was explained away, but problems remain. I concluded that four armed men could storm the plant without too much difficulty. I suggested this to a colleague who is with the CIA, and he was rather frank. His answer was, quote, "I think they could do it with pea-shooters," unquote.'

The director-general's glance betrayed his scepticism. Sheehan continued, unperturbed.

'Page twenty-three, gentlemen. Fully enriched uranium

is shipped in ten-litre bottles from the uranium plant in Portsmouth, Ohio, to conversion plants across America. Each ten-litre bottle contains seven kilograms of uranium-235. Often there are twenty bottles in a shipment. And those shipments go by plane, train and even, sometimes, by truck. Many times, two truck drivers have been entrusted with a cargo of a hundred-and-forty kilograms of uranium-235. Frankly, some of those cargos could have been hijacked by a pack of boy scouts.'

The director-general snorted.

'You're surely dramatizing this, Sheehan. Over the last year or two big changes have been made.'

'Not big enough,' Sheehan persisted, his voice maintaining the same level tone. 'Page forty-three. This section deals with nuclear processing plants under the control of private industry. I have to say it's terrifying. Guards with guns but no bullets. One union official protested to me that his members were not paid sufficient to throw down their lives for "bits of tin". The chairman of another company confessed that it would be "very difficult" to prevent systematic pilfering of nuclear material if two men in appropriate departments acted together.'

'Sheehan, we've all had an opportunity to read your report,' the director-general said. 'I hope you're not going to read it out word for word.'

'No, but I must add that things are no better in other countries. Security arrangements just aren't keeping pace with increased production of these materials. In Britain we're even running out of storage facilities for radioactive waste, but the stuff keeps piling up.'

The director-general nodded to the American delegate, who had been waving for attention.

'Sorry, but I can't buy all this,' the American said. 'I think you've exaggerated the problems. In the States over the last few years security has been improved considerably. We need to investigate much further before being stampeded into any dramatic action. It would take an army to raid one of these places, and then they'd be blasted to smithereens.'

Sheehan remained impassive.

'I think not. Those guards are civilians. They're not trained fighting men. They're worried about pensions and how to live long enough to collect.'

'So where's this leading?' the director-general asked impatiently. 'I remind you that our budget is well accounted for. We can only do so much.'

'We have to find a way to do more,' Sheehan insisted stubbornly. 'We're all aware that the techniques of nuclear weapons assembly are widely known. My view, and that of many scientists, is that any intelligent physics graduate could acquire the know-how of atomic bomb assembly from published material which, sadly, is available in public libraries. We can't risk this stuff getting into the wrong hands.

'My Minister of Trade and Industry has instructed me to put forward the following resolution:

> That the International Atomic Energy Agency request the United Nations General Assembly to approve an immediate allocation of further funds to the agency to enable the urgent institution of effective worldwide security of nuclear materials.

'In a word, let's shut the stable door before the horse bolts. The amount of these funds could be worked out in committee. I suggest that this is a matter of extreme urgency.'

The Soviet delegate was the next to be given an opportunity to speak.

'My government's view is that nuclear authorities in non-Soviet countries are criminally negligent. We . . . ' He paused to allow murmurings of protest to die down. 'We are mystified by the fact that the Soviet example has not been followed. All our nuclear installations are guarded by the Red Army. Our troops would be well able to handle any contingency.

'Accordingly, there will be no money from my country to put this resolution into effect. We have put our house in order. Others must do the same.'

Mutterings of disapproval reverberated across the room.

The American tossed aside his headphones on hearing the last of the translation.

'That reaction is just what we'd have expected,' he said sharply. 'I say we kill this resolution for different reasons.'

He turned to face Sheehan.

'This report leaves me cold. It's mostly opinion and comment. It's too general, and takes insufficient account of recent improvements.'

'I agree things are better than they were,' Sheehan admitted patiently. 'But every day the nuclear industry gets bigger, and so do the risks.'

From a jacket pocket he withdrew a misshapen chunk of brownish metal the size of a golf ball.

'I think this should prove the point.'

He held the metal in view on the palm of his hand.

'This is surprisingly heavy, gentlemen. It's a memento of my recent travels. A small piece of uranium-235. Weapons-grade nuclear material.'

The uranium made a dull thud as he dropped it on the desk. Several astonished delegates stood involuntarily. All stared at the innocuous-looking piece of metal.

Sheehan surveyed them one by one.

'It won't bite,' he teased. 'It's quite safe to handle in this form.'

'Let me see that,' the director-general snapped.

Sheehan walked to the director-general's desk with the uranium and handed it to him.

'Good God, Sheehan. Where the hell . . . ?'

'I got it with the connivance of the chief security officer at a nuclear storage facility in upstate New York. Admittedly, he wouldn't be so obliging to a terrorist. But until this moment only the chief security officer and I knew that this metal had been taken. Its absence has not been detected. With a little more of this stuff, I could make a nuclear bomb.'

The director-general sighed.

'I shall have this returned immediately under guard. Meanwhile, I suggest that we can do without further discussion. This is clearly a matter of extreme gravity. Is the resolution seconded?'

The American delegate slowly raised a hand. The resolution was approved on a show of hands.

3

Denning was alert the instant he awoke. He reached down to the side of the bed and picked up his chest expander. He grunted each time he forced the expander wide apart, fully stretching his arms. Thirty-five . . . thirty-six . . . He continued tugging the expander. It was invigorating to feel so strong. Forty-nine . . . fifty . . . He tossed aside the expander, threw himself to the floor and began a series of push-ups. A vein on the left side of his forehead stood out and his face reddened with the exertion. Forty-six . . . forty-seven . . . He tightened his stomach muscles and delighted in the feeling of power his strength gave him. Fifty. From a drawer he took a pair of briefs and slipped them on. Making no more noise than a snake slithering across sand, he entered the living room. Wanda was deeply asleep, her slight frame covered by a grey blanket. He switched on the TV. Lines rolled back and forth across the screen, then came a high-pitched buzz. The buzz gave way to the voice of a news announcer.

'. . . had been shot. The body of his wife was slumped beside him. She had been garrotted . . . '

Denning whooped with excitement.

'They've found them,' he yelled. 'They've found the bastards.'

Wanda stirred and hauled herself to a sitting position. Denning impatiently fiddled with the dials of the TV in the vain hope that the set would produce a picture.

'. . . body of a mailman, also garotted, was found in a ditch near the house. His motorcycle and uniform were discovered in another ditch some distance away.'

Denning squatted by the sofa and grabbed Wanda's hands. His hazel eyes, sparkling with exhilaration, probed her face.

'You've made the TV, sweetheart. They're talking about the bums you helped me wipe out.'

Wanda shuddered and let her hand fall limp in his grasp.

' . . . at least two people are believed to have been involved. Detectives believe that, after garrotting the mailman, one of the killers wore his uniform and approached the ambassador's home. The ambassador was shot, probably by the second killer, as he stood in the doorway. Mrs Packer was then garrotted, presumably to ensure that there would be no witnesses to the assassination.'

Denning whooped.

'Clever bastards, aren't they? Three cheers for the finest police force money can buy. Wanda honey, they'll never get onto us. We're clean, honey.'

' . . . The only clues so far are a bloodstained handkerchief and a telegram addressed to the ambassador, both of which were found near the scene of the crimes. Detectives have refused to reveal the contents of the telegram.'

Denning slapped a fist into the palm of a hand.

'They're up shit creek without a paddle.'

The handkerchief was one of millions made from identical material and sold in hundreds of stores throughout the United States. And when dictating the telegram he had given a false name and address. He chortled on remembering the words of the telegram. They read, 'In recognition of your services, you are to receive the reward you deserve.' Subtle that, Denning congratulated himself. Ingenious.

The newscaster went on to outline the ambassador's career. He had recently been expelled from Moscow. He was one of a group of diplomats who had been accused of spying. On returning to the United States he had spoken out against oppression of Soviet citizens. His remarks had received widespread publicity and drawn protests from the Kremlin.

Denning flicked off the TV as the newscast ended and

let out another whoop. Wanda continued to gaze at the blank screen as though in a trance.

'But we killed two other people, Earl. . . . Why did we kill the other two?'

He stared at her like a cobra about to pounce on a mouse. She lowered her head.

'We did it because we believe we have something important to do, and those people were in the way, for Christ's sake.'

He picked up a jacket that had been draped over a chair.

'You stay here. When I get back you'll see just how much we've achieved.'

She made no reply. She looked upward and found him still staring at her.

'I mean it, Wanda. You stay here. OK?'

'Yes . . . yes. I suppose I will.'

'You'd better do that, baby. By Christ, you'd better do just as I say.'

Denning slammed the door behind him.

Denning walked up and down several blocks of Fifth Avenue, seemingly ignoring the USSR Purchasing Commission offices. They were like to many nondescript offices in the same skyscraper block except for the red flag outside, wafting gently in the cool morning breeze.

He had searched the Manhattan directory in vain for the address of a Soviet embassy or consulate. The Purchasing Commission was the only official Soviet organization based in New York, but Denning was confident that the staff would include at least one diplomat. If not, he would simply have to phone the Russian embassy in Washington.

He was reluctant to make a direct approach to the Purchasing Commission building. Intuition warned him that it was likely to be kept under surveillance by the Americans. He decided to think out his next move more carefully and wandered into a breakfast bar. Only one other customer was in the restaurant and a waitress approached immediately. Denning ordered pancakes and milk, strolled to the public phone in a corner of the room and dialled.

'I want to contact the KBG.'

A short laugh greeted Denning's request.

'I'm sorry, sir. This is the USSR Purchasing Commission. We aren't able . . . '

'Look, this isn't a crank call. I have some information about the former American ambassador to Moscow. You'd better put me in touch with someone who knows what's what. And fast. I don't want to walk into your offices in case the place is being watched.'

'I see.' After a pause the voice at the other end added, 'Wait a moment, please.'

The tone of the voice indicated to Denning that at last he was being taken seriously. He watched the waitress set down the pancakes and milk at his table. The other customer ambled to the cash desk, paid his bill and left the restaurant.

The voice at the other end of the phone asked, 'Where are you?'

Denning gave the name of the restaurant.

'You're right. It would not be good for you to come here. Wait for a short while. Make yourself known to a man in a blue tie who will enter shortly.'

Denning felt his cheeks burn with the flush of excitement. This was to be the moment of truth. He returned to his table and almost immediately a man wearing a vivid blue tie entered. Denning nodded at his inquiring glance and the man joined him at his table.

'Well?'

Denning, suddenly calm, gazed into the man's eyes.

'Well . . . I represent the group that did in the ambassador. We're anxious to serve the Soviet Union.'

The waitress returned to the table and stood beside the Russian, her pencil poised above a notebook.

'Coffee. Black, no sugar.'

'Coffee you've got,' the waitress answered. 'Big spender, eh?'

The Russian ignored the taunt. As she left the table he said, 'You have begun badly.'

Denning flushed again, this time in anger. What the hell did the damned fool mean? Denning sipped his milk and glowered at the Russian as the waitress delivered the coffee. When she turned to leave, Denning asked in a low, frantic voice, 'What do you mean? He was an enemy of the Soviet Union, no?'

'No.'

The blunt answer hit Denning like a blow to the stomach.

'But . . . '

'But nothing. The ambassador was not an enemy. Give me your name and address.'

Denning lowered his fork and placed it beside his plate.

'I don't think I will.'

'I think you will.' The Russian assumed an air of one extremely bored with a troublesome child. 'If not, you will be followed and a call will be made to the police. If you co-operate, we might consider your proposition more favourably.'

'I . . . we thought the ambassador . . .'

'You were wrong.'

Denning needed no further explanation. Suddenly it dawned on him that the ambassador could have been a double-agent. The expulsion from Russia might have been a ploy.

'You mean the ambassador was . . . '

'I mean simply that I want your name and address.'

Denning mumbled in reply.

'And phone number.'

The Russian scribbled the information in a diary.

'You may be hearing from us.'

He pushed the bill across the table to Denning. Without drinking his coffee he left abruptly.

Denning was confused and afraid. Obviously, he could not expect financial backing from the Russians. What would happen to the group? How could he tell the others he had been treated like a wayward schoolboy? Damn the bloody Russians. Damn the Americans, and everybody. He threw three dollar bills on the table and strode into the street.

Karl Vorishilov, Soviet United Nations delegate and consultant to the USSR Purchasing Commission, sat at his desk and smiled. He stubbed a half-smoked cigar into an ashtray.

'I take it that this young man is being followed to enable us to confirm his information.'

The inquiry was addressed to the Russian who had recently left Denning in the restaurant.

'Yes, sir. But I think he was telling the truth.'

Vorishilov toyed with a pencil.

'Do we report this to the police?' the other man asked.

Vorishilov thoughtfully tapped the pencil on his desk top.

'No, I think not. Put him on the workers' list. He might be useful.'

'Yes, sir.'

The 'workers' list' contained the names of people who might be of value in unusual circumstances. It was a file of men and women who had committed some crime or indescretion, apparently without being detected. Several high-ranking UN government officials were among those named. On occasions, the workers' list would be scrutinized. Often, an approach to some unsuspecting citizen would follow. Usually, cooperation could be solicited without undue difficulty.

Denning was unable to find a seat on the crowded subway to Queens and clung to an overhead strap. He kept tightening his grip on the strap, exercising his powerful fingers and forearm. There was no familiar release of tension through his flexing muscles. The idea that his offer of help would be rejected by the Russians had not occurred to him. His dreams of power were shattered. He would probably lose the support – certainly, the respect – of the few members of his group when they learned of his failure.

The train lurched to a halt and as the doors opened he stubbornly maintained his stance, forcing passengers who wished to leave to struggle around him. As the doors began to close he bustled his way to an empty seat and jostled an old woman who had moved ahead of him toward the same seat. Ignoring her frown, he picked up a newspaper. The thrill of the killings returned as he scanned the headlines. 'Ambassador and wife murdered'. Another headline read, 'Mailman found garrotted nearby'. Police had no clues to the identity of the killers, the newspaper reported. It had been established that the sender of the telegram found in the ambassador's hallway had given a fictitious name and address. Denning turned to page three of the newspaper, where a fuller account of the discovery of the bodies was given. Details of the ambassador's career were also outlined.

He read three times the report of the killings. At least he had been right when he had assured the others there was no way any one of the group could be suspected. He dismissed his earlier fear that the Russians would report his approach to the police. It would be uncharacteristic. They would be more likely to try to blackmail him later. If they did, they would find they had a tough customer.

He idly scanned another news story at the foot of the page. It was headlined, 'Nuclear materials fear'. Nuclear authorities were asking the United Nations for more money to ensure adequate security at nuclear installations, the report announced. The last sentence of the four-paragraph story quoted the director-general of the International Atomic Energy Agency as saying, 'We are particularly concerned about security in view of the widespread dissemination of information on the structure of nuclear weapons. Given some knowledge of physics, the manufacture of nuclear weapons would not be an impossible task for anyone who had the right materials.'

Denning slowly folded the newspaper lengthways, then crossways. 'Given some knowledge of physics . . . ' He pondered the words and a wave of elation swept over him. Henrick had more than 'some' knowledge of physics. He was expecting to secure a degree the following year in physics and higher mathematics. Denning twisted the newspaper and crammed it between his seat and the side of the carriage.

Jesus, if it could be done . . .

His idea so obsessed him that he was startled to find himself suddenly at his home. He had no recollection of leaving the train, or of the walk from the station to the house.

He walked to the rear of the house and looked thoughtfully at the ferrets he kept in a long, low wooden hutch. Two ferrets, one white and one with sandy fur, were in a long compartment of the hutch. A larger white ferret was kept apart from the other two in a smaller compartment. The supple bodies of all three writhed and twisted as they darted to and fro. They expectantly pushed their pink rat-like noses and the sharp claws of their forelegs against the wire mesh on the front of the hutch. The pink shining eyes remained fixed on Denning. He stared back at one of the ferrets until it turned away its gaze.

A vet had periodically supplied ferrets to Denning since he had been a young boy. He had read that they could be trained to catch cottontails and jack rabbits, and the sport appealed to him. He seldom ate or sold what he caught. The excitement of the chase was the only fulfilment he sought. He thumped the top of the hutch in the manner of a judge calling for order in court.

'Yes, we just might be able to do it. We just might.'

He bounded through the front door, up the stairway and into his living room. Wanda, on her way to the kitchen, turned to face him timidly. He ran to her, picked her up by the waist and spun her around in a circle.

'Wanda, we're going to catch a few cottontails. I want to think. You can drive.'

She looked quizzically at him as he placed her on the floor.

'Earl, what's happened? What's going on?'

From his bedroom Denning grabbed a wooden toolbox.

'Come on. Just be patient.'

He flung the two ferrets which shared the same run of the hutch into a canvas sack. He placed the third ferret in another sack. Wanda, clearly bewildered, started the engine of his Chevrolet as he slumped into the passenger seat.

'Hit the Long Island Expressway.'

She drove in silence until he directed her to turn off the expressway down a narrow lane leading to the south shore. At a patch of open grassland he ordered her to pull up at the side of the roadway.

'Wait here. I'll be half an hour. I just want to think a few things over.'

Denning had visited the area previously. Spotting the rolling grassland as a likely spot for cottontails, he had investigated and found a cluster of burrows. He made his way toward them, the sacks flung over his shoulder. He counted nine small holes. For several minutes he wandered around looking for other entrances to the burrows. Cottontails, he knew, had a cunning knack of hiding an escape route with loose vegetation. Eventually, he found a tenth hole, cleverly camouflaged.

From his toolbox he counted out ten large string nets and staked one over each burrow entrance. He then took the two smaller ferrets from their sack and held one in each hand. He slipped the white ferret under one of the nets. It sped down the mouth of the burrow. Immediately he was rewarded with a high-pitched squealing from below the ground. He pushed the sandy ferret into another burrow and three nets bulged simultaneously as half a dozen cottontails fled in panic. The white ferret hurtled into one net among three cottontails and grabbed one victim around the throat. Denning leapt to the net, held off the ferret with one hand and killed the three cottontails with a series of sharp blows with his free hand. Other nets now bulged with squealing cottontails.

He returned the white ferret to its sack. Moving slowly but methodically, his prey without hope of escape, he selected cottontails at random, strangling them by pinching their throats between a thumb and middle finger. When the task was finished he glanced around in search of the sandy ferret. It was nowhere to be seen.

'Goddamn,' he snarled.

The ferret had obviously caught a cottontail below ground and was enjoying a feast. It could be hours before it emerged. He would have to send the third ferret into action. This creature was kept constantly apart from the other two to encourage its antisocial temper. Denning enjoyed prodding it from time to time to make sure it was suitably ferocious. Its purpose was to drive other ferrets away from a kill in precisely such circumstances as this.

From his toolbox he drew a wristwatch-sized transmitter and secured it to a collar around the large ferret's neck. Attaching a strong line to the collar, he pushed the ferret down a nearby hole. He followed its progress by holding a small electronic receiver a foot or so above the ground. The length of line was soon exhausted. Denning decided to let the ferret continue its hunt and released his hold on the end of the line. Soon the bleeping emitted by the receiver remained at constant strength while he held it stationary. The large ferret had found the kill.

A net bulged once more and the sandy ferret struggled vainly. Denning put a hand beneath the net and the ferret bit a finger. His face remained expressionless, even though the creature's teeth pierced the flesh down to the surface of the bone. With his uninjured hand he grabbed the ferret's neck and squeezed. The animal's struggle for life lasted only an instant. Denning thrust it into a burrow.

He returned to where the receiver continued its bleeping. The third ferret had remained below ground to finish off the meal. Denning selected a hunting knife from his toolbox and began to dig. After a few minutes of digging, the roof of the burrow collapsed and the ferret could be seen squirming below the fallen soil. Denning grabbed the ferret from its victim. He ignored the mutilated cottontail, wiped some of its fur from around the ferret's bloodstained mouth and returned the animal to its sack.

Kicking the dead cottontails back into the burrows, he collected his nets.

Denning's ideas now shone with startling clarity. The

hunting always cleared his head. When it was over, problems usually assumed a new perspective. Once again the exercise had worked.

He returned to the Chevrolet, flung the sacks and tool-box into the rear seat and climbed into the passenger seat.

'You're hurt,' Wanda said, seeing the blood trickle from his wounded finger. Denning disinterestedly dabbed at the wound with a handkerchief.

'It's nothing. Let's go. We'll round up the others.'

Wanda started the engine and shifted the gear lever.

'Wanda honey, we're going to hit the big time. And I mean big.'

Denning and Wanda collected Henrick and Sarah Jane and drove to Gallagher's home. His mother worked in a super-market and would not return for several hours.

All accepted Gallagher's offer of a glass of white wine.

Denning eyed the others in turn while assessing their aptitudes for the jobs that lay ahead. Of Henrick he was confident. The son of a small-time grocer, Henrick had seen his father's business sunk by competition from the capitalist-backed supermarkets. His parents survived on social security and he was able to continue his studies at the University of Columbia only because his brilliance had enabled him to obtain several large grants. Henrick's hatred of capitalism was as intense as his own, and he was equally ruthless. When the foot had been amputated he had also lost the last lingering traces of compassion.

Gallagher was a less promising revolutionary. Denning contemptuously studied his feeble, gangling frame and weak facial features. He looked like an unfinished waxworks dummy. The fool was sensitive and burdened by conscience. Nevertheless, he was easily led and responded readily to any show of kindness or friendship. Now he was implicated in the killings he would be infinitely more corruptible.

As for the girls, they could be bullied to act if necessary. Sarah Jane would do precisely what Henrick ordered her to.

And Denning was sure he could control Wanda.

Denning stood, walked to the fireplace and turned to face the others. He grinned.

'We have an assignment. Here's to us.'

He swallowed his wine at a gulp.

'My approach to the KGB was a success,' he lied. 'Before I report further, we need to agree on our purpose. We are part of a force whose aim is to establish a world food council. The council will be set up to ensure a fair distribution of food worldwide, according to need, not wealth.'

Henrick snickered.

'You've got to be kidding, Earl. It's a great idea, but how the hell . . . ?'

'Shut up.'

Henrick shrugged as Denning frowned at him.

'I'll explain how in due course. We will also work for the setting up of a standard world currency. The unit will be the Russian ruble. A world prices council will establish standard worldwide prices. A world wages council will establish standard worldwide wages. The result will be an end to inflation.'

Henrick looked at the ceiling and whistled a tuneless melody. He barely suppressed another chuckle.

'For now,' Denning continued, 'those details will have to be sufficient. I'll elaborate at some later stage. Meanwhile, does anyone disagree with our motivation? If anyone doesn't approve, speak now.'

The other four exchanged glances.

'It's Utopia, Earl.' It was Sarah Jane who had spoken. 'An end to poverty and an end to capitalism. But how could we possibly hope to bring this about?'

'I will explain later. Does anyone want to dissociate himself from the group?'

No one spoke.

'Right. Next, we need an identity. Soon we're going to have to communicate with the authorities. To do that, we need a name. I've chosen one which should have some appeal to the masses. We will be known as ACE.'

The others surveyed him dispassionately.

'The letters stand for, "A Chance to Eat". That's what we're all about. Right?'

He waited in vain for some approving comment. He waved his glass to Gallagher. All five glasses were refilled.

'We have behind us the might of the Soviet Union,' Denning continued. 'Success will be rewarded generously. Failure will be punished severely. A mistake, or treachery, could be fatal. Are you still with me?'

Henrick nodded. Concern over the involvement of the KGB had persuaded him to conceal his scepticism.

'Sean?' Denning asked.

Gallagher blushed at finding himself in the full glare of the spotlight.

'Yes, I am.'

'Wanda?'

She hesitated only momentarily. 'Yes.'

'Sarah?'

She placed a hand on Henrick's wrist, smiled at him and mentally rehearsed her reply. At length, she said, 'I'll do whatever Wayne wants me to.'

'So. We're all in. As of now there can be no dropping out.'

Denning downed the last of his wine.

'As for how we're going to achieve our aims, well, we're going to do it with blackmail. ACE is going to hold the whole bloody world to ransom.

'We're going to make an atom bomb.'

4

The Minister of Trade and Industry had insisted that Sheehan should meet him at the House of Commons immediately on returning to Britain. The order had irritated Sheehan. He was wary of politicians, and the minister in particular. They all had too much cunning and not enough common sense, Sheehan thought cynically. The minister's interest in nuclear security had increased dramatically with the approach of the forthcoming general election.

A British Airways official introduced himself to Sheehan as he stepped from the plane at London's Heathrow Airport.

'Welcome, sir. Your baggage is being collected.'

Sheehan followed the man away from the main stream of passengers and through a side door. A bored-looking customs official lounged behind a desk.

'Special diplomatic clearance,' the airways official announced.

The customs officer touched his cap.

'Sure.'

Recognizing Sheehan, he added, 'Welcome back, sir. This gentleman is your driver.'

Sheehan smiled at the uniformed chauffeur standing beside the desk. This pomp always slightly embarrassed Sheehan, but he was grateful to be spared the risk of customs officials prying into his suitcase. He never packed neatly, and his papers, including vital documents, were stuffed inside at random.

A porter arrived with his three cases and the chauffeur led the way to a nearby exit, outside which was parked a black Daimler.

'Straight to the Commons, sir?'

Sheehan paused at the limosine.

'No. Lock it up. Let's have a quick one first. I need a pint. of good old English bitter.'

'Yes, sir,' the chauffeur agreed woodenly.

He was unlikely to be the liveliest of drinking companions, Sheehan thought, but he would have to do. Sheehan tipped the porter as the cases were locked in the boot, then led the chauffeur back through one of the airport's electronically operated doors and headed for a bar behind the check-in desks.

'What's yours?'

'Tomato juice, sir.'

'Come on, man. I won't tell.'

'Not while I'm driving sir. Tomato juice, thank you.'

Sheehan fumbled for money to pay for the drinks. He silently cursed politicians, the Minister of Trade and Industry and House of Commons drivers, and hurriedly swallowed the pint.

'That was terrific. That Austrian beer is devil's brew.'

'Yes, sir.'

'OK, let's face the music.'

Sheehan walked back to the car as the chauffeur muttered the inevitable, 'Yes, sir.'

Sheehan sank in the luxurious leather rear seat of the Daimler. His father had travelled only once in such a car – the hearse that carried his coffin on the day of his funeral. Sheehan was born to poor parents in the Yorkshire mining town of Barnsley. They lived in a four-roomed terrace house which they shared with the occasional field mouse and, in summer, the bugs. On hot nights his mother would place a large dish, partly filled with water, on his bedside table. A smaller dish was put upside down in the centre and a candle fixed on top. Bugs, attracted by the light, would head for the candle and drown in the water. His mother's ingenuity thus saved the cost of bug powder. In the kitchen of the house was only one tap, and the water was unheated. He would bathe every Saturday night in an aluminium tub placed in front of the sitting room fire. It had seemed that he was destined to follow his father into a career in the coal mines. But at eleven Sheehan won a place at a local grammar school. He was a talented student, and won a scholarship, with a reasonable grant, to Cambridge University. His mother took a job at a laundry to enable him to complete his education.

At twenty-five Sheehan entered the diplomatic service. His parents would have almost died with pride, but hard work and poverty had killed them earlier. In the diplomatic service Sheehan found his plain speaking a handicap. He successfully applied for a post with the administrative board of the Special Air Services, a corps of elite soldiers trained for secret missions throughout the world. His common sense enabled him to solve complex problems boldly and decisively, and his achievements came to the notice of the Defence Ministry. He began to be spoken of in the corridors of power. The previous Minister of Trade had chosen him for the job of special delegate to the International Atomic Energy Agency.

As the Daimler pulled into the House of Commons car park Sheehan rubbed each shoe in turn against the back of a trouser leg in the hope of restoring some semblance of a shine. His crumpled suit bore evidence of the neglect it had also suffered on his travels.

He was ushered into the minister's private office. It was a musty, white painted room with a Victorian moulded fireplace. A Persian rug partly covered the polished oak floor. The minister rose from behind an antique rosewood desk.

'Welcome back. You've made quite a hit. Take a seat.'

He handed Sheehan a copy of that day's *Times* and pointed to a double-column story on the front page. It detailed Britain's role in urging an evaluation of security at nuclear installations. The Minister of Trade and Industry was quoted extensively. He had obviously planted the story.

Sheehan grunted, seemingly pleased. Privately, he reminded himself never to forget that the minister was a self-promoting career diplomat. He might be useful in getting things done, but his motives would have to remain suspect.

'One more time, Ken. How real are these dangers you've been on about? I know you were hot under the collar before the IAEA meeting, but how do you feel now that you've confronted the others? Are they as worried as we are?'

Sheehan groaned, recognizing that the minister was simply fishing for more information to enable him to push himself once again before the press. Still, at least his frequent press conferences were helping to keep the issues alive. And they certainly needed an airing.

'Minister, I repeat, there are three very real dangers. One, a nuclear plant could be sabotaged by an assault force. Two, many unstable countries with nuclear reactors can readily produce weapons-grade material and put together some sort of nuclear bomb. Then comes revolution. A bunch of hotheads are in power, and . . . whoosh. Three, weapons-grade nuclear material is being produced in increasing quantities every day and security is bloody awful. On those three points all sane people agree.'

The minister grinned.

'Good. I may bring this up once again in the Commons. I'm sure you won't mind helping me with a little more detail. Sabotage, for instance. How might that be done?'

Sheehan swallowed in an attempt to ward off a bout of hiccups. He had refused the plastic-textured lunch that was offered on the plane.

'Well, let's say we have a kamikaze pilot. Or a hijack. Most nuclear plants are designed to take the impact of a 200 000-pound aircraft arriving at something like 150 miles an hour. A Boeing 747, if I've got my facts right – and I bloody well have – weighs about 365 000 pounds without passengers and travels a lot faster than 150 miles an hour. The idea's a bit way out, maybe, but sooner or later some nutter might give it a try.'

'And the consequences?'

'Immeasurable. The nuclear core would go berserk. Radiation alone would kill thousands.'

The minister wrote on a notepad.

'Next, point number two. You mentioned unstable countries with nuclear reactors. What kind of country did you have in mind?'

Sheehan sensed he was losing the battle with the hiccups. He held his breath for several seconds.

'How about Argentina? They have a nuclear reactor, and the present government's pretty daft. The people are even dafter. After the next coup heaven knows whose finger might be on the button.

'As for point number three, surely you're not going to quiz me again on security at nuclear installations. I could think of a dozen ways to nick weapons-grade material, and I wouldn't need an army to do it.'

'Probably. You've already given a convincing demonstration on that score and I'm not asking for an encore. I think we can keep matters on the boil with this lot.'

Sheehan lost the battle with the hiccups. The minister winced.

'Sorry. I skipped lunch.'

The minister's apparent disgust made Sheehan feel like a schoolboy who had been too late in asking for permission to leave the room.

'Another thing,' he added, 'I'm not sure a small assault force couldn't steal a nuclear bomb from store. Just a thought, but how do we know that every nuclear bomb ever made is still where the authorities think it is? I'm not saying any have been nicked, but I wouldn't take any bets.'

'You're not serious.'

'I certainly am. We've all got our heads in the sand and we're in for one hell of a kick up the rear.'

'Yes . . . ' The minister gave a short laugh. 'Well, I shan't quote that last bit, but you've been very helpful. What are your plans before the UN punch-up?'

Sheehan had been instructed to present the IAEA appeal for funds in person at the United Nations annual General

Assembly meeting. As ever, it was to be held on the third Tuesday of September, just two weeks away.

'I'd like some time at home with the little woman. I need some decent home-cooked grub.'

The 'little woman' was how Sheehan usually referred to his wife. She was small and dumpy, nagged him unmercifully but was devoted to him. They had married young and she was the only woman with whom he had made love. He had not sought affairs, and none had presented itself to him. All in all, he was not dissatisfied with marriage. At worst, it was a means of acquiring clean shirts and shoes.

'Then I'd like to get to New York a week or so before the UN meeting,' Sheehan continued. 'I want to make sure the boys on the Nuclear Regulatory Commission are on our side.'

The NRC had been set up only recently to develop a system for safeguarding nuclear materials in the United States.

'Yes, of course. As for your report on the Vienna meeting, and your expenses . . . '

'Oh, hell. Do we have to go into that boring bit?'

Sheehan was notoriously unmethodical with paper work. He had not submitted an expense account for months. By now he had lost half the receipts he had meant to file.

The minister smiled tolerantly.

'I've some good news, Ken. I want a lot of feedback on your activities, and I want you to keep on the straight and narrow. I'm going to give you a travelling secretary. It's a "she", top-security clearance and all that.'

'With a face like the back of a smashed-up bus, no doubt.'

The minister peered down his nose and focused on a beer stain on Sheehan's tie. He was baffled at how someone so slovenly in appearance and manner could be so incisive in dealing with major issues.

'She hasn't been chosen for her looks. You'll let me know when you plan to leave for the States?'

'Of course.'

The hiccups seemed to have cured themselves.

'I'll get you and your secretary together before the flight. Perhaps we can have dinner.'

The interview over, the minister rose from his desk and shook hands.

5

The early-morning rays beamed through the curtainless, soiled windows of Denning's flat. On waking, he watched the dust particles dancing in the wide shaft of golden-yellow light. He flung back the covers and launched into an exhausting physical workout. Finally breathless from his exertions, he showered, dried himself vigorously and sprawled on the sofa to review the reactions of the other members of the group to his plan.

Henrick had showed no emotion. His response had simply been, 'Well, I suppose it could be done.' Denning had instructed him to learn what he could of nuclear weapons assembly and design a suitable bomb. As a physics student, he would have access to a wealth of technical data and could determine how effective the bomb was likely to be.

Gallagher had flinched nervously and dropped his wine glass on the carpet. He had blushed when confronted by Denning's icy stare. Denning had ordered him to visit the *New York Times* clippings library to obtain copies of any news reports indicating poor security at particular nuclear plants. He was to pretend he was a freelance journalist obtaining background information relevant to the forthcoming meeting of the United Nations.

Wanda, silent, had glanced furtively at the others. Sarah Jane had permitted herself an astonished gasp.

Denning returned to the bedroom and began to dress. He was uneasy about the women and Gallagher, but felt that appropriate threats would keep them in line. The women would be involved gradually, Denning decided, and given only such information as was vital for the success of the operation.

A bigger problem was the lack of financial backing. Sooner or later the others would become suspicious at the absence of KGB funds.

Denning collected his toolbox. He would exercise the ferrets. Perhaps inspiration would come to him during the hunt.

Henrick had returned the green van to his parents' lock-up garage and spent the night at their ground-floor Bowery flat. His room had once been his father's food store. The window overlooked a terrace of grey buildings as drab as the one in which he lived. An L-shaped wooden counter ran underneath the window and parallel to the wall furthest from the doorway. As a child Henrick had helped his father set up vegetable displays on the counter. Now it was littered with chemical equipment, much of it pilfered from Columbia University. The walls were painted dull green and the shelves were crammed with books and magazines on physics, philosophy and history. Behind the counter was Henrick's single bed.

He lay awake, assessing Denning's plan. It certainly seemed practical. Henrick had been curious why the KGB simply did not present them with weapons-grade nuclear material and a design for an atomic bomb – or even a bomb itself. Denning had explained that contact with the Russians must be kept to a minimum. In the event of a bomb being exploded and the Russians being implicated, worldwide repurcussions could be catastrophic. If no link with any world power could be established, retaliation would be impossible.

'We keep the group small, stay low and we must win, Wayne,' Denning had insisted passionately. 'How can anyone fight when they don't know who the enemy is?'

Denning had just as convincingly dismissed Henrick's concern about their ability to obtain weapons-grade nuclear materials.

'Just you leave that to me,' Denning had said. 'You design the bomb and we'll take it from there. I don't intend to be idle in the meantime.'

Henrick reached to the bottom of his bed for his artificial foot. Mechanically he secured the straps to his stump and stood gingerly. He experimented with a few steps while leaning a hand on the counter. The foot did not hurt too badly. He walked around the counter, sat on the chair placed in the middle of the bare wooden floor and began to dress. He made his way to the bathroom and hoped the sound of running water would not awaken his parents. He avoided them as much as possible. Their heroic acceptance of squalor and oppression revolted him.

He let himself out of the front door. An old brass shop bell above the door clattered. He cursed, reminding himself for the umpteenth time to dismantle the bell. But it no longer mattered if his parents awoke. Once again he had made an unhindered escape from his mother's cloying possessiveness.

Henrick limped to Second Avenue and hailed a cab.

'Public Library.'

As the cab pulled away he found himself counting the diamond shapes on the steel mesh guard between the driver and the rear seat. Since he was young Henrick had been fascinated by mathematics and was forever creating puzzles to solve. He would count the squares on a wall of patterned wallpaper, the number of windows in an apartment block. He persuaded himself that the exercises helped to keep his mind alert.

The cab turned north onto Park Avenue and he felt the familiar resentment of those who owned such sumptuous apartments. This was the world cesspit of capitalism and its vulgar symbols . . . the Empire State, Chrysler and Pan American buildings . . . that sick joke of misguided idealism, the United Nations headquarters.

'Drop me here.'

Henrick halted the cab at the junction of Park Avenue and

East 40th Street. The library was a short walk away and the foot felt comfortable enough. He crossed Madison Avenue and Fifth Avenue and noted sullenly that the exclusive shops were crowded with customers. To Henrick, these were the human filth among Manhattan's eight million people. He calculated . . . twenty-five square miles, eight million people . . . three hundred and twenty thousand people to the square mile . . . the Grand Central terminal was within this particular square mile so the figure would be higher. He chortled. Yes, this would be a great place to set off a nuclear bomb.

He mounted the wide stone steps to the ornate frontage of New York Public Library. The low, squat building contrasted oddly with the surrounding skyscrapers. He pushed through the revolving doors and headed for the non-fiction section. He selected an armful of books and settled in a leather chair beside an oak desk.

Flicking through a book entitled, *Nuclear energy: its physics and its social challenge*, his attention was caught by a chapter headed, 'Nuclear explosives'. The text was basic enough and contained little that he didn't know. But that little was vital. It referred to two drawings, both explicit. One detailed a simple gun-type atomic bomb assembly. The other showed an implosion type of atomic bomb. Both designs were foolproof.

'Jesus . . . '

He had muttered softly. This was going to be easy. Painstakingly, he copied both designs in a notebook.

The bibliography of another textbook contained the information that *The Los Alamos Primer*, which had been declassified in 1964, detailed the mathematical fundamentals of fission bombs. It was available from the Nuclear Regulatory Commission for two dollars and six cents. Henrick wrote the details in the notebook. He noted another title, *Manhattan District History, Project Y, the Los Alamos Project* – a textbook of declassified technical information which had been discovered during the manufacture of the first atomic bombs. It was available from the Office of Technical Services of the United States at four dollars a copy.

But he would need still more information. He cursed the fact that the next semester was some weeks away. The Columbia University library would have much helpful data but was closed during the vacation.

He was rewarded by further searching. One manual referred readers to its two main sources, the *Plutonium Handbook*, published in two volumes by Gordon & Breach, New York, and available for $81.50, and the *Reactor Handbook*, published in four volumes by Wiley, New York, and on sale for $123.

Henrick whistled through his teeth in excitement. No wonder so many nations had nuclear weapons. Snatching up his notebook, he limped hurriedly to the library exit. He took a cab to a Second Avenue bookshop, pencilled a list and handed it over the counter.

'Would you order these for me?'

The assistant raised his eyebrows on reading the titles.

'I'm a physics student,' Henrick explained. 'We need them for Columbia.'

'That's fine by me, just so long as you don't want me to read the junk. When I was a kid it was two and two make four. Now they're into real crazy stuff. Soon they'll be teaching kids how to make an atom bomb.'

Henrick laughed obligingly.

'How long before you can get them?'

'Oh . . . a day or two. I can pick them up. That OK?'

'Fine.'

Henrick handed over a fifty-dollar deposit.

'I'll pay the rest when I collect the books.'

'Fine.'

The assistant began to scribble a receipt.

'Name?'

'Put it down to Columbia.'

He accepted the receipt, thanked the assistant and limped through the door.

Whispers in the hallway awoke Gallagher. His mother's

laughter rose above the sound of a man's voice. She suddenly stopped laughing as though fearing that her son might hear her. More murmurings came, then the click of the front door. A floorboard creaked as she returned to her bedroom.

Gallagher had come to despise this house of whispers and secrets. He remembered the whispers of his childhood. His parents obviously hadn't realized that often he was awakened by their bedtime mumblings. Once there was a low, angry conversation about a boarding school. Some weeks later he was dispatched with suitcases to a school in Connecticut. His father explained that he would live in the school until the end of the semester. Shortly afterwards Gallagher received a letter from his parents telling him that they had moved to a new home in Queens. At the end of term, a strange new house would await him. His father wrote often, but the letters were a poor substitute for the cosy, intimate chats that Gallagher remembered with such anguish. He missed the advice, even the stern rebukes. Growing up was no longer playing football with his father, going fishing and to the movies; it was a correspondence course. Finally came the phone call from his mother. His father had died after a heart attack. Those last, wretched months had begun with whispers. Gallagher was taken by hire car to the new house for his father's funeral. Soon there were more whispers as his mother began to smuggle in a succession of men friends. There were more secrets that apparently had to be kept from him, and more secrets of his own that he longed to share but had to bear alone. The whispers of a sad, lonely young boy were heard only by his pillow.

Now, through ACE, he was being heard at last. He had a voice in a small but powerful group. His secrets were real and vital. And because of ACE people would sit up and take notice. And squirm. The whole lousy world would squirm.

Gallagher remained in bed while his mother prepared to leave for work. She entered his room and softly spoke his name, but he pretended to be asleep. Eventually he heard the front door close once again.

Within minutes he was on his way to the nearby subway.

He caught a train to Manhattan, then took a cab to the *New York Times* building. To the commissionaire he gave the name of a reporter who used the bar where he worked. After a short while the reporter joined him in the spacious marble foyer. Gallagher asked the reporter to help him get access to the clippings library.

'Why, sure. That's no big deal.'

'I'd like them to think I'm a reporter.'

The reporter laughed.

'You want them to think you're a big shot, eh? Well, why not?'

'It's not that. I just don't want anyone wondering why I'm nosing around. You know . . . '

'No problem.'

The reporter regarded Gallagher as an odd individual and gave no thought to his behaviour. At the library Gallagher was introduced to the girl on duty.

'This is a buddy of mine,' the reporter said. 'Help him out with a few clips, honey.'

She looked up disinterestedly from her desk.

To Gallagher the reporter said, 'That's all there is to it. That's a drink you owe me.'

The two shook hands and the reporter left.

'What are you after?'

Gallagher turned to the girl and self-consciously brushed his long hair down over his ears with his palms. He hoped that his protruding ears weren't showing.

'Er . . . nuclear installations. You know, power plants and all that . . . Security.'

Not realizing that the library staff would be accustomed to dealing with an infinite variety of bizarre questions from reporters, Gallagher had expected to be greeted with suspicion. But the girl simply pulled out a draw of index cards and wrote down a lift of reference numbers.

'Follow me.'

She led the way to a series of desks, on each of which was placed a television screen. She manipulated several knobs beneath one of the screens and a reproduction of a *New*

York Times page came into focus. Checking her list of reference numbers the girl pressed several digits and the screen flickered through a host of pages before coming to rest on one which detailed a prominent senator's recent criticisms of security at nuclear installations.

'Is this any good?'

Henrick had briefed Gallagher to concern himself primarily with plants producing or using either uranium-235 or plutonium-239. He scanned the text and the word 'plutonium' caught his eye.

'Er . . . yes.'

At the touch of a button a photocopy of the page thrust its way through a slot at the side of the desk. The girl handed it to Gallagher, who stood by as another page was brought into focus. One article referred to a statement by the Nuclear Regulatory Commission expressing concern about the systems for the accounting of weapons-grade materials. The girl looked inquiringly at Gallagher.

'Yes, please.'

By the time she had exhausted her reference numbers he was in possession of more than twenty photo reproductions of *New York Times* pages. Officials of the government and nuclear authorities had obligingly put a finger on nearly fifty installations at which security was suspect. In some cases, specific ways in which it was feared nuclear materials might be stolen had even been detailed. Gallagher was delighted. In his hands he held a mass of virtual blueprints on how to steal nuclear materials.

He thanked the girl, returned to the lift and pressed the ground-floor button. The girl was already preoccupied in dealing with another of the paper's reporters.

It was a poor morning's hunting. Denning searched for hours on Long Island's south shore before finding a cluster of likely burrows. His one small ferret went to ground eagerly, but without success. The burrows were deserted.

Denning sat disconsolately in the meadow. He was unable

to free himself of thoughts of his elder brother. Tim had shared his passion for hunting with ferrets and had been the one member of the family he loved. Their parents were dull, grasping and had no thought of the hunger and poverty of others as long as their own bellies and wallets were well stuffed. But Tim had been different. He had concern for others, and a lusty sense of humour. He had joked even when called up for duty in Vietnam.

'I've always fancied one of those oriental chicks," he told his brother. 'I'll bring one home for each of us.'

Tim was killed in a mortar attack within a week of arriving in Asia. Denning regarded his brother's death as murder by American imperialists. Repeatedly he pledged that one day those murderers would have to pay.

He drove home to Queens, returned the ferrets to the hutch and strolled up the staircase to the attic. He flopped on the sofa, his depression taking a firmer hold as he weighed the problems ahead. So they were going to make an atomic bomb. Just like that. How were they going to get the stuff? If they did, could Henrick make a bomb that would work? And they'd need money.

'Dammit,' he cursed softly. 'We will do it. By Christ, we'll do it.'

He answered a knock at the door and Gallagher, grinning broadly, stepped briskly into the room. He held a wad of photostats.

'I've got the goods, Earl. How to rip off a nuclear power plant, by the top brass themselves.'

Denning returned to the sofa and waved Gallagher to the chair.

'Earl, it was a cinch. The girl at the clippings library never batted an eyelid.'

Denning made a conscious effort to suppress his ill-humour. At the slightest hint of rebuke Gallagher's sunken pale eyes would reflect hurt and he would clam up.

'Christ, Sean. Let's hear it.'

'Wayne says we need uranium-235 or plutonium-239. Right? Well, there's tons of the stuff lying around just asking to be picked up. It's all over the place. No wonder they're so worried about security.'

Gallagher sat on the edge of the chair, his gaunt angular frame crouched over the photostats on his knees.

'All nuclear power stations use uranium in some form or other. So far we've got more than fifty reactors in the United States, and security is giving the government the shakes. Then there's the fuel reprocessing plants. The left-over junk from the reactors is sent there and converted to uranium and plutonium. From the fuel reprocessing plants it's shipped back to reactors or storage plants.'

Gallagher's eyes glinted as he studied Denning's face. 'When they're shipping this stuff about, Earl, it goes by plane, train or truck. We're going to be able to do it, Earl. I know we are.'

Denning, stimulated in spite of his gloomy mood, slapped a fist into the palm of his other hand.

'And how do the maestros suggest we get our hands on a few samples?'

Gallagher laughed.

'It's crazy, man. They've outlined more than twenty possible ways in which the stuff could be grabbed. Take uranium. Chunks of the raw metal are dumped at the fuel reprocessing plants, but at that stage it's too mixed up with other crap to be any use. They start extracting the best of it – the bombs stuff. Some plants are not that well guarded. Then there's problems with staff. If we could get one of those workers with us, Earl . . .'

'Too risky. The fewer of us there are the better. What about shipping the stuff?'

'Well, for instance, pure uranium is made at Portsmouth, Ohio. It's shipped out in . . .'

He paused to flick through the photostats.

'Here we are. It's shipped in ten-litre steel bottles. Each bottle contains seven kilograms of uranium-235 and there are up to twenty bottles in a shipment. If we could hit one of those trucks . . .'

'What about guards?'

'That's what the government's worried about. Some fuel plants are run by private industry and the government is complaining that they're too damned profit-conscious to guard the shipments properly.'

Denning fetched two beers from the fridge.

'Thanks, Earl.'

'What about storage depots?'

'Some are just sitting up asking to be hit. There's one here with only one guard at night. Course, there's all sorts of fancy electronic stuff there, too.'

Gallagher handed a photostat to Denning.

'Marvellous, isn't it?' Denning said. 'They're all worried about security so the damned fools spell out exactly what the problems are. Crazy. Here's to the freedom of the American press.'

Gallagher joined in the toast.

'Here's another beauty, Earl. The International Atomic Energy Agency have been mouthing off about the Atomic Energy Act. It gives the public the right to certain information about the private use of nuclear materials. If you want a plan of a nuclear depot all you have to do is go to the Nuclear Regulatory Commission reading room at . . . let's see.'

Again he checked the photostats.

' . . . 1717 H Street in Washington, good old DC. They'll give you the works, capacities of storage rooms, details of shipments, the whole bloody works.'

'Give me that.'

Denning snatched the photostat Gallagher had been reading, hurriedly read the article and flung the photostat into the air. He moved as though to slap the frail Gallagher on the shoulders, but held back his hand.

'It's terrific, Sean. You're a genius. What about plutonium?'

'It's the same story. It's dodgy to deal with, but not when it's all wrapped up for shipment.'

A rapping on the door startled both men. Denning was relieved to find that the caller was Henrick. He limped into the room and winked at Gallagher. Denning fetched a third beer and handed it to Henrick.

'Sean's been filling me in on how we might get the stuff. Baby, it's going to be a walkover.'

Henrick grinned and looked inquiringly at Gallagher.

'That's right. Uranium and plutonium is shipped all over the States. It's all here.'

He slapped the pile of photostats.

'We want plutonium,' Henrick said emphatically. 'Uranium's good, but plutonium's better.'

'Does it make much difference?' Denning asked.

'You bet your sweet ass it does. With uranium we'd knock off, say, maybe a hundred thousand people.'

Henrick took a long drink from the beer can, then continued.

'With the same amount of plutonium . . . well, let's say ten times as many if we hit the right place. A cool million stiffs.'

Denning let out his cowboy whoop and crushed his empty beer can. The whoop became a wild shriek.

'You mean you can do it, Wayne? You can design an atomic bomb and build it?'

'I reckon so.'

He pulled his notebook from an inside pocket.

'In fact, it's designed already. How do you fancy one of these little beauties?'

Denning grabbed the crude drawings Henrick had made in the library. Gallagher moved swiftly from his seat to look over Denning's shoulder.

'You mean that this is all there is to it?' Denning asked incredulously.

'Not quite. Those designs aren't quantitative. There are a whole lot of calculations to be made and I'll need a lot of equipment. It'll cost a lot of bread.'

Henrick sat on the sofa and sighed with relief as he took the pressure off his aching stump.

Denning was subdued again, alarmed about the lack of cash. Gallagher looked expectantly at the other two.

'What will you need?' Denning asked.

'A glove box for a start – that's like a glass box with gloves fitted into one wall so you can handle radioactive stuff. A furnace . . . a Geiger counter . . . a few other things. I can get them, but we're talking about thousands.'

Denning wheeled around and glared at Gallagher.

'Are you serving in the bar tonight?'

'Yes, but . . . '

'Who'll be with you later on?'

'Hey, come on, Earl. You're not serious.'

Gallagher blanched at the realization of what Denning had in mind.

'Who'll be with you, Sean?' Denning repeated threateningly.

'Well . . . just Mike.'

'How much cash will there be?'

'I suppose a fair bit,' Gallagher said reluctantly. 'Mike said last night that he hadn't had time to go to the bank for the last few days.'

Gallagher mentally added a few figures.

'Maybe three thousand or so in the cafe.'

'Can you fix the alarm?'

'Oh, shit, Earl . . . I . . . '

'Can you fix it, for Christ's sake?'

'Well, yes.'

'OK. Here's what you do. First, give me a list of those plutonium plants named in the clippings. Then just go to work and, when we get to the bar, turn off the alarm. And don't worry about another thing. We'll make it look good.'

Gallagher hung his head and slumped back in the chair. Denning strode towards him, placed a hand underneath his chin and forced his head upward.

'Look at me, baby. Don't worry about a thing. I know what I'm doing. And when the cops question you, just act like an outraged victim. Shop us and you're a dead man.'

'I won't shop you, Earl.' His voice faded to a whimper. 'I won't shop you.'

6

'Yes, dear.'

Of the dozen or so phrases Sheehan had uttered within the last ten minutes the majority had been, 'Yes, dear.'

'And you've got your pills?'

'Yes, dear.'

'And your diet chart?'

'Yes, dear.'

'And . . .'

'Oh, do stop fussing, woman.'

He kissed her lightly on the cheek. His wife was as fastidious as he was slapdash. Despite his success, she had remained down-to-earth. She liked to boast that she was 'pure Yorkshire – straight talking and straight living.'

'And you've got all your papers?'

'I bloody hope so.'

She had spent an hour the night before smoothing out the crumpled documents which had been stuffed in his cases. They were stacked neatly in plastic sandwich boxes, but in no particular order. Notes on security at various power plants were shuffled among receipts and personal letters.

'A secretary is travelling to New York with me. She'll help me get things sorted out.'

Mrs Sheehan stretched herself primly to her full five feet two inches at the mention of a 'she'.

'Just make sure she remains a secretary, and nothing more.'

Sheehan laughed, flattered by her anxiety.

'Little woman, didn't I give you your conjugals back last night? That'll keep me going for a while.'

'Ken, don't be vulgar.'

Sheehan often joked about 'giving the little woman her conjugal rights back'. The glibness disguised the real pleasure he derived from their sex life. Over the years they had adjusted well to each other. The little woman was quite a performer under the sheets.

The Sheehans lived in a picturesque cottage in the Kent village of Shoreham. It was three hours from Heathrow Airport, and Sheehan planned to spend the night in London before catching the early morning Concorde flight to New York. But before checking into the hotel there was to be dinner with the Minister of Trade.

'And you haven't replaced that washer in the downstairs toilet. It still won't flush properly.'

'Yes, dear. I'll do it when I get back.'

The door bell chimed. The Ministry chauffeur had arrived. He carried Sheehan's cases to the Daimler.

Sheehan put his arms around his wife and kissed her.

'You'll miss me, Ken, won't you?'

'Course I will. I always do.'

As the car pulled away she stepped through the doorway onto the spotlessly clean tiled step and waved. Sheehan was fumbling for his cigarette lighter. He cursed, remembering he had left it in the breakfast room.

Denning led the way into Mike's Place at a few minutes before one a.m. Wanda and Sarah Jane followed into the long narrow bar with Henrick, carrying his blue suitcase, at the rear. All four sat at the table nearest the door. Gallagher, drying glasses behind the bar, looked up anxiously.

Amid loud shouts and drunken laughter, a group of men and women lurched out of the bar. The only other customer was a man, obviously in a stupor, at the far end of the room. His head lay on his arms, which were stretched across the table.

'I hope you lot aren't planning to make a night of it,' Mike said. 'Some people have homes to go to. I'm just about to close up.'

Denning waved a fifty-dollar bill.

'Gin and tonics all round. Have one yourself – and one for your long-haired mate.'

Mike eyed the fifty-dollar bill.

'OK. One round then.'

As he turned to the bar Denning glanced at Gallagher and silently mouthed the word, 'Alarm'. Gallagher put down the glass he was drying and walked to the furthermost corner of the bar. He returned a few seconds later and gave Denning a surreptitious thumbs-up sign.

Shielded by the other three from the view of Mike, Henrick opened his suitcase, drew out the automatic and snapped the gun barrel onto the stock. He held the gun under the table.

Mike approached with the drinks.

'On second thoughts, we'll have these on the house,' Denning said.

Henrick produced the rifle and pointed it at Mike's midriff.

'The safe, buster.'

Mike looked hopefully at the front door. Wanda rose from her chair and secured the two bolts which locked the door from the inside.

Mike raised his arms, turned and walked to the bar. As he neared the safe, which was hidden from the sight of customers, he pressed his foot on one of six rubber buttons placed strategically on the floor behind the bar. There was no answering clanging of the alarm. Mike frowned. Slowly, he turned and looked at Gallagher. For a moment Gallagher looked as though he were about to speak, then lowered his head. He continued to polish an already sparkling glass.

'You bastard, Gallagher. You've turned it off. You lousy dirty . . .'

Mike was silenced by a prod with the rifle barrel.

Denning held out a hand.

'Look, Mike, let's be buddies, eh? There's no reason for anyone to get hurt.'

Mike instinctively half accepted the offered handshake. Denning smiled. Exerting as much strength as he could, he crushed the bartender's hand. The bones crunched sickeningly and Mike slipped to the floor.

'Now get up.'

Mike stood, gently massaging the injured hand.

'The safe. Now.'

Mike crouched in front of the safe and twirled the combination lock. After four turns the safe door fell open.

In a flash Denning drew a wire from his pocket, looped it around Mike's neck and tugged. The bartender slumped sideways. Denning cleaned the wire with a handkerchief.

'You fool,' Gallagher shouted. 'You've . . . '

'Shut up. And switch the alarm back on unless you want to advertise that this is an inside job.'

Gallagher crossed to the alarm control box and returned the master switch to the 'on' position.

Denning gestured to the two women and pointed to the safe. Henrick repacked the automatic and started to help the women stuff the notes beside it in the suitcase.

'Let the girls do that,' Denning said. 'You put our buddy to sleep.' To Gallagher Denning said, 'When you wake up, buddy boy, remember who your friends are. Two masked men came in. OK? One wrong word and you're a dead man. If we don't get you the KGB will.'

Henrick sidled up to Gallagher, picked up a full whisky bottle and crashed it onto Gallagher's skull. He crumpled to the floor.

Sarah Jane was fastening the suitcase.

'How much?' Denning asked.

'More than we thought,' Sarah Jane said. 'Maybe five thousand.'

'Good. OK, let's go.'

Wanda unfastened the bolts, then Denning removed her fingerprints with his handkerchief. He looked quickly around the room, suddenly remembering the whisky bottle with which Henrick had hit Gallagher, ran behind the bar and wiped the broken neck of the bottle.

The drunk at the far end of the room snored loudly. Denning grabbed the man's hair and pulled back his head. The man didn't flinch. His head thumped the table as Denning, satisfied that he was oblivious of all around him, released his grip. The man grunted protestingly, then continued snoring.

Denning walked to the table nearest to the door, wrapped his handkerchief around one of the glasses and gulped down the gin and tonic. With a final look around the bar he ran after the others into the street.

The four walked one block and hailed a cab. Their departure from Mike's Place had gone unnoticed.

Twice Denning insisted that the group should change cabs on the journey back to Queens. In the unlikely event that they had aroused suspicion it would be difficult for any association to be made between the four who had hailed a cab near Mike's Place and those who now arrived near Denning's flat.

In his room he grabbed the suitcase from Henrick and tipped its contents onto the table. The other three gathered around the table and looked greedily at the pile of notes.

'Let's count.'

Denning flung the rifle onto the sofa and sorted the money into four heaps. They began to count. Denning whistled when the final amount was determined.

'Six thousand two hundred lovely smackers. That guy's an idiot for keeping so much money in the safe.'

'Was an idiot,' Henrick corrected.

'Yeah, was.' Denning laughed and slapped Henrick on the back.

Denning fetched four beers and handed them around. Henrick sat on the solitary chair and Denning squeezed between the girls on the sofa.

'Me and Wayne split the cash,' he said. 'Half each. Wayne,

you go ahead and buy what you need. Where are we going to set up the workshop?'

Henrick had already given the problem some thought. 'Sarah's and Wanda's place. The basement is ideal.'

Denning looked at Sarah Jane. She folded her hands in her lap and crushed her arms against her breasts.

'It's all right with me. Wanda?'

'Suppose so.'

'In that case,' Denning said, 'once we get the stuff let's make sure someone's always in the house. Wayne, Sarah and Sean can take turns – once Sean gets clear of the cops. Wanda's coming with me. We're off to Washington to look into ways of getting hold of the stuff. OK?'

No objections were raised.

'Meanwhile, Sarah, you keep Wayne happy. I don't want any of us to mix with outsiders. You'll have to keep Sean happy, too. I don't want anyone running around chasing broads.'

Henrick's freckles merged into a mottled flush as he blushed in anger.

'If you're suggesting I should share Sarah, forget it.'

'That's just what I'm suggesting. If it's necessary, Wayne. You handle it, but I don't want anyone cracking up. This whole deal's a lot more important than a quick screw. OK?'

Henrick decided not to pursue the matter. Privately, he resolved that if Gallagher made any approach to Sarah Jane he would thrash the life out of him.

'OK, Sarah?' Denning asked.

'That . . . well.' She blew Henrick a kiss. 'I'll do anything Wayne wants me to. Anything.' Her eyelids fluttered and she let her gaze fall to her lap.

'OK, Wanda?'

She was uneasy at being sentenced to spend so much time with Denning, but excited at the prospect that the real business was about to begin.

'Suits me.'

'We'll leave in a day or two. We'll make out we're on a

camping trip. Tonight, Wanda stays here in case we decide to make a quick start. Wayne, I'll keep in touch by phone.'

Henrick replaced the rifle in the suitcase. Denning sorted the cash into two equal piles, placed one in the suitcase and fastened the catch.

Sarah Jane smoothed her skirt.

'Let's go, Wayne. I've got to keep you happy. Right?' She laughed provocatively. 'So let's start tonight.'

Henrick picked up the suitcase and limped toward the door.

Gallagher regained consciousness in the ambulance. Instantly he longed for the merciful oblivion of sleep. His head throbbed excruciatingly, the pain more severe than he would have believed he could tolerate. The ambulance siren screamed at full pitch, its sound waves drilling into his skull like a thousand fiery needles. Flashing lights pierced his brain and exploded into a host of burning sparks.

'He's awake.'

The voice seemed to float from some great distance away. Gallagher realized that the flashing lights came from buildings on either side as the ambulance sped onward.

'How are you feeling?'

Gallagher groaned. The face of the ambulance attendant came into focus. A red blanket, similar to the one wrapped around Gallagher, covered a still form on the opposite side of the ambulance.

'Is that . . . ?'

Gallagher needed no answer. Suddenly, he remembered the raid . . . the killing . . . the crashing blow on his head.

'You'll be OK, buddy.'

Gallagher groaned once more, his memories more painful than his injuries. He tried to sit up.

'Where are we going?'

He saw the attendant's lips move in reply but heard no words as he sank into unconsciousness.

The next time he awoke he was covered in crisp white

sheets in a hospital bed. The sweet, sickly smell of disinfectant stung his nostrils. A nurse turned from a wall cupboard and smiled.

'Hi. How are you feeling?'

'Hell, what a question. Like death. It hurts . . . '

'I'm preparing something to take away the pain. The X-rays are clear.'

She lifted his arm and daubed a small area with a cotton swab. He felt the sharp prick of a hypodermic needle.

A doctor entered and checked a chart hanging from the foot of the bed.

'You'll be feeling better soon.'

Gallagher laughed stupidly, grateful that at least the doctor hadn't asked some dumb question about how he was feeling.

'It bloody hurts,' Gallagher complained. 'When will this injection start to work? My head's killing me.'

'It'll work soon. In cases of suspected brain injury we can't give pain-killers until we know the extent of the damage. It might be important to judge the patient's reactions.'

'I want to go home,' Gallagher said listlessly, uninterested in the doctor's explanation. 'When can I get out of here?'

'Well, there's no serious injury. There'll be a little concussion and shock, but otherwise no problem. Maybe in a day or two.'

'A day or two,' Gallagher repeated loudly. 'But that's no good. I want out. My mother . . . '

'We've contacted your mother. She knows you're OK.'

The doctor declined to add that he had been told Gallagher's mother seemed only mildly interested in her son's health.

'There's somebody here who wants to see you,' the doctor added. 'Do you feel up to making a statement?'

Gallagher caught his breath and began to tremble. A statement. That could only mean the police.

'Oh, God. Do I have to?'

'Sooner or later, yes. But I suppose we can leave it for

a while.'

The doctor turned to leave.

'No.'

Gallagher shouted the word as the doctor reached the door.

'No. I mean, I'll see them now. I want to get it over with.'

The doctor hesitated, reconsidering Gallagher's condition. The odd behaviour was probably a result of mild shock, he decided.

'Very well. I'll bring them in.'

A police lieutenant and a sergeant, both in plain clothes, introduced themselves to Gallagher and drew two chairs to the bedside.

'How are you feeling?' the lieutenant asked.

Gallagher cringed. He felt that if anyone else asked that question he would scream.

'Like a million dollars.'

'Yes. Well, what can you tell us about what happened?'

Gallagher felt an overwhelming need to tell the truth. Perhaps he could do a deal. He could explain away his part in the murder of the ambassador, and how he had been blackmailed into agreeing to the raid on the bar. It was no part of the plan that anyone should get hurt. On the other hand, Denning was a vindictive and patient man. Then there was Henrick, and even the girls. That crazy bird Wanda sometimes showed an intensity of fanaticism that was scaring. And there was the KGB.

Conflicting thoughts tumbled through his mind as he answered straightforward questions about his name, address, age, how long he had worked at the bar.

'How many of them were there?' the lieutenant asked.

This was the moment of decision. Gallagher heard himself reply before he had consciously decided to do so.

'Two. They wore masks.'

'What kind of masks?'

Panic gripped Gallagher. He hadn't thought out the details.

'Er . . . stockings, I think. Yes, women's stockings, tied

on top of their heads, sort of.'

'Were these men tall, short or what?'

'Sort of medium. A bit smaller than you, and well built.'

'Both of them?'

'Yes. They were about the same size.'

'Anything unusual about them? How one of them walked? Or anything?'

'I don't think so. No.'

The lieutenant paused, allowing the sergeant to complete writing down Gallagher's replies.

'Were they armed?'

'One had a rifle. The other had . . . that wire thing. He killed Mike.'

Gallagher looked appealingly at the doctor and nurse, who had remained in the room. The nurse smiled encouragingly.

'OK, let's hear it from the beginning,' the lieutenant said. 'Everything. Every little detail from the moment they came in. There you were, standing at the bar . . . '

'Yes. I was drying glasses behind the bar. Mike was clearing up on the other side. A crowd had just left and Mike was going to close up. There was only one customer and he had passed out, blind drunk. They burst in, pointed the gun at Mike and said something like, "Touch the alarm and you're a dead man". They made Mike open the safe and . . . that man pulled a wire round Mike's throat and . . . It was . . . He just fell. Then something hit me on the back of the head. That's all I remember.'

Gallagher was trembling uncontrollably. The doctor came to the rescue.

'I'm sorry,' he said to the policeman. 'That's it. The patient is clearly in shock.'

The lieutenant shrugged, then went carefully through Gallagher's story once more.

'There's nothing else?'

'No . . . that's everything.'

The lieutenant rose to leave. As the sergeant opened the door he was faced by a third policeman, who had been reaching for the door handle.

'Something from forensic, lieutenant,' he announced breathlessly.

'What is is?'

'That handkerchief we found in the bar. I don't get it. It had blood from the victim soaked into it and something else. It's weird.'

'For Christ's sake . . . ' the lieutenant began impatiently.

'Rabbit's blood.'

The lieutenant and sergeant exchanged astonished glances.

'That's right. It's covered in rabbit's blood, lieutenant.'

'Ken, meet Sheila Duncan.'

The minister's voice was matter-of-fact. It could hardly have betrayed less interest if he had been reading aloud the minutes of a dull committee meeting. But the woman he introduced to Sheehan was sensational. In her mid-thirties, she was stunningly beautiful, with immaculately groomed mid-length black hair and deep blue eyes. She wore a buff plaid skirt, plain beige jumper and slightly raised brown shoes. The clothing was simple, but expensive.

'Miss Duncan is going to be your secretary on the trip.'

On closer inspection Sheehan noticed that her nose tilted slightly to one side, as though it might at some time have been injured. He decided he would forgive her this one small imperfection. His heartbeat accelerated as he shook her slender, warm hand. He held on to her hand just a fraction longer than decorum required.

'I'm delighted . . . Nice to meet you, Miss Duncan.'

Her cream features rippled into a smile.

'Call me Sheila, please.'

Efficient and dedicated, Sheila had worked in a succession of ministry departments. A love affair in her late teens had ended disastrously and she had devoted her considerable energies to her career. She was unashamedly ambitious. As the wounds of the love affair healed she developed other relationships. It was inevitable that one so sensuous would have many romances, but never again had she fallen in love.

'Shall we dine, then?'

The minister sat at the head of the long table and gestured to the two seats next to him. The dining room at his Whitehall office was cold and impersonal, though furnished with several priceless antiques. The mahogany dining table was laid with crystal glassware and heavy old silver.

Sheehan's gourmet taste was revolted by the first course, a powdered variation of pea soup. He noticed Sheila also approached the soup cautiously. The minister finished his soup heartily.

'As you no doubt know, Ken, my speech went down well. I think people are really taking notice of this security business at last.'

'About time, too.'

A waiter served the main course. Sheehan's nose twitched in protest. A plate of lumpy potatoes was heaped with carrots and peas from a can. He probed a small portion of meat which might have been a cross between an old hen and a polyethylene bag. The minister assaulted the food as though afraid his appetite would run out.

'How big a task would it be to draw up worldwide safety standards, Ken?'

Sheehan gratefully took the opportunity to put down his knife and fork.

'It would be tough. Solutions we draw up today are immediately out of date because the industry is growing so fast. Nuclear power plants are sprouting up everywhere. The world is running out of the fossil materials like coal, so the growth will go on and on. You know the story. We have to have power. That means more plants and more weapons-grade nuclear fuel being shipped back and forth.

'In America the problems are particularly acute because so many nuclear facilities are in the hands of private industry. The old profit motive rears its ugly head and the companies cut costs to the bone. Also, they don't like having guards all over the place. It puts off the customers, alarms local people and is thoroughly bad for the image of a so-called peaceful nuclear industry.'

Sheehan took a sip of red wine. Too late, he noticed Sheila's warning look. The wine was no better than the rest of the meal.

'Well, I want you to keep thinking about it, Ken. We're going to win this one, and we want to be ready for victory.'

The minister daubed his lips with a napkin.

'It's a good idea to get those boys of the Nuclear Regulatory Commission on our side,' he added. 'They'll be keen to start off by making a big impression. And I know you'll put the case well at the United Nations. Lay it on heavy. Don't be shouted down, and just keep talking.'

A bowl of what Sheehan supposed was meant to be rice pudding was placed in front of them. Sheila smiled at the waiter.

'Er . . . no dessert, thanks. I'm on a diet.'

'Me too,' Sheehan added.

'Sheila here will keep me in touch,' the minister added, rapidly spooning the rice into his mouth. 'I don't want to keep you tied up on the phone.'

Sheehan was to be spared the ordeal of having to drink an inferior brandy.

'Forgive me,' the minister said, 'but I'll have to dash. I need to be at the Commons early in the morning. Have a good flight, and a successful trip. Both of you.'

The minister shook hands with Sheehan and the secretary and was gone.

'Well, Miss . . . sorry, Sheila. I hope you're looking foward to our assignment.'

'I am. I love America. I hope it's a long stay.'

Sheehan checked his watch.

'Look, it's a bit early to check into the hotel. I've got an idea.'

'Yes?'

'Let's go and have a meal. I'm bloody ravenous.'

She laughed and followed him through the door. Her new boss, she thought, was quite something.

7

The doctor listened patiently to Gallagher's frantic pleading.

'I insist. I know my rights. I want out. Now.'

'Concussion can be dangerous. I must advise against it.'

'Thanks for the advice. Now get my bill and my clothes.'

The doctor shrugged.

'I must ask you to sign a form indemnifying the hospital against any responsibility.'

'Sure, sure. I'll sign anything. I just want to go.'

Gallagher dressed hurriedly and was escorted to the reception area. He handed his Blue Cross medical card to a woman clerk and signed the papers she pushed across her desk. He took a deep breath as he walked through the hospital's main entrance. His bandaged head throbbed painfully but at least he was free. He had to get to Denning.

Pausing repeatedly to gaze in shop windows and steal a glance behind him, he walked to the Grand Central railroad terminal. He felt reasonably confident that he was not being followed. The police had given no indication that they were suspicious of his story.

Only a dozen or so passengers waited on the subway platform – it would be another hour before the morning rush started. He remained seated on a subway bench as his train arrived. When the doors began to close he slipped quickly on board. He glanced through the train windows to left and right along the platform. No one seemed to have noticed his dash to the train. He was certain now that he was not being followed.

As a final precaution he walked twice around the block

where Denning lived before letting himself through the unlocked front door and making his way to the attic.

Denning, wearing only shorts, answered his knock. Gallagher could not suppress the envy he felt on noting the other's magnificent physique. Denning yawned, his biceps rippling as he raised his arms above his head. Gallagher pushed past him into the room.

Wanda lay asleep on the sofa.

'That handkerchief, Earl . . . You must have dropped the handkerchief.'

Gallagher shuddered at the significance of what he had overheard in his hospital room.

'You've left your bloody autograph, Earl. The handkerchief you dropped at the ambassador's place . . . the handkerchief at Mike's.'

Wanda sat up and Gallagher slumped wearily onto the sofa alongside her.

'Cool it, Sean,' Denning snarled. 'Cool it, man. So what's the big problem?'

Gallagher felt a futile desire to strike Denning in frustration.

'You haven't heard the worst of it. The handkerchief at Mike's Place . . . it's got rabbit's blood on it. I heard the cops . . . Don't you see, Earl? Rabbit's blood. Cottontails. The ferrets. If someone tells the cops about your ferrets . . . '

He almost sobbed with relief as the colour drained from Denning's cheeks. The message had got through.

'They'll know it was the same man who killed the ambassador's wife and the mailman, Earl. They were all killed the same way. And those handkerchiefs . . . '

'Shut up.'

Denning desperately sought relief from Gallagher's frenzied blabbering.

Wanda, fully alert, looked anxiously from one man to the other.

'Let's keep this cool,' Denning said, stalking the room. 'So just what are they going to think about the rabbit's blood, eh? They might look for a butcher. We've still got time.'

He clenched his fists and flexed his arm and back muscles.

'So they know it's the same guy, but they still don't know who. No sweat . . . '

Gallagher leapt to his feet.

'The ferrets, Earl. The fucking ferrets. Don't you see? If someone reports to the police that you've got ferrets, they'll be nosing around here.'

His voice trailed away as he slumped back onto the sofa.

'Look, Sean, cool it – for Christ's sake. Thanks for the warning, but I won't be here if anyone does come nosing around. Me and Wanda are going to Washington to check out one of those power plants. And I'll get rid of the ferrets. Now just tell me exactly what you told the pigs.'

Gallagher recounted his interview with the lieutenant and the sergeant.

'And did they seem to buy it?'

'I think so. And I made sure I wasn't followed here.'

'Good. Now listen, Sean. You did great. We've still got plenty of time to clear out. You just go home and stay there. The cops may want to question you again. If they do, stick to the same story. Word for word. And stay cool, for Christ's sake.'

He gave Gallagher a playful punch on the chest.

'You did great, Sean. Stay home. OK? Either me or Wayne will be in touch when you're needed. After a few days you can move in with Wayne and Sarah at her place.'

Gallagher forced a smile.

'OK, Earl, but for God's sake get rid of those ferrets.'

'I will, I will. And me and Wanda will be on the road just as fast as we can get you out of here.'

Gallagher pulled open the door, then paused uncertainly.

'So long, Earl, Wanda.'

The girl waved a hand. Denning slammed the door as Gallagher trudged down the staircase.

'So, smart ass, you're not exactly infallible after all?'

Wanda threw off the grey blanket that had covered her and stood naked, stretching the sleepiness out of her slim, soft-boned limbs. Though nondescript in the loose-fitting casual clothes she usually wore, when naked she was startlingly attractive. Denning longingly studied the small breasts and firm thighs. He wondered if he would ever make a pass at her. If so, it would have to be after this was all over. No woman had ever returned to him for seconds, and he couldn't afford to alienate Wanda any more than necessary.

'We're home free, baby. Don't you worry about a thing.'

' "We're home free",' Wanda mimicked. 'The great revolutionary says, "We're home free", so nobody worry about a thing.'

She wiggled her hips and sneered.

'You've been reading too many of your biographies, Earl. You've got delusions of grandeur. I reckon we're in big trouble.'

Denning scowled.

'I tell you, everything's going to be OK. I'm going to pack.'

'You don't fancy me, then,' she taunted, delighted to see that for once his confidence was shaken. She cupped her hands underneath her breasts and spun tantalizingly in a circle.

Denning grabbed a suitcase from beneath the sofa and strode to the bedroom.

Within half an hour the boot of his Chevvy was crammed with his camping gear. He carried the hutch containing the ferrets to the car and placed it on the rear seat. Wanda, in jeans and a loose sweater, slipped into the front seat beside him as he turned on the ignition.

Sheehan was awakened by a tapping on the door between the two adjoining rooms of his suite in the Tudor City Hotel on East 42nd Street. A faint light filtered through the heavy drapes. He squinted at the luminous dial of his watch. Twelve o'clock! Midday! He sat upright, then relaxed as he realized he hadn't adjusted his watch to American time. It was only seven a.m. He threw back the covers, remembered he hadn't unpacked his dressing-gown and hastily pulled the covers back in place. He tried to smooth his hair.

'Come in. It's not locked.'

The door opened and Sheila was framed in the doorway, the light from behind her glinting around the outline of her hair, which hung loosely to her shoulders.

Her pink robe rustled as she stepped to the window and pulled back the curtains. While her back was turned he fastened the buttons on his pyjama jacket and tried again to smooth his hair. She walked to the bathroom and he heard the sound of gushing water as the taps were turned on. Sheehan caught the scent of her cologne as she returned.

'I'll have breakfast ready by the time you've had your bath.'

She smiled and he admired the sheen on her cheeks. He smoothed the sheets and wondered if he looked as ghastly as he felt.

She returned to her room and allowed him to escape from the bed. He snatched one of the still unpacked suitcases from the foot of the bed and scampered to the bathroom. Ten minutes later he re-emerged dressed in trousers and a sweater. The bath had refreshed him and he felt slightly less bizarre.

Sheila had made his bed and had wheeled in the breakfast trolley, which had been delivered to her room. She had found time the previous evening for a talk with the head chef. The result was a superbly displayed breakfast of kippers, peaches, french toast, coffee and orange juice.

'I hope you're not one of those people who skip the first meal of the day.'

'Er, no. Especially when the British government is paying. This looks terrific.'

Sheila wore a trim grey skirt and a blue V-necked blouse. As he sipped his orange juice he stole a glance at the rise of her breasts, revealed by the plunging neckline.

'And what's the programme for today?' she asked.

He sampled the kippers and murmured appreciatively.

'I'm going to look up one of the NRC guys who's hanging out here at the UN, then there's an old Russian buddy I want to see.'

'Shall I come along?'

Sheehan was tempted to accept the offer. She would at least be decorous, even if her presence wasn't strictly necessary.

'No. I don't think so. Have a day off and I'll rejoin you in the evening. I can give you a rundown if anything crops up.'

'OK. I'll go through your cases and sort out the paper work.'

She poured the coffee and handed him a cigarette. He fumbled in his pocket for his lighter.

'You left it at home. Remember?'

'Damn. So I did.'

'Never mind. I've something for you.'

She smiled and handed over a gift-wrapped package. He unwrapped a silver-plated lighter.

'Hey, you shouldn't have done this.'

'It's OK. I bought it duty free at the airport. It didn't cost as much as all that.'

He adjusted the flame of the lighter and lit her cigarette.

'I'm grateful,' he said, hoping she hadn't been offended by his surprised reaction. 'Thanks.'

He gave her a fatherly peck on the cheek.

Sheila busied herself removing the breakfast trolley to her room. Sheehan decided it was time to leave and grabbed a raincoat.

'See you later,' he called.

She returned, smiling.

'Have a good day.'

He wondered fleetingly if any one man was important in Sheila's life. If not, it was a shame for such delicious equipment to go to waste. If so, he was one hell of a lucky guy, whoever he was. Sheehan cautioned himself to try to regard her as more of a daughter than a possible bedmate.

At nine a.m. officers of the homicide bureau of New York's 17th Precinct were assembled in the conference room. The lieutenant and sergeant who had questioned Gallagher at the hospital sat at a table on a raised platform. The lieutenant lit a cigarette, rose to address the meeting, then was seized by a coughing spasm as he gulped too much smoke into his lungs. The officers chuckled at his discomfort.

'OK, OK. Joke over.'

The lieutenant frowned at several officers in turn.

'We're here to weigh what we've got on the killing of the bartender. You've all got your orders, but first you're going to tune in on an update. We've got a psycho on the loose, and the chief wants us to get him. Fast.'

The lieutenant flicked ash from his cigarette into a plastic cup on the table.

'We're reasonably sure that the group who killed the bartender is also responsible for the killing of the ambassador, his wife and the mailman. All the wounds were probably made with the same, or a similar, length of wire. All agreed?'

A murmur of assent greeted the question.

'Then we've got a couple of handkerchiefs, both identical, one of which was found at the scene of each crime. Unfortunately, they're also identical to millions of others sold at countless stores. The first handkerchief was smeared with blood which matched that of the ambassador's wife and the mailman. The second was smeared with the bartender's blood and – I don't get this – rabbit's blood. The first guy who comes up with a bright idea on how we get rabbit's blood on the handkerchief receives my personal genius-of-the-week award. I just don't get it. Maybe we're looking for a butcher or a butcher's assistant. Maybe a chef. I just don't know. Perhaps someone who works in a pet store, but I doubt it. They don't go around carving up animals in the normal course of events. This guy just could be so crazy that he goes around garrotting cottontails as well as people. All we know for sure is that he likes to clean his tools after each job. Let's hope he hasn't got too many handkerchiefs.'

The lieutenant drew on his cigarette and blew the smoke

through his nostrils.

'We also need ideas fast on why the same group of people might have carried out both crimes. The telegram found at the ambassador's home indicates that the motive for his killing was political. The mailman and the ambassador's wife were probably taken out just because they were in the way. The killing of the barman has all the signs of a homicide during the course of armed robbery. There was certainly no robbery motive for the killing of the ambassador, and no political motive for the killing of the guy who ran Mike's Place. Maybe we've got a crazy nut who likes garrotting people for the hell of it. Maybe we've got some political nut who needed cash to finance some other job. Either way, it's bad news. There's no way of knowing where this freak and his cronies are going to turn up next.'

An officer waved for the lieutenant's attention.

'That telegram, lieutenant . . . '

The lieutenant interrupted.

'It doesn't help. Not a lot, anyway. The sender used a false name and address. No prints. On its own, it doesn't mean much at this stage. But we do have a couple of things going for us.'

He crushed his cigarette into the plastic cup.

'We've got the Winchester-Magnum .303s that perforated the ambassador. They're the soft-nosed type, longer than the regular .303s, and are the sort used in a modified .303 automatic. That's a fairly distinctive and dangerous weapon. Sooner or later this guy is going to need more ammunition and we've alerted gun dealers to contact us immediately if anyone asks for bullets of this kind. We could be lucky, but don't hold your breath.

'We also know that our friend the psycho has at least two accomplices. The first killings probably involved at least three people. There's our psycho, the guy who did the shooting and a driver. The raid at Mike's Place also probably involved three people. Again, we've got the psycho. The second bartender was hit with a bottle, and the two methods of attack suggest two different people on the raid. Also, there'd be too much going on for one guy to handle. And there was probably a driver. There's also the bartender's statement that there were two bandits, but I'm not taking too much account of his evidence at this stage. More about this character later. But for the record, it seems we've got two guys who do the handiwork and a getaway driver. I'm taking bets that when we grab these punks we'll find that at least three people are shacked up together somewhere.'

The lieutenant signalled to an officer seated behind a slide projector. The lights in the room were put out and the blinds drawn. A photograph taken from behind the bar at Mike's Place was projected onto a screen behind the lieutenant.

'This shot shows us the alarm buttons at Mike's Place,' the lieutenant explained. 'And here's where we've got a problem. Note, there are six buttons, all placed on the floor within a step or so of each other. What I want to know is, why the hell wasn't the alarm used? Presumably, both barmen had an opportunity at some stage to slide a foot over one of those buttons and bring New York's finest on the scene. The buttons are out of sight from anyone on the customers' side of the bar. Yet – no alarm.

'The alarm control box had been dusted, and fingerprints were found. Surprise, surprise, they belong to the second bartender. So, there's no genius-of-the-week award for any officer who decides that this guy is something fishy.'

The lieutenant turned on the lights and the projector was switched off.

'Let's see, then, what we know about this guy. Name, Sean Gallagher. Age, twenty-three. Single. Columbia dropout and barman. He signed himself out of hospital in a highly agitated state against the advice of doctors. In one respect he's a bit special. He's the only man who's confronted these people who's survived.

'They clearly don't like leaving witnesses about. So, the departure of the ambassador's wife and the mailman. So, curtains for the guy who ran Mike's Place. Yet Mister Gallagher gets a good look at these people, though they were supposedly wearing masks, and he lives to tell the story. And it really isn't much of a story he has to tell. We all have his statement, and it's very brief. After this meeting I'm going to have another talk with Mr Gallagher.'

The lieutenant looked around the room.

'Anyone want to raise anything else?'

No one took up the invitation.

'OK, let's move. The sergeant here and I go to see Gallagher. Meanwhile, I want the lowdown on this guy from the time he left the cradle. I want to know about the guys he goes around with, the women he's been with and the old woman who stopped to pat his head when he was being pushed around in a baby carriage. Anything and everything. Question his teachers, neighbours and everyone who's ever known him.

'I'll brief the press. We can rely on them to make the most of this gory clue about the rabbit's blood. That's the sort of thing they like. OK. You've got your assignments. Good luck.'

Chairs scraped on the floor as the officers rose to leave the conference room. The lieutenant winked at his sergeant.

'Let's you and me give this guy Gallagher the works.'

Henrick vigorously thrust a cleaning rod down the muzzle of his automatic. He sat against a wall of Sarah Jane's living room. The floor was littered with newspapers, on which were placed cleaning patches, gun solvent and gun oil.

He had bought the gun, complete with false registration papers, from a fellow student at Columbia. The price was $500. At the time Henrick convinced himself that he would use the gun only for hunting, though he acknowledged that its possession gave him a strange sense of power.

He examined the patch he had pushed through the muzzle. The cotton was soiled with gun powder. Still the barrel was not clean.

'Another patch, honey.'

Sarah Jane, sitting beside him, poured gun solvent on a patch and handed it to him. With the cleaning rod he pushed the new patch down the muzzle. Working automatically on the gun, his attention returned to the nuclear physics manual which lay on his lap. Suddenly he laughed loudly.

'Know something, honey? We're going to be a nuclear power.'

He laughed again and threw back his head, tossing his ginger curls. Sarah Jane smiled at his enthusiasm.

'We're going to be a nuclear power, Sarah. That makes the States, Russia, China, Britain, God knows who else and me and Earl and the rest of us. Look out, world. Here we come.'

Grinning broadly, he checked the second patch. It had emerged clean.

'One more, honey, with the gun oil.'

Sarah Jane daintily lifted the bottle of gun oil as if she were raising a bottle of champagne. She soaked a patch with oil and handed it to him. Once more the cleaning rod was thrust down the muzzle and he continued reading. Sarah Jane examined her soiled fingers and frowned.

'It can't be this easy, Wayne. Surely you can't make an atomic bomb just like that.'

His freckles danced as his face creased into a grin.

'It ain't easy, honey. Look at it this way. It took nature about a hundred million years to make coal. It took man a million years to invent the automobile. Once they'd cracked the secret of splitting the atom it took the greatest scientific brains in the world another three years to make a nuclear bomb. But you're in love with a genius, honey. It's going to take me about three weeks.'

He patted her thigh but caught his breath as the movement sent a stabbing pain shooting up his leg from his bandaged stump. Sarah Jane kissed his cheek.

'We don't have to learn how to split atoms, honey. Given the right materials and the right conditions, they'll split themselves.'

He repacked the gun in the suitcase. Sarah Jane carried

the case to the bedroom and returned to find him scribbling figures on a sheet of paper. He had begun to amuse himself by creating a series of puzzles on the structure of atoms.

'You know, Sarah, it really isn't going to be so tough. I reckon I could even teach you how to do it. Lesson one. Everything is made of atoms. Every atom is like a mini-universe, with tiny planets whizzing around a sun. Most of the inside of every atom is space. So if we took all the space out of the atoms in your body it would shrink to a tiny speck one thousandth of a centimetre tall. And that would be Sarah Jane Kaye, and you'd still weigh the same as you do now. Got it? What little tits you'd have.'

She curtsied with mock respect.

'If you say so, sir. Brilliant. But I think I'll leave the clever work to you.

'You're dumb, Sarah, but you're terrific in bed.'

'Thank you, sir.'

She began to feel uneasy at the frivolous way in which he seemed to regard the task of making the bomb. She faced the window as he returned to his book.

'Wayne, you remember why we're doing this?'

She continued to look absently out of the window.

'Why? What do you mean, "why"? Why what?'

She turned and sat beside him.

'It's not just a game, is it? I mean, what we hope to achieve and all that.'

Henrick chuckled.

'You mean . . . what was it Earl said we'd be called . . ? ACE. A Chance to Eat. Stupid bloody name. But no, of course I haven't forgotten why we're doing this.'

He ignored the hand she placed affectionately on his shoulder. He was only partly convinced by his reply. Since he had begun to tackle the problems of the bomb assembly he had become like a child obsessed with a favourite jigsaw puzzle. He had thought of little but computations, quantities, explosive effects.

'Of course I haven't forgotten why,' he repeated, more to himself than to Sarah Jane. 'They'll have to give in to us, you know. They'll have to. This bomb's going to work. A fair share of food. A fair share of money. Sarah, I'd give a lot to achieve that.'

'You wouldn't do all this just . . . well, if we didn't have a good reason, would you?'

He sighed, irritated by the questioning.

'Honey, what do you think I am? I'm not crazy. Earl might be, but I've got all my bits and pieces in the right places. Of course I wouldn't. But if somebody doesn't do something, millions are going to keep on dying every day. The stupid bomb doesn't have to go off for us to get what we want.'

She put her arms around his neck and hugged him.

'Really, Wayne? Do you mean it . . . that we don't have to set off the bomb?'

'Yes, I mean it. Now help me draw up the shopping list. Get the Yellow Pages.'

She kissed him, then fetched the directory. He picked up his pencil and the scrap of paper.

'Look up under "laboratory supplies". For a start we're going to need the glove box and furnace.'

She flipped over the pages.

'There's dozens of these places, Wayne.'

'OK, let's pick six in Manhattan. Go for the bigger ads. Those firms will be the big ones.'

'Right. Here's the first one . . . '

The Chopin tape played softly. Gallagher's thin, lanky legs dangled over an arm of the chair. He placed a cushion behind his bandaged head in the hope of easing the painful throbbing. The pain persisted. He reached to the floor for a glass filled with white wine.

Once again, he thought, Denning had got it right. He had promised that the raid would go smoothly, and it had. If only Henrick hadn't hit so hard with that bottle. Still, the injury should divert suspicion. And by now Denning should be well on his way to Washington.

'Damn that smart ass,' Gallagher muttered. He resented Denning's domineering manner, and the offhand way he had received the warning that the police had found rabbit's blood on the handkerchief left behind at the bar. That tip had probably kept them all out of jail. And there'd been no kudos for getting injured and facing the cops.

The door bell startled him as he refilled his glass. It was unusual for anyone to call while his mother was at work. It couldn't be Denning, and it was unlikely to be Henrick. Gallagher nervously sipped the wine. He decided not to answer the bell. Perhaps whoever was there would go away.

Again the bell rang.

'Who is it?'

'Police. Mr Gallagher?'

'Yeah. Just a minute.'

He felt his normally pallid cheeks flush with fear. He swallowed another mouthful of wine, switched off the stereo tape and released the door catch. The lieutenant pushed the door back on its hinges.

'OK, OK, don't shove,' Gallagher said sullenly. 'I'm going to let you in.'

He returned to the chair. The lieutenant and sergeant entered the room and remained standing opposite him. Gallagher topped up his glass.

'I thought we'd been over everything at the hospital. What's this all about?'

'We've one or two loose ends, sonny boy. I'm sure we can count on your help. Yes?'

Gallagher was emboldened by the wine he had drunk, but uneasy at the lieutenant's cynical manner.

'Sure you can. What do you want to know?'

'For a start, why did you sign yourself out? The doctors tried to get you to stay, didn't they? My buddy here thinks you got the jitters just because we talked to you.'

Gallagher evaded the sergeant's sneering look.

'Why shouldn't I sign myself out? I'm OK, and I don't like hospitals. It's a free country, isn't it? I want to be home. It was only a knock on the head.'

The lieutenant looked at Gallagher for several seconds without talking. It was a trick calculated to make a suspect feel uncomfortable during questioning.

'I see. But the doctors tell me you were very agitated. Like a bear with a sore head. A frightened bear. Now why should an innocent, heroic citizen like yourself be so twitchy?'

'What do you mean, "twitchy"? Why not? So would you be. I saw a guy killed who wasn't just a boss. He was a friend. A good friend. And those bastards could have killed me, too. I was lucky to get out alive. Hell, anyone would be twitchy who'd been through all that jazz.'

Gallagher's voice had risen almost to a squeak. He drained his glass and refilled it with the last of the contents of the bottle.

'Yes, I suppose so.'

The lieutenant's eyes moved from Gallagher's face to the glass, then back to his face.

'Must have been quite an ordeal, sonny boy. But even worse for Mike. I wonder why they rubbed him out, and not you. I wonder why he never used that alarm. Strange, that. My buddy here thinks that's very suspicious, don't you sergeant?'

The sergeant grunted. Gallagher spilt some wine into his lap.

'What do you mean? Hell . . . there just wasn't any time, was there?'

'My buddy thinks there was. Six buttons on the floor, and you and Mike must have had lots of chances to hit one of them and our boys would have been all over the place. Or didn't you want our boys all over the place?'

'Course I did. You don't understand, do you? Mike didn't get a chance to hit the alarm, did he? I told you, he was on the other side of the bar. He was trying to wake up that guy who was smashed out of his mind. They just barged in, pulled the gun and that was it. They forced him to open the safe, and . . . It was horrible. It happened so fast. He didn't get a chance.'

Gallagher sniffed and blinked. He felt an irrational need

to cry, more in fear than grief.

'And meanwhile, you stood by and watched the show. Behind the bar, I think you said you were. According to your statement you were behind the bar drying glasses – with your feet no more than inches away from one of those alarm buttons. Why didn't you press the alarm?'

'I told you. It happened so fast. If I'd hit the button they'd have shot Mike straight away, wouldn't they? It makes such a noise, that alarm. What good would it have done? They might have shot me, as well. I didn't know what to do. Hell, I was all mixed up. I couldn't think. It was all over so fast. I was hit on the head and passed out.'

'Yes . . . yes.'

The lieutenant casually interrupted the flow of words.

'Yes, I see. But there's something else that bothers my buddy here, and I don't like it either. We dusted the alarm control box and, you know, that thing was smothered in prints.'

Gallagher realized he had been drinking too rapidly. For an instant he felt he was going to be sick. The unnatural redness drained from his face, which was suddenly more waxen than usual. His loose bottom lip trembled.

'Well, it would have prints on it, wouldn't it. I mean . . . why not?'

'They were your prints, sonny boy. I want to know why the alarm wasn't pushed by Mike, or by you. Or was it pushed by Mike but didn't go off? I want to know why your prints were all over that box, sonny boy.'

'Hell . . . I mean, we clean the joint, don't we? I always turned it off while we cleaned the floor. Mike didn't clean the floor, did he? That was one of my jobs and I always turned the alarm off when I did it, then turned it on again when the job was done, didn't I?'

'I hope so. And the alarm was switched on during the raid?'

'The alarm was switched on during the raid. I told you . . .'

His voice trailed away as he took another gulp of wine.

'I got to tell you, sonny. I don't think my buddy's going

to buy that. Are you, sergeant?'

The sergeant grunted.

'Now here's what he thinks,' the lieutenant continued. 'He doesn't claim to be the brightest cop in the world, but he thinks the alarm didn't go off because you switched it off, then you switched it on again after Mike was wiped out. Then your buddies gave you a gentle knock on the head to make things look good and marched off with the loot.'

Gallagher made as if to leap to his feet, but remained seated.

'Look, that's dumb. I want a lawyer. This isn't fair. After all I've been through . . .'

He let the glass fall to the floor and lowered his head into his hands.

'Why are you putting me through all this?' His voice wavered. 'You've got to be kidding if you think I had anything to do with it. Shit, the bastards might have killed me. If they'd been trying to make it look good they needn't have made it look this good.'

He pointed to his bandaged head.

'They could have killed me. I told you the way it happened. Me and Mike never had a chance to press that alarm. I didn't dare push the alarm. They'd have shot him if I'd done it. After they'd killed him, well . . . I don't know. Things just happened so fast. I just didn't think. You don't know what it's like to see your buddy . . .'

He choked on a sob. He wondered if he were acting brilliantly, or simply scared witless.

'Well, look. I'll talk to my buddy and see what he thinks. I don't know what to think. One more thing. Did you read about the murder of the ambassador?'

'The ambassador . . . ?' Gallagher found the courage to look directly at the lieutenant. 'Sure, I read about it. What's that got to do with all this?'

'Oh, I don't know. I just wondered if you'd read about it.'

'Sure I read about it.'

'What was your job – to drive the getaway car?'

Gallagher looked at the lieutenant and the sergeant.

God, they were warm. Too damned warm.

'Back off, will you? I've had enough. Why can't you believe me? I've told you all I know.'

'Sure, sure. I guess that's it for now. You're not thinking of going anywhere for the next day or two, are you? Or is there another job lined up?'

'What's that supposed to mean? No, I'm not going anywhere. There's nowhere to go to. I just want to rest and get well.'

'Good. If you change your mind, let me know.'

The lieutenant placed his card on the table. At the door he turned on his heels.

'I'd stay by the phone if I were you, sonny boy. You might need help. You know, in a way you're a lucky guy. You're the only guy who's met these killers and lived to talk about it. But you're an unlucky guy, too. If you're telling the truth, that makes you a real danger to them, and they might want you out of the way. If you're not telling the truth, well, you've got me and my buddy on your tail. You know, sonny, you should have stayed in hospital. It might have been a lot safer in there.'

The lieutenant and sergeant stepped into the street. Gallagher began to close the door, but the lieutenant forced it wide open.

'By the way, sonny. How do you like rabbit pie?'

Gallagher spluttered. The significance of the question hit him like another blow to the head.

'Rabbit pie? What is all this? What . . . ?'

'Forget it. I just wondered if you liked rabbit pie. Maybe someone drops one off at the bar for you now and then.'

'What's that supposed to mean? Are you crazy or something?'

'Forget it. It doesn't matter. Stay by that phone. And go easy on the booze, sonny.'

At last they had gone. Gallagher pushed on the door with both hands.

In the police car the sergeant uttered his first words since he and the lieutenant had arrived at Gallagher's home.

'Think we should watch him, lieutenant?'

The lieutenant deftly swung the car around a corner and into the stream of traffic.

'Like a hawk. Put a watch on him for, say, a week. Right now, you and me are going to get a search warrant to hit that guy again. I think he'll crack into little pieces.'

Sarah Jane answered the phone, then held it out to Henrick. He heaved himself onto his good foot and hopped over to her.

'Yes?'

'Wayne? Thank Christ. The cops, Wayne. They're onto us.'

Gallagher had almost shouted. His voice was barely recognizable.

'For God's sake, cool it, Sean. The cops can't be onto us. Now let's hear it. Slowly.'

Gallagher stammered out the details of the visit by the lieutenant and the sergeant. Henrick made him repeat most of the questions and the answers he had given.

'Listen, Sean, and hear me good. The cops have got nothing. They might smell a rat, but they've got nothing. They don't have a clue about Earl, me, Sarah or Wanda. They know nothing. All you have to do is stick to your story and keep cool. Just sit it out on your sweet bony ass. Don't go anywhere. Not anywhere. And don't call any of us. Stay off the phone and on your ass and we'll be in touch when we need you.'

'But . . . I tell you, they know something.'

'Jesus, Sean, if they knew anything you'd be inside. Now get off the phone and sit it out, and don't ring again. If you blow it, Sean . . . '

'I know. I guess you're right. When will I hear from you?'

'Let's wait till the heat's off. Now get off the phone.'

'So long.'

Henrick slammed the receiver into its cradle.

'That bastard's going to blow it. I know he is.'

Sarah Jane had watched him anxiously throughout the conversation.

'What is it, Wayne? What's happened?'

'Oh, forget it. It'll be OK. The cops have just given Sean a roasting. It'll blow over. Let's go out and check those labs. While we're in Manhattan I'll see if the books I ordered have arrived.'

On leaving the hotel Sheehan decided to walk to the United Nations building, in which an office had been set aside for the Nuclear Regulatory Commission. He had neglected his doctor's advice to cut down on drinking and eating, and periodic stomach pains warned him that his ulcers were acting up.

The air was crisp and, for Manhattan, relatively fresh. He skirted Central Park and the towering skyscrapers on his left gave him the illusion of walking along the bottom of a massive cliff. Steam gushed from manhole covers in the roads as a Niagara of hot waste water from business offices and homes tumbled into the cold sewage system. Traffic hurtled through the columns of steam; cabs would be engulfed, then reappear, the drivers apparently unconcerned at being momentarily blinded.

On a platform above the main entrance to the UN headquarters a workman carried on the interminable cleaning of the countless windows. The walk had tired Sheehan and he paused to watch idly and allow his breathing to return to normal. He reflected sorrowfully on the deterioration of his condition since the days of the rigorous training he had undergone with the SAS.

He introduced himself to an assistant at the information desk and asked for Pete Stoddart to be told of his arrival. Stoddart had been appointed chairman of the NRC after an adventurous career with the CIA. He and Sheehan had become friends in Angola during the mid-1970s when both had been involved in a covert mission to inhibit the recruitment of Cuban mercenaries. Since the Nixon debacle and exposure of questionable CIA involvement in foreign affairs, Stoddart and his colleagues had found their freedom to act severely curtailed. Sheehan and the SAS suffered no such inhibitions. When the two men had stumbled on a plot led by a Cuban recruiting agent to assassinate a moderate Angolan military leader, Stoddart found his hands tied and Sheehan seized the initiative. The Cuban was kidnapped, drugged and regained consciousness to find himself on a slow cargo vessel to Argentina. Stories were planted with the media to the effect that he had turned tail and deserted his compatriots. Stoddart had conceded that Sheehan's action had been just as effective, and more humane, than traditional CIA methods of eliminating such activists.

The information desk assistant spoke briefly into a phone and directed Sheehan to a lift. He rode to the fourth floor and the doors opened to reveal the tall, grinning figure of Stoddart. The face was still handsome, though not as nature had intended it to be. A blue-tinged scar ran above the right eyebrow and a broken tooth was capped with gold. The numerous lines that creased the sun-parched skin had been sculpted by hard living, eighteen months of deprivation and torture in a Vietnamese prisoner-of-war camp and an irrepressible sense of fun. His wiry, dark hair ran rampant over his forehead. He wore a neat grey suit, but the garish tie gave a hint of his flamboyance.

'How goes it, Ken?'

Sheehan was enveloped by the American's massive arms and crushed in an exuberant greeting.

'I'm fine, unless you've just broken a few ribs.'

Stoddart responded by loudly slapping the Englishman on the back.

'It's great to see you, Ken. How's the little woman?'

'Terrific. Nags a lot and screws a little, but I'm not complaining. How's yours?'

'Mine? No one told you, then. She's gone off with a banker who promised to spend every evening at home.'

'I'm sorry.'

Sheehan shrugged apologetically.

'Forget it. It was great while it lasted. Anyway, Manhattan's fantastic for broads. I'm not doing too badly.'

Stoddart's grin returned and he entered his office. He took a bottle of bourbon and two glasses from a cabinet.

'I haven't had time to make this place look like home, but we've got the basic essentials of life.'

He filled both glasses, handed one to Sheehan and toasted, 'Here's to the old SS team – Stoddart and Sheehan.'

'Cheers. And here's death to my ulcers.'

'You worry too much. And I hear you're trying to worry everyone else, too.'

'That ruckus in Vienna was just the opening shot. I hope I can count on your backup at the UN meeting. Security of nuclear materials is lousy, and you know it.'

'I sure do. Of course I'm with you. Frankly, I'm glad you're calling the shots. Politically, things are a bit sensitive here. At least the old Atomic Energy Commission guys had control of the whole works, even if they did balls it up. Now the NRC and this bloody Energy Research and Development Administration are constantly at each other's throats over who does what.'

Sheehan was aware of controversy over the division of responsibility between the two groups, formed following the breakup of the AEC. The issue was complicated by overlaps. ERDA had been given the job of devising safeguards for military or classified programmes. The NRC was responsible for security at nuclear installations operated by private industry. The two bodies were far from agreement on what safeguards were necessary in their respective areas, and on what should be classified and what should not. Further clashes arose because ERDA had to negotiate safeguards agreements with other countries, and the NRC was in charge of security within the United States.

'It's the old story,' Sheehan sympathized. 'While officialdom goes on with its ponderous squabbling, we're wide open.'

He accepted another bourbon. The ulcers were taking a rest.

A secretary entered and dropped a typed memo into Stoddart's in-tray. He glanced at it and despairingly shook his head.

'The latest brainwave. Congress seems determined to sell a nuclear reactor apiece to Israel and Egypt. Christ knows where this madness is going to end.'

'In Armageddon. Each side will be racing to stockpile bombs and wipe out the other.'

'Why we don't provide one massive reactor between them, place it in the Sinai and let equal numbers of Israelis and Egyptians staff it, God knows. Try suggesting that to anyone around here.'

'I admit I'm more worried about problems nearer home. Thanks for agreeing to help.'

'No problem. I'll talk to one or two other people, too. You're not fighting alone.'

Sheehan rejected another bourbon.

'No thanks. I've got to do more lobbying. Perhaps if you could get over to the hotel for dinner tonight . . . '

'Done. A pleasure.'

'More so than you think. I've got a secretary who'll knock your eyeballs out. Just keep your hands off.'

Sheehan took a cab to the USSR Purchasing Commission. The bourbon had anaesthetized his resolve to exercise more frequently.

An official in his early twenties examined Sheehan's identification papers.

'I'd like to see Karl Vorishilov.'

'One moment, please.'

The official vanished through a rear door and left Sheehan to speculate how many hidden guards had him in view. The official returned, directed Sheehan to an upstairs office and opened the door. Vorishilov rose smilingly.

'Welcome.'

'Hello, Karl. It must be years . . . '

Vorishilov was no taller than Sheehan, but trimmer around the middle. Though greying at the temples he had worn well. His immaculate pinstriped suit contrasted starkly with Sheehan's crumpled raincoat.

The handshakes over, Vorishilov produced the inevitable vodka. Sheehan guiltily eyed the bottle. Whenever he had to choose between what he enjoyed and what was good for his ulcers, the ulcers usually lost out. Vorishilov studied the long grass stem placed inside the bottle to indicate the purity of the vodka.

'The grass thrives, so the vodka is good,' he explained. He grinned and added, 'If the grass dissolves, the vodka is very, very good.'

The two men had met a dozen or so times during the last twenty years, usually in some unlikely corner of the globe. While in the SAS Sheehan won Vorishilov's grudging respect by detecting the infiltration of a Russian agent into his unit. For months the agent was fed with false information about the activities of the SAS. By the time the Russians realized the agent had failed in his mission, Sheehan had ordered his arrest. Like Sheehan, Vorishilov continued to appear periodically at many of the world's trouble spots. They had met in Korea, Vietnam and Egypt and at various diplomatic conferences. Sheehan was well aware that Vorishilov's influence extended far beyond the upper echelons of the USSR Purchasing Commission.

'I hope I can take your vodka as well as the grass can. Salud.'

'Cheers,' the Russian answered.

Newspaper clippings covered Vorishilov's desk. Sheehan's eyes rested on a headline, "Rabbit's blood clue in riddle of crazed assassin".

'I see you're catching up on current events, Karl.'

The Russian laughed, shuffled the clippings together and returned them to a folder. His attention had been drawn to newspaper reports linking the murder of the bartender at Mike's Place with the assassination of the ambassador. The 'workers' list' entry on the youth who had approached the commission after the ambassador's death would have to be revised.

'Like your people do, we file information on all sorts of happenings. Most of it's useless. But I'm sure this isn't a social call.'

'No, Karl. I want your support at the UN. We've got to stop the risk of nuclear materials falling into the wrong hands.'

The Russian frowned.

'The dangers are not so much of it "falling" into the wrong hands. Your friends seem to be inviting people to come along and help themselves.'

'I couldn't agree more. So are you with me?'

The Russian rested his elbows on the desk and held his glass in both hands.

'Up to a point, perhaps. I've read the report from our delegate in Vienna of your recent meeting, and I must say I agree with your conclusions. But frankly, and I'm sure I can rely on your discretion, if our American friends wish to make themselves look foolish, it might not be in our best interests to prevent them.'

Sheehan angrily finished his drink.

'For God's sake, Karl. While we're all battling for position it's mankind who's in danger of going under. If a bomb can be made covertly here, or in Britain, or India or wherever, it's as likely to be set off in Moscow as anywhere else. The bloody things don't have to be as big as a house, you know.'

The Russian smiled patiently.

'Be assured that Moscow is secure, but I will converse with my colleagues. We ourselves have been very concerned lately about the activities of various terrorist organizations. These people are no longer the pawns of political groups. They're getting out of hand. If such people should exploit the lack of security here . . . '

'Exactly, Karl. Terrorism is just about the only fashionable growth industry these days. We're no longer looking for a guy with a banner or a Che Guevara hat. We don't know who the hell we're looking for. A terrorist is any crack-pot who can get his hands on a weapon. The only way we can keep them down is to keep the weapons from them. For God's sake, back me, Karl. Or at least, don't rock the boat.'

'Perhaps. Perhaps. I can say no more.'

Sheehan angrily ran a hand through his hair.

'Damn you, Karl. Damn everybody. I'll see you around.'

As the Russian rose Sheehan added, 'No, I'll see myself out. I'd hate to be under obligation.'

'Ken . . . '

Sheehan didn't wait to hear what the Russian intended to say.

Denning and Wanda drove with only sporadic comments for more than two hours until they reached a forest-lined roadway running west through New Jersey. Denning pulled onto the shoulder, removed the hutch from the car and carried it a short way into the forest. Placing the hutch on the ground, he lifted the roof. The smaller ferret instantly leapt over the side of the hutch and with a rapid snake-like rhythm writhed over the undergrowth. The larger ferret stood on its hind legs and sniffed the air. Denning stroked its back.

'Good hunting, old buddy,' he murmured.

As he stood upright the ferret scampered off.

Without bothering to return the roof of the hutch Denning walked back to the car.

His next stop was several hundred yards beyond a small town. He wandered to a used car lot and pointed to a pale blue two-seater Dodge pickup truck as a salesman approached. The two haggled for some five minutes before Denning counted out eight hundred dollars in used notes. In an office at the rear of the lot he signed the registration slip. The salesman handed over a set of keys and a wad of papers, and Denning was on his way.

He tooted as he passed the spot where the green Chevy

was parked. Wanda moved behind the steering wheel, followed him for a further five miles west and into a multistorey car park. On the fifth floor Denning transferred their belongings to the truck and drove away, abandoning the Chevy.

'With luck it'll be weeks before anyone gets too curious about the car,' he said. 'And by then we'll be miles away. Washington, here we come.'

Sheehan called in at the hotel restaurant and ordered a light salad and a bottle of Nuits St George. The wine improved his temper and compensated for the frugality of the lunch. He signed the tab and took the lift to his suite. He was surprised to find Sheila at the desk. The room smelled pleasantly of her perfume.

'Hi. I thought you might be seeing the sights by now. A nice girl like you shouldn't be locked up in a dump like this.'

'I've been busy. I wasn't expecting you back so soon.'

She smiled and pointed to a stack of folders on the desk.

'Security reports, documents from the meeting in Vienna, preliminary draft address for the UN, receipts . . . they're all filed in order for you to check through.'

'You're a sensation.'

'I know.'

'How did I ever manage without you?'

'The papers were in these sandwich boxes. What do you want me to do with them?'

Sheehan chuckled as he thought of his wife's futile attempt to help.

'I'll take them home to the little woman. She stores odds and ends in them.'

Sheila returned the boxes to a suitcase.

'What kind of morning was it?'

'Terrible. Those bloody Russians . . . everyone's sitting on their backsides while the whole world goes to pieces. I feel like packing in the whole bloody works.'

Sheila tactfully busied herself with a blank piece of paper

on the desk.

'Get my wife on the phone, will you?'

He had suddenly remembered that he hadn't called the little woman to let her know he had arrived safely. She would have been expecting a call.

'Ken?'

'Yes. Hi.'

'How is everything?'

'Lousy. The Russians . . . '

'I called the plumber about the toilet. He can't come until next week.'

'Fine. It's going to be tough here. The . . . '

'Tibs misses you,' she interrupted.

Great. So the cat missed him. This conversation was going to be a big morale-booster. He decided to wrap it up.

'So everything's all right at your end?' she was asking.

'Yes, everything's terrific. Bye. I'll be in touch.'

'Bye.'

He turned to Sheila.

'If anyone wants me I'll be in the downstairs bar – or maybe the Hudson River.'

8

Henrick's first call in Manhattan was to the store from which he had ordered the technical manuals. The same assistant was on duty and looked up from a batch of receipts as Henrick and Sarah Jane entered.

'Columbia University,' Henrick said. 'I ordered some books.'

'Oh, yes.'

A smile of recognition flashed across the assistant's face.

'You're the guy who's going to blow us all up.'

Henrick and Sarah Jane laughed at the joke.

'The stuff's all here,' the assistant added.

He hauled a cardboard box from beneath the counter and began to check off the titles listed on a label attached to it.

'*The Los Alamos Primer, Manhattan District History,* etc., *Plutonium Handbook* and *Reactor Handbook* . . . that's two hundred and ten dollars and fifty-six cents, less the fifty-dollar deposit. I'll settle for one-sixty.'

Henrick counted out the notes.

'Sure you don't want me to deliver? That's one hell of a parcel.'

Henrick had been surprised at the size of the box. The two handbooks were among the fattest books he had seen.

'No, it's OK, thanks. We'll manage.'

He felt less certain when he lifted the box.

'If you're sure then,' the assistant added.

He walked around the counter and held open the door. Henrick limped outside with the box, followed by Sarah

Jane.

'Happy reading,' the assistant called. 'Don't stay up all night.'

Laughing, he returned to the store.

Henrick hailed a cab, dumped the box of books on the floor and gave the address of his parents' home in the Bowery. As the driver pulled away Henrick leaned forward to shout above the noise of the traffic.

'I want to drop off this parcel, then you can bring us back to Manhattan.'

'Sure thing. You're paying.'

Henrick asked the driver to stop a few doors away from his parents' house and limped to the front passenger door.

'I'd appreciate help with the parcel. I've got a bad leg.'

'Sure thing.'

Henrick placed the key in the lock as quietly as he could, hoping not to disturb his parents. The shop bell clattered loudly. The driver followed him into the room and placed the box out of sight behind what had been the shop counter. Henrick cursed softly as the shop bell tinkled again when he closed the door on leaving.

'Used to be a shop,' he explained to the driver.

'Yeah. What did you call it? Bloomingdale's?'

Henrick ignored the joke.

'Let's go, I don't want to bother my folks.'

He directed the driver to the address of the first laboratory on the list Sarah Jane had drawn up. He paid off the cab when they arrived.

Sarah Jane followed Henrick into a brightly lit salesroom. A counter, heaped with catalogues, ran the length of the room. Henrick chose one at random and flipped through. He whistled softly. Everything was there . . . glove boxes . . . furnaces . . . the lot. He decided to order no more than one item from any laboratory so as not to arouse more suspicion than might be necessary.

'Can I help?'

Henrick was delighted that the assistant was a bored-looking girl in her early twenties. She didn't give the impression of being the inquisitive type.

'Er . . . Columbia University. We're replacing some of our equipment. This glove box.'

Henrick pointed to a drawing in the catalogue.

'Certainly, sir.'

The girl went through a door at the rear of the salesroom. She returned with an older man.

'You want a glove box?'

Henrick silently cursed his luck. This was almost certainly one of the senior assistants. He was obviously curious.

'That's right. Just a small one. Columbia University. The one we have isn't big enough and we're going into radio-activity in a big way.'

'Which one was it you wanted?'

Henrick showed him the same drawing he had pointed out to the girl.

'That's a good choice. Portable, and easy to assemble. Fourteen hundred and ninety-five.'

'That'll be fine.'

'Very good, sir. It'll take about a week. We'll have to order from our depot.'

'OK.'

The assistant opened an order book.

'Name?'

Henrick hesitated for an instant, then gave the name of his university physics professor.

'Address?'

'The University, of course.'

'Account?'

'No, we don't have an account. I'm authorized to pay a five-hundred dollar deposit and the balance when we collect.'

'We normally like to deliver this sort of equipment, professor. We like to make sure we know where it's going, you know.'

'Certainly. Cash on delivery, then.'

'Yes, sir.'

Henrick obtained a receipt for the five hundred dollars and followed the assistant to the door.

'About a week, then?'

'Yes, sir. Thanks for the order.'

'I'll call you to arrange delivery.'

When the door closed behind Henrick and Sarah Jane the assistant searched the Manhattan directory for the number of Columbia University. He dialled and let the phone ring for almost a minute. There was no reply. He was about to dial a second time when another customer entered. The assistant made a mental note to try the call later.

On leaving the salesroom Henrick hauled Sarah Jane into the nearest bar and ordered two beers.

'That bastard smells something,' he said.

'I know, Wayne. And he said they'd deliver to the university. How can we get round that? And you paid him five hundred bucks.'

The experience had robbed Sarah Jane of her poise. A frown creased her forehead.

'I'll think of something. In fact, I think I already have. Don't worry your pretty little head. Let's get to address number two.'

They finished the beers and hailed another cab. The salesroom was another impersonal, plainly furnished room with catalogues placed at strategic intervals. Henrick checked the indexes and turned to 'furnaces'. He found what he was looking for and approached the counter.

'This furnace. It's reliable?'

'Certainly, sir. Those maximum temperatures are guaranteed.'

'I'd like one, please.'

'Yes, sir.'

The salesman began to fill out a sales slip.

'Name, sir?'

'Columbia University. We're replacing some equipment.'

Henrick had no intention of offering any identity if none was requested.

'Oh, I see. When would like us to deliver?'

'We'll collect.'

The salesman looked up hurriedly from the sales slip. 'That's a bit unusual with this stuff. Delivery's no problem, sir.'

'I'm sure, but the university's closed for vacation. I'll send our van round so I can be sure I won't have to spend a whole day waiting for your boys to turn up. I want to get the furnace set up before the new semester.'

Sarah Jane gave the salesman her most dazzling smile.

'I'll be paying cash,' Henrick added.

'That will be fine, sir. In that case you can collect, say, any time after three days. If you're sure you don't want us to . . . '

'No, no. We'll collect. I'll give you a call before our van sets off.'

Henrick handed over a hundred-dollar deposit and agreed to pay the balance of four hundred and twenty-nine on collection.

The purchase of the Geiger counter went without incident. Again Henrick explained that he represented Columbia University. He handed over the cash price of a hundred and forty-four dollars while the salesman wrapped the parcel.

Henrick then took Sarah Jane to a clothing store. She watched, puzzled, while he bought two full-length white coats similar to those worn by laboratory assistants. He simply grinned in answer to her look.

Once again he caught a cab to his parents' home, collected the books and loaded them and the Geiger counter into the green two-seater van which he had left at his father's garage.

Henrick rejected his mother's offer of a meal and set off for Sarah Jane's home in Queens.

'Things didn't go exactly without a hitch, did they Wayne?'

He reassuringly patted her knee as he drove off.

'Things went fine. There's nothing to worry about. Believe me, it's all going great.'

9

For the second time within hours Gallagher was confronted by the lieutenant and sergeant.

'What now?'

'We've got a search warrant. My buddy and me want to take a look around.'

The lieutenant waved the document underneath Gallagher's face.

'My buddy thinks the money's here,' the lieutenant added.

Gallagher was surprised to find that he felt composed. He wondered if there was a sort of panic peak, beyond which the human mind returned to normal. Or perhaps his courage came from the white wine which he had continued to drink throughout the day. He was now half way through his third bottle.

'If you find any cash, let's split it three ways. I'm going to want more wine.'

The policeman stepped past Gallagher and began to search the living room. Gallagher slumped into a seat and surrendered himself to the indignity of the experience. He hadn't felt so degraded since the time at school when he had been told to strip for a medical examination.

'You're wasting your time, you and your sergeant. There's no money here because I haven't done anything. Perhaps after this you'll believe me.'

The search of the room over, the sergeant looked at the lieutenant.

'You take the rest of the house,' the lieutenant said.

'I'll have a word with the wino here.'

The sergeant turned into a nearby bedroom. The lieutenant picked up the half-empty wine bottle from the floor, walked across to Gallagher and filled his glass.

'See how nice I can be,' the lieutenant added. 'Why don't you tell the whole story and I'll be even nicer?'

'You're really slow on the uptake, aren't you? I've told you the way it was. Get on with your search, then get out.'

Henrick's advice had been sound, Gallagher reassured himself. All he had to do was remain cool and stick to his story. These cops were just fishing.

'Now let's not get too fresh, sonny boy. Overdo it and I'll put that wine glass where it'll take a surgeon a month to find it.'

'Look, lieutenant, I'm glad you're here. I really am. You didn't have to get a search warrant. I'd have let you do the place over without one. I just want you to check out all the angles and then get on with the business of catching whoever killed Mike. The sooner you believe me, the sooner you can get some real detective work done.'

Gallagher could tell from the silence that followed that his pleading had made some impression. This time the lieutenant wasn't keeping silent in the hope of trapping him into saying something incriminating – this wasn't his little gimmick. He simply didn't know what to say.

'Lieutenant.'

The sergeant had called from Gallagher's bedroom. The lieutenant smiled as Gallagher flinched.

'So you've got nothing to hide? I wonder what my buddy's found.'

The lieutenant joined the sergeant and left Gallagher to speculate about what had caught the sergeant's interest. Both policemen returned to the living room, the lieutenant holding Gallagher's walkie-talkie. Gallagher laughed with relief.

'What do you use this for?'

'Come on, lieutenant. I've had that thing since I was a kid. So I've got a walkie-talkie. You can buy them anywhere.'

'They're also pretty useful for anyone involved in crime. This is an expensive one, too.'

'Look, my parents bought me expensive presents to make up for bringing me up in this crummy dump. That walkie-talkie doesn't mean a thing. Why don't you stop wasting your time and get on the trail of the bastards who killed Mike?'

'What's the range of this thing?'

'Maybe two miles. Yes, I'd say two miles. But what the hell . . . ?'

'Is this all we've found, sergeant?'

'I guess so. Nothing else but a heap of tapes.'

The lieutenant placed the walkie-talkie on the table and shrugged. Gallagher flung open the door.

'I guess you'll be on your way, then. No hard feelings, lieutenant. Good luck.'

'We're not relying on luck, sonny. I think we'll meet again.'

In the police car both officers remained thoughtful for a while.

'Sergeant, what do you think?'

'I don't know, lieutenant. I just don't know. Do we keep the heat on?'

'Yes. I think that snivelling bastard's as guilty as hell.'

10

Denning and Wanda reached the outskirts of Washington after driving through the night. They had shared the driving, and each had slept for about five hours. Wanda now dozed fitfully in the passenger seat.

'This is it, babe. Washington, DC. Idiot centre of the universe.'

She awoke as Denning drove over the mud-brown Potomac and headed for the city centre. This was her first visit to the capital. Though movies had given her some idea of what to expect, she was surprised at the vastness and openness of the administrative area.

Denning pointed out some of the sights.

'The Washington Monument . . . he was such a clever bloody liar he convinced everyone he was honest; the Jefferson Memorial . . . amateur musician, astronomer, inventor and professional capitalist – the first of the stinking breed; Arlington Cemetery . . . home of the only good Kennedys – the dead ones.'

The pristine whiteness of the administrative buildings gave way to the drab, pollution-soiled stonework of a seamy residential area. This was a part of Washington avoided by tourist coaches. None of the ethnic groups had yet claimed it as their ghetto. Even to the very poor, this squalid area was not worth fighting too hard for.

Denning pulled up the Dodge in front of a news-stand and bought several newspapers. When he returned to the car he kept one and handed the rest to Wanda.

'Apartments to let,' he said. 'Let's see what we can find.

I want a basement and garage. I'd rather not have windows peeping in on us. And ignore realtors. They're too damned nosey.'

They had soon marked off more than half a dozen addresses. Denning chose a particularly likely prospect and asked for directions. The address he had chosen was no more than several blocks away.

The house seemed to have begun as a skyscraper destined not to make it. Three nondescript storeys brooded above the street and ended abruptly in a flat roof, as though builders had abandoned the project in disgust at its ugliness. Metal railings around the basement gave it the gaiety of an ancient tomb.

A speaker fitted alongside the door crackled in answer to Denning's knock.

'Who is it?' a woman's voice asked.

'We've come about the rooms to let.'

'Come in. Top floor.'

The front door clicked as the locking mechanism was released by remote control. A blast of stale cooking smells escaped into the street. A fat woman, a naked boy no more than three years old clinging to her stained pinafore, met them at the top of the stairs. She smiled fleetingly and revealed a set of broken, discoloured teeth. Her eyes narrowed as though she had difficulty focusing on Denning and Wanda. She carried a thick-lensed pair of glasses in her hand. He noticed that one of the lenses was broken.

'Help yourself,' she said, handing over a key. 'Second floor or the ground floor basement.'

'We'll take a look.'

Though the second floor was reasonably furnished, Denning grunted disapprovingly.

'Only one way out, and that's down the stairs. And there's not enough room to work. I'm going to want the others over here at some stage. This is no good.'

The ground floor was more to his liking. A large living room led off to a bedroom, bathroom and kitchen. Patio doors in the kitchen provided an exit to the rear. The basement was a large, undecorated room covering the ground area of the entire house.

Wanda sniffed the musty air.

The fat woman had waddled down the stairway. The child yelled on the top landing.

'You the agent?' Denning asked.

'Yes.'

'Garage?'

'There's one at the back. It's never used.'

'We'll take the ground floor, basement and garage.'

'That's a hundred a month.'

'I'll give you three hundred – three months in advance. And nobody, but nobody, enters our part of the house. We'll move in now.'

Denning peeled off six fifty-dollar notes and handed them to her. She held them only inches from her eyes as she counted.

'Well, first I'll need to make enquiries.'

'Honey, you wouldn't know where to make enquiries. We move in now and we'll sign the lease when you've got it ready.'

Denning held forward an extra twenty-dollar note. It was smothered by the woman's podgy hand.

'If you want to see me, leave a note in the mailbox,' Denning said. 'I don't want to be disturbed.'

'I hope you enjoy . . . '

'Do shut up, woman. Let's have none of that crap.'

He pushed Wanda into the living room and locked the door behind him.

'So, home sweet home. Reckon you can make this place habitable?'

'I suppose so.'

Wanda ran a fingertip through the dust on the table.

'Well, carry on. I've got to do some shopping. Lock the door after me. And stay in until I get back.'

Denning parked the Dodge in the garage at the rear of the

house and waved down a cab.

'H Street,' he ordered. 'Number 1717.'

The Nuclear Regulatory Commission had inherited the old Atomic Energy Commission offices to which Denning had directed the driver. The letters 'AEC' outside the building had been replaced by 'NRC', but otherwise the premises were much the same as they had been before. The reading room was still a mine of information, all available to the public since Congress had approved the Atomic Energy Act.

'I'm a journalist working on background for the UN meeting.'

Denning flashed his wallet to the girl receptionist. She didn't bother to look at it.

'I'd like what you've got on this place.'

He passed her a slip of paper on which he had written the address of a nuclear fuel storage plant about fifty miles north of Washington.

'Ground plan, capacity, security . . . all that dope.'

'Sure. Take a seat.'

Within minutes she returned, her arms laden with files.

'It's all here somewhere. If you'd like to browse through . . .'

'Thanks.'

Denning was rewarded with a detailed ground plan of the plant. Two fences were marked. A recent entry showed that the number of guards on duty around the clock had been increased from two to four. Another folder gave information about deliveries of reprocessed fuel. Denning found enough information about material flow to calculate with some accuracy the probable quality and frequency of the deliveries.

Denning, busy taking notes, was startled when the assistant reappeared at his shoulder. Guiltily he turned over the page on which he had been writing.

'What is it?'

'You seem to be doing a lot of writing. I thought perhaps you didn't know . . .'

'Didn't know what?'

His muscles tensed. He clenched his fists. The pencil,

forgotten as it rested in his right hand, snapped. Surely the girl wasn't spying on him.

'The Xerox,' she explained, a puzzled smile on her face. 'It's over there.'

He followed her pointing finger to the photocopying machine.

'You can make as many copies as you want for ten cents a time,' she added. 'It would save you all that writing.'

'Of course.' Denning laughed. 'I'm sorry. I was concentrating on what I was doing. Thanks.'

The girl returned to her desk. Denning took the files to the Xerox machine.

For four dollars and ten cents he collected all the information he needed to prepare his plan for robbing the plant.

On his way back to the flat Denning called in at a camera shop and studied a display of binoculars. A salesman praised a Zeiss set that Denning seemed to admire.

'Are these the best you've got?' Denning asked.

'No, not exactly. But they're . . . '

'Let me see the best you've got.'

'Certainly.'

The salesman drew another set of binoculars from the glass showcase.

'These are excellent. They . . . '

'They're the best you have?'

'Yes. They can also be used at night. They . . . '

'How much?'

'Well, they're expensive. Three hundred and forty.'

'I'll take them.'

Wanda was asleep on the one double bed in the flat when Denning returned. He decided not to waken her, closed the bedroom door and backed into the living room. Stimulated by the success of his expedition, he stripped to his pants and began a strenuous physical workout. After fifty push-ups he ran on the spot for five minutes. The thudding of his feet on the floor awoke Wanda and she stole to the bedroom door. She opened it an inch or two and watched surreptitiously as he lay on his back, supporting his weight on his shoulders and pedalled furiously in the air. Finally he went to the bathroom and she heard the shower being turned on.

That brute, she thought, has one hell of a physique.

He re-emerged with a towel around his waist. Wanda was rolling cigarettes.

'The grass can wait,' he said sternly. 'We've got work to do. I want us to find a campsite.'

'Today?'

'You bet your sweet ass it's today, honey. Things are moving. Is the camping gear still in the truck?'

'Yes.'

'Great. The keys are in my jeans. Bring it to the front. I'll be waiting.'

Wanda drove while Denning gave way to one of his zany moods. Suddenly he would let out a wild cowboy whoop to the consternation of passers-by, and Wanda. Once he pointed to a passing motorist and shouted, 'We're gong to bomb you, baby. We're going to bomb you.' The motorist, unable to hear, grinned. Denning collapsed into a fit of hysterical laughter.

To Wanda's repeated requests for information about their destination he would only say. 'Keep heading north, baby. Just head north.'

He consulted a map after she had been driving for about an hour and directed her down an approach road to a camping ground. A hoarding at the entrance advertised sites with electricity and running water for a dollar a night. He handed seven dollars to a young boy at the reception hut.

'We may stay longer. I'll let you know.'

The camping ground faced west toward a breathtaking view of rolling hills and intermittent small lakes, but Denning led Wanda to the most easterly site. The view was less attractive than from elsewhere, but the site was the most isolated of all.

'Get some grub, will you, honey? I'll set up house.'

Soon the three-man tent was up, mattresses inflated and Wanda was serving two large helpings of frankfurters and beans bought from a shop on the camping ground. Water bubbled in a pan on Denning's portable stove.

'We'll leave the dishes,' he said, switching off the stove. 'We've only got a couple of hours before sunset.'

'OK, I'm ready. Am I permitted to know where we're going?'

'Sure, honey.' He smiled. 'We're going hunting for some plutonium.'

He slung his binoculars around his neck and handed a sketch pad and pencil to Wanda.

'Hang on to these. You're going to be artist of the outfit.'

He strode off at a scorching pace toward the north-east, where a wood vanished over the horizon of a small hill. Wanda was thankful that he cleared some sort of path through the wood.

Over the hill the wood swung south. A weird conglomeration of buildings a mile or so further east swept into view. Denning raised the binoculars to his eyes.

'Here she is, baby. This is the joint that's going to give us the plutonium. Check against this map and draw everything you see. Every strand of wire or whatever.'

Wanda's pulse quickened. She accepted the glasses and map from Denning. She adjusted the focus of the lenses and the fuel storage plant, surrounded by two high wire fences, leapt into view. The only road from the plant threaded through a small collection of houses three-quarters of a mile from the plant entrance and linked with a main highway.

'I'm going for a look-see around town,' Denning said.

He pointed to the same three hundred or so houses that Wanda had already seen through the glasses.

'I'll be about an hour. That should give you time to finish the sketch.'

He sped downhill and slowed to a walk when he was

within two hundred yards of the houses. On the main street were a general store, a post office and a bar. Denning called in for a beer. Behind the bar was a poster which announced, 'The end of the world is down the road.'

'That's good, that poster,' Denning said.

The bartender merely grunted in reply.

'Get many visitors here?'

'Not many. A few rubbernecks and garbage from the camping ground.'

Denning nodded to two customers seated in a corner away from the bar and crossed toward them.

'Sociable guy, our host, ain't he?'

The men grinned.

'There's only one bar around here and he knows it,' the older of the two answered.

Denning downed his beer.

'Can I get you guys a drink?'

Two glasses were raised and emptied in unison. Denning took all three to the bar and returned with refills.

'That plant over there . . . plenty of jobs, eh? Is that where you work?'

'It is.'

The older man was apparently going to be the spokesman.

'Brother, you're at the deadest hole on earth,' he added. 'Most of us just waste away here while we're stockpiling enough arms to blow the world to bits. The sooner they get on with the shooting match the better.'

Denning remained with the two locals for half an hour. By the time he left he knew that the morale, dedication and discipline of at least two of the plant's work force were at rock bottom.

He wandered boldly up the access road toward the plant. Nobody approached him. Suddenly, the road dipped and the fuel plant was out of sight. Denning slammed a fist into an open palm. This was more than he had dared to hope for. He ran foward for fifty yards before the plant came once more into view. Then he ran back and paced the area which was out of sight from the plant.

'Oh, beautiful,' he muttered. 'Jesus, this is beautiful.'

He checked the distances and, avoiding the town, ran across the hillside to rejoin Wanda. He was annoyed to find she had taken up another position a hundred yards below the wood.

'You should have stayed under cover,' he complained.

'Oh, I've only been admiring nature, haven't I? I had a much better view from here.'

'And they'd have a much better view of us, if they happened to be looking. Not that . . . '

Denning tensed on hearing the distant chattering of a helicopter. Wanda gasped in amazement as he leapt on top of her, thrust his knees between her legs and pulled up her skirt.

'What the . . . ?'

'Spotter patrol. Keep the binoculars and sketch pad between us. They might be taking pictures.'

Wanda laughed.

'And a fine picture this is going to make.'

The helicopter skirted the wood, returned beyond the point from which it had approached and, finally, could no longer be heard.

'Must have been a spotter patrol,' Denning said anxiously. 'I read about them at H Street.'

He moved as though to heave himself back to his feet. Wanda kissed him quickly on the lips.

'Don't overdo it,' he growled. 'This is just for the guy with the camera, remember?'

'He might come back . . . '

She laughed provocatively, fumbling for the zip of his jeans and pulled slowly. She thrust a hand through the opening and stroked the stiffening flesh.

'Come on, big boy. Let's see what you're made of.'

'Wanda . . . I . . . '

His protest was too late. Wanda removed her hand, arched her hips and removed her briefs with a slick, practiced movement. With her fingers she guided him inside.

'Let's make this look really good,' she said softly. 'Just in case the chopper comes back.'

Denning's head reeled as he thrust forward in a frenzy.

An hour later they walked back towards the wood. The sun had dipped below the horizon and moonlight glinted on the trees and the distant buildings of the fuel plant.

A new sound alerted Denning. This time it was the faint but unmistakeable growl of a heavy truck. Powerful headlights swept around a bend of the access road leading to tl storage plant. Denning snatched the glasses.

'Time?' he snapped.

'Eight forty-two.'

'Write that down.'

The truck's rear lights illuminated two lines of large red letters on the tailgate. Through the glasses Denning was able to make out the words:

DANGER
PLUTONIUM

He adjusted the glasses and was able to read the company name on the truck. From his enquiries at H Street he was confident that this truck was carrying twenty ten-litre bottles of partly reprocessed spent fuel, each bottle containing up to two-and-a-half kilograms of plutonium. If Henrick could convert the contents of those bottles to fully enriched weapons-grade material . . .

The lights of the truck vanished temporarily as it swung into the dip below the power plant. At the first fence the truck was halted by a guard with a rifle. A second armed guard stepped from a sentry box. The first guard examined papers handed to him by the driver. The second guard stepped toward the passenger door. It opened and the driver's companion walked to the rear of the vehicle, pulled open the doors and stood by as the second guard made a cursory examination of the truck's contents.

'These are the ten-litre bottles, all right,' Denning hissed.

The second guard followed the driver's companion as he returned to the cab. The large double doors in the fence opened and the truck inched forward. This area was guarded by alsatians. Again, the driver handed some papers to a guard at a sentry box; another guard accompanied the driver's companion to the rear and examined the cargo; the driver's companion returned to the cab and the truck was allowed to proceed.

A host of workmen swarmed around the truck as it backed toward a low, squat building which was obviously an unloading area.

The first of the ten-litre bottles was lifted from the truck and rolled into the storage building. Denning noticed that two men were able to carry the container without apparent discomfort.

Half an hour later the truck left the complex. Guards at the two outer checkpoints again examined inside the vehicle.

Wanda was dismayed by the seemingly foolproof security measures.

'Earl, it's going to be impossible. They have radio links, too . . . all sorts of electronic stuff. There's no way, Earl. No way.'

'Don't you believe it, honey.'

'But we'd need an army . . . '

'Rubbish. I think I've got an idea. We need to check out some more, but trust me.'

They followed the headlights of the truck as it returned from the access road to the main highway.

'Yeah,' Denning repeated. 'I think I know a way.'

Back at the campsite he lay subdued on a mattress. As Wanda undressed he was reminded of their lovemaking.

'Wanda . . . before . . . was it any good?'

The darkness hid her smile. She had found his Achilles' heel.

'I won't tell. Anyway, you weren't too bad. With practice . . .'

'I don't want to practice. I don't want any complications during this operation – for you or me.'

She drew a cigarette from her purse, placed it in her mouth and turned to face him. The flame of her lighter reflected on her smooth skin.

'Smoke?'

He shrugged his wide naked shoulders.

'Why not?'

Wanda lit the cigarette, sucked deeply and handed it to him.

The marijuana began to take hold. Denning laughed as she flapped her arms and hooted like an owl.

'I can fly . . . I can fly . . . I . . .'

She kneeled alongside him and slid her hand inside his sleeping bag.

'Come fly with me, lover boy.'

That night Wanda became the first woman with whom he had made love twice. Afterwards she grinned in the darkness. Her suspicion that Denning was not too hot in the love stakes had been confirmed.

11

The lieutenant angrily rechecked the report on Gallagher. An intensive three-day investigation had drawn a blank. He seemed to be a man without known contacts, political affiliations, police convictions or vices of any kind.

'I'm sorry,' the sergeant said, 'but that seems to be it. Not even a parking ticket. His teachers at Columbia say he kept very much to himself. They were all surprised when he dropped out. He hadn't discussed his plans with anybody. He wasn't a bad student, by all accounts.

'We also spoke to teachers who knew him in high school. Same story. He was just a plain, fairly bright, rather boring loner. Since he got the job at Mike's Place he seems to have been sleeping by day and working well into the night. His mother's a bit of a pain in the ass and he probably took a bar job to get out of her way.'

'And how's the watch going?'

'Well, we've only been keeping watch for three days. So far, nothing. He's been out once – to a liquor store.'

Throughout the rest of that week the sergeant's reports on the watch at Gallagher's home were no more promising. By the end of the seventh day Gallagher had been to the liquor store twice more and to the hospital once for a prearranged appointment. Meanwhile, the department had been hit with four new homicide investigations.

'I guess we call off the heat, lieutenant.'

'I guess so. Christ knows, the old NYPD does have other

problems. What do you really think of this creep, sergeant? I mean, in your gut. Do you think he's our man?'

'I don't know, lieutenant. I did, but he just could be telling the truth. He's got no spunk, that's for sure. Maybe he reacted badly because he's scared of cops, or because of the shock. I don't know. But if I was a psycho I wouldn't want him on my side.'

'I suppose it could add up either way. Damn, blast and shit. OK, sergeant. The heat's off.'

12

Henrick had spent an anxious week. He had immersed himself in problems of the bomb assembly, but was frequently distracted by concern over the purchase of the glove box and the furnace.

At last it was time to phone the labs. On his first call he asked for the salesman who was named on the sales slip.

'Columbia University. Is the glove box ready?'

'Oh, yes, professor. Yes, it's here. When would you like us to deliver?'

'I'll work something out and let you know.'

As the salesman hung up he remembered that he had meant to make a check call to the university. He checked the number and dialled.

'Columbia University.'

'Hello. I'm inquiring about one of your professors. He's professor . . . '

'Look, I'm just the caretaker here. The university's on vacation.'

'Of course. But you probably know the professor. He's Professor Ryan Fitzgerald. Physics.'

'Sorry, I'm not authorized to say nothing. He mightn't like it, might he?'

'But you do know him?'

'Course. Everybody does. But I'm saying nothing.'

'Oh, that's OK. You've told me all I need to know.'

The salesman turned to a girl assistant.

'Draw up the invoice for that glove box. Looks like we'll be delivering some time today.'

Henrick checked the second sales slip for the salesman's name and dialled.

'Columbia University. The furnace?'

'Yes, sir. It's here.'

'Our van will be along shortly. We'll pay the balance when we get there.'

'Very good, sir.'

Henrick whistled through his teeth.

'Sarah, baby, so far so good. Help me fasten these straps.'

She secured his artificial foot while he made another call, this time to Gallagher.

'Sean, how's it going?'

'Wayne? That you? Thank Christ. I feel like I've been buried alive.'

'Any more visits from the cops?'

'You bet.'

Gallagher told of the lieutenant's return with a search warrant.

'And since then?'

'All quiet. I think they cooled off when they found nothing.'

'Great. Get over here as fast as you can. I'm at Sarah Jane's. Oh, and bring your walkie-talkie. Sooner or later we're going to need that again.'

'OK. I'll leave a note for the old lady. When shall I tell her I'll be home?'

'Christ, do you have to tell her anything? Next thing you'll be asking her if we can set off the bomb.'

'I have to let her know something. She might tell the cops I've gone missing.'

'Tell her you're taking a vacation. A long one. You'll be in touch. Now get your ass over here.'

Henrick cut short Gallagher's effusive greeting.

'Put this on.'

Henrick flung one of the white full-length coats to Gallagher and slipped into the second coat. On the breast pocket of each Sarah Jane had embroidered the words, 'Columbia University.'

'Wayne, what's going on?' Gallagher asked. 'What's this all about?'

'We're just going to pick up some lab gear, that's all. Don't worry about a thing and leave the talking to me.'

Henrick handed Gallagher the keys to the van and lightly kissed Sarah Jane on the cheek.

'Have the basement cleared out by the time we get back, honey. Today we're going to set up the bomb factory.'

On reaching Manhattan, Henrick directed Gallagher to the first lab.

'Pull up here.'

'We'll get a ticket, Wayne. Sure as shit.'

'Just stay at the wheel. Talk your way out of trouble if any cop comes along. Say we're picking up some stuff and we'll be away in a flash. If you have to, drive around the block.'

Gallagher blanched as he realized what Henrick had in mind.'

'The plates, Wayne. The van's plates. They're a dead giveaway. The cops will know this is a private vehicle.'

'Oh, fuck . . . '

Henrick gripped his forehead. He was going to have trouble enough in persuading the lab to hand over the glove box. On the phone the salesman had again indicated that he expected to make delivery direct to the university.

'We have to chance it, Sean. Keep the engine running. And hope.'

Henrick was approached in the salesroom by the girl assistant he had met on his first visit. He gave the name of the salesman who had taken the order.

'I'm afraid he's at lunch.'

Henrick almost laughed with relief at such an unexpected

stroke of luck.

'No problem. We've got out van outside. I'd be grateful if you could get us loaded up before we get a ticket. Here's the rest of the money.'

'I thought we were going to deliver, sir.'

'That's right, but we changed all that on the phone.'

Henrick handed over the balance of nine hundred and ninety-five dollars, all secured with an elastic band, and his copy of the sales slip. The girl began to count.

'Look, honey. Can you get your guys to help with the loading while you do that? I did arrange all this on the phone, you know. Your boss's lunch break is going to get me a ticket.'

'Er . . . yes, sir. I'm sorry.'

She picked up a phone and summoned a workman from the rear of the building. Henrick intervened after she had explained what had to be done.

'Please hurry, buddy, will you?'

Henrick handed him five dollars.

'We want to get our van out of the way before we get a ticket.'

'Sure thing.'

The workman pocketed the five dollars and hurried to the rear of the room. In less than ten minutes the girl had counted the money and handed Henrick a receipt, the glove box was loaded into the van and Henrick and Gallagher were on their way.

At the second lab a salesman directed Henrick to a loading bay at the rear of the building. He returned to the van just as an advancing policeman approached within fifty yards of the vehicle. Henrick hurriedly gave directions to Gallagher and grinned at the policeman as they drove past. The salesman was waiting in the loading bay with a group of uniformed workmen. Henrick handed over the outstanding four hundred and twenty-nine dollars.

The salesman counted the money and nodded to two of

the workmen, who hauled a large cardboard box into the van.

Without waiting for a receipt, Henrick moved into the passenger seat and signalled to Gallagher to drive off. The salesman hurried with the receipt to the passenger window.

'You might need that for the taxman.'

'Buddy, you got something there,' Henrick said jovially. 'I just might at that.'

Gallagher drove back to Sarah Jane's without incident. She ran to the van as it pulled up outside and looked anxiously at Henrick. He raised both thumbs.

'No problems, honey. We're in business. Let's set up the workshop.'

13

Denning and Wanda had completed a week's vigil at the campsite. They had arranged sleeping hours to enable them to keep a twenty-four hour watch on the plant each day.

Two more trucks had arrived and the same procedure had been followed. One had been escorted by motorcycle outriders and an armoured car. Denning had guessed that this truck had contained enriched, weapons-grade material.

Only one truck had left the plant.

Denning joined Wanda at her lookout point beyond the wood.

'Another truck left an hour ago, Earl. Armoured car, motorcycles. These people are waking up. In the clippings it says a lot of this stuff used to go out by unescorted truck.'

'I know, I know. We're going to have to get a move on, but there's still time. Tonight I'll know if we're on the right track.

'Tonight? What happens then?'

'With luck . . . no, let's wait and see. I don't want to tempt fate. We'll know when it happens.'

At eight p.m. he and Wanda were keeping watch together on the edge of the wood. He alternately gripped each hand with the other and flexed his muscles.

'Relax, Earl. Relax. What are you waiting for?'

Without replying he reached for the glasses and looked toward the main highway.

At eight-thirty Wanda's eyes were still fixed on the highway.

'It was about this time last week, wasn't it?' she asked. 'You're expecting another truck to come.'

'Yes. If I'm wrong . . . forget it. From all that stuff I worked out at H Street I reckoned there should be three deliveries a week. Well, there were three deliveries last week, and now the new week starts today. I'm just hoping this guy keeps to the same timetable. If so, we're laughing.'

Denning leapt to his feet as headlights swept from the main highway down the access road to the fuel plant.

'The stupid, stupid bastards. What time is it?'

'Eight forty-one . . . forty-two, maybe.'

'Right on the button. The stupid bastards.'

The headlights vanished for several seconds as the truck dropped into the dip three-quarters of a mile before the plant entrance. The same security checks were carried out.

'I've seen enough. And I've had enough of life under canvas. Tonight we sleep in the apartment.'

Denning re-booked the site for another week before they left.

'We're going on a tour. Might be away a day or two, but keep an eye on the tent for us. Keep the change.'

The boy at the reception hut eagerly accepted the twenty dollars offered to him.

'Thanks. Thanks a lot. I'll keep an eye on your stuff. Yes, sir.'

On reaching the flat Denning left Wanda to prepare a meal while he set out in search of a phone. Some instinct made him hang up after asking for a collect call to Sarah Jane's. A reverse-charge call would be recorded. That might turn out to be an embarrassment. He dialled thc call direct and pumped a fistful of quarters into the box when Sarah Jane answered.

'Hi, lover. Get me Wayne.'

'Earl? Sure.'

An instant later Henrick was on the line.

'Earl? How's things?'

'Terrific. You first. Have you got the gear?'

'The big stuff, yes. I still need a couple of items, but they won't be any problem. Have you got the other stuff?'

'No, but I know how it can be done. First, I need everybody over here. This will have to be the base of operation.'

'But that's crazy, Earl. Crazy, man. I've got everything set up at Sarah's. Are you asking me to break this lot up, load it into the van and haul it all the way there? Suppose . . .'

'Cool it, Wayne. Are you asking me to bring the big stuff all the way there? Listen, when all hell breaks loose I want everyone together. And right now, I need help. And what's more, I've had further instructions. Surely to Christ I don't have to remind you that others are involved. There's a big reason for coming here, Wayne. A very big reason. So get over here fast and pick up the other bits you need on the way.'

Denning's formula of fact and fiction helped to decide the issue.

'OK. If that's the way it has to be. We'll take a detour to pick up the rest of the stuff, but we'll be there some time tomorrow morning.'

'Great. Come straight to the apartment. The address . . . No. On second thoughts I'll wait for you in the parking lot of the last McDonald's on the turnpike before the city centre. Be there between eleven and twelve. If there's any problem, ignore me.'

'Fine. See you soon.'

'For Christ's sake don't let anything go wrong.'

'I won't.'

'One more thing. Get yourself a three-man tent and sleeping bags.'

'You're kidding. I thought you said we'd got an apartment.'

'And so we have. Don't cross-examine me over the phone, Wayne. Just get the gear. I'll explain when I see you. So long.'

Sarah Jane and Gallagher were even less enthusiastic about going to Washington than Henrick had been. She preferred to operate on her own stage, where she was more familiar with the responses of the audience. She sensed, rightly, that in Washington she would be given a minor role. Gallagher typically, began to think of various problems, likely and unlikely, that might arise.

'What if we get stopped with all that stuff on board? What if . . . ?'

'Sean, you're wasting your time,' Henrick interrupted. 'Washington it has to be. Let's load the van now and get everything ready for the road. OK?'

Sarah Jane pursed her lips, raised her eyebrows and shrugged in a grand gesture of submission. Gallagher looked from one to the other.

'Suppose so . . . '

In the basement Henrick sighed at the thought of having to dismantle the superb laboratory he had built up.

'Do we still have all the packing?'

'Yes, I think so,' Sarah Jane said. 'The garbage men don't call until tomorrow. I'll go and get it.'

Gallagher wandered to the glove box and reverently touched the outer screen.

'I can't believe this is all happening to us, Wayne. We're really going to make that bomb, aren't we? It's really going to happen.'

'You bet your life it is. The world out there is going to hear about you and me, buddy.'

Sarah Jane returned with a cardboard box.

'It's all still here. If you could help, Sean . . . '

'Sure.'

Gallagher followed her from the basement as Henrick began to loosen a section of the glove box.

In less than an hour the equipment was loaded into the van.

'Great. Sarah, make some coffee. Sean, get the map out of the van. I'm going to rest this blasted foot.'

Henrick was eventually joined in the living room by the

other two. He accepted the map from Gallagher and spread it on the table.

'You'll drive, Sean. Me and Sarah will get some rest in the back of the van. If we're stopped, we're going on vacation. I'll have the automatic in case of emergencies.'

'I want you to drive here, Sean.'

Henrick indicated a group of small towns to the south-west, approximately half way between New York and Washington.

'This place is a warren of quarries, and that means explosives. I worked there once during a vacation and the stuff's just lying about asking to be ripped off. We're going to need quite a bit. We could buy it, but if we can get it free . . . If we can get there, say, around three in the morning, it should be a cinch.'

'You mean . . . we're going to load that van with explosives?'

Gallagher disbelievingly shook his head.

'You can't do that, Wayne. You can't.'

'For Christ's sake, the stuff's harmless. It's not going to go off just because you drive over a bump. I've worked with the stuff, Sean. I know what I'm doing.'

'I hope so.'

Henrick limped to the door.

'Come on,' he called. 'Let's hit the road.'

'Wayne. Wayne!'

Henrick groaned and shifted his position in the back of the van as he awoke. His artificial foot caught a corner of the package containing the glove box. The familiar stabbing pain shot from the stump to his scalp.

'What the . . . what is it?'

'I think we're here – where you said all the quarries are. We've just passed one.'

Henrick checked his watch. Four a.m.

'Pull over.'

When the van was stationary he painfully manoeuvred

himself onto the bench seat. Sarah Jane had also awoken and squeezed onto the seat between the two men.

'Drive on,' Henrick ordered. 'We're looking for a mobile work hut near any of these quarries. Preferably one that's unguarded. Just drive on the side lights.'

A half-mile down the road Gallagher slowed on approaching a likely hut. He accelerated as the van's side lights picked up the outline of an alsatian chained to the hut. A mile further along he cut the engine and coasted to a halt beside the gateway to another quarry. Beyond was a similar hut.

Henrick left the van and fumbled with a chain which tied both gates together. It was looped through the two gates and tied loosely. Soon the gates swung open. He held a torch against a window at the rear of the hut, then signalled to Gallagher to pull off the road. He drove behind the hut and switched off the side lights. A passing motorist would be unlikely to notice anything suspicious. Henrick was already busy with a penknife on the hut's door lock. In seconds the door creaked open.

'Stay in the van,' he called softly.

He re-emerged after several minutes.

'We've hit the jackpot. These places are so used to explosive they leave it lying around like candy. Give me a hand.'

Henrick had found not only a large store of explosive, but also a supply of detonators – enough of both to trigger off the nuclear explosion when the bomb was assembled. He recognized the trade name of the explosive as one he had worked with during his vacation job. It was extremely stable and could be worked easily with the fingers, no matter how hot or cold the hands might be. It was not likely to explode accidentally even if dropped on the floor. Henrick selected a large box packed with eight-ounce packages of the explosive and passed it to Gallagher.

The detonators were also ideal for the job. Again, Henrick recognized the brand name. The detonators contained a reliable fulminate in aluminium tubes an inch and a half long by a quarter of an inch in diameter. Henrick had calculated that he would need about two dozen. The box he selected contained a gross.

He limped back to the van as Gallagher closed the rear door.

'I'll drive, Sean. Take a rest.'

'Sure. Thanks.'

Gallagher stretched himself full length as comfortably as he could in the crowded rear of the van. Henrick coasted for a short way downhill, then turned the ignition key.

After driving for two hours Henrick pulled into a hamburger restaurant. Gallagher was given the job of bringing breakfast to the van. He picked his way with excessive care from the rear.

'I told you, Sean. That stuff's pretty stable. It's not going to blow up in your face, man.'

'Well, I don't know. I don't like it.'

Gallagher returned with hamburgers and coffee. As he struggled over the bench seat Henrick winked slyly at Sarah Jane.

'Watch that coffee, Sean. If you spill any you could blow us to bits.'

'Wha– . . . ?'

Henrick and Sarah Jane laughed. Gallagher reddened.

'If that's supposed to be funny . . . '

Henrick drained his coffee, tossed the plastic cup into the back of the van and teasingly mouthed the word, 'Boom'. With arms outstretched he drew the shape of a mushroom cloud.

'Funny, very funny,' Gallagher said with a scowl. 'Are you going to act the fool all day or do we move on?'

'In good time, Sean. We're also going to have to get more gear. By the way, can you re-tune your walkie-talkie?'

'Sure I can.'

'Well, do so. I want it tuned beyond the normal range of channels. That little set is going to explode the bomb. Keep well away from emergency and cab bands or we'll have the cops blowing us to smithereens.'

'No problem.'

'Also, we want to be two miles away when we send the signal. Is your set effective over that distance?'

'Provided the batteries are OK, just about.'

'Well, they'd better be OK. We'll stop at a shopping centre and you can pick up plenty of spares. At the same time pick up a roll of insulating tape and a length of wire for a radio antenna. We want that signal to get through loud and clear. Oh, and a soldering iron. I'm going to have to solder each connection.'

'No trouble. I can pick that lot up at any Radio Shack.'

'Fine. Then there's the timing device. We're not going to want to have to keep running back to the bomb to replace batteries once it's stashed, and we might need weeks to negotiate after the bargaining starts. To play safe, I'm going to put in a timing device that will bring the bomb live for just two hours a day, from, say, twelve till one. That means we'll only be able to set off the bomb between midday and one p.m., or midnight and one in the morning. It also means only a two-hour burn each day, so the batteries will last for months.

'Sarah, I want you to get me a watch called a Bulova Accutron. It's ideal for the job. It'll run for a year on a tiny transistor battery that fits into the back. It has a fancy movement without a tick, so we don't have to worry about the bomb being found with a listening device once it's hidden. I'll insert a simple make-and-break points system through the face and connect it to the rest of the mechanism. Clever, eh?'

He handed her a hundred-dollar note.

'Bulova what?'

'Accutron, darling.' He spelt it out. 'Don't come back with an alarm clock. I'll need a few other bits and pieces but I'll pick them up myself. Anyone think of anything else?'

'Yes. I need a pharmacist,' Sarah Jane said coyly. 'I need some more . . . You know.'

Henrick exploded into laughter.

'Just like a woman. "Go ahead and save the world, boys,

but first there's a delicate little matter . . . " Sarah, you're priceless.'

'I can't help it . . . '

Henrick was still laughing as he pulled onto the highway.

Henrick whistled the McDonald's TV jingle. The meeting place was in sight. As he parked the van he saw Denning and Wanda in the blue Dodge truck. Soon all five were boisterously exchanging greetings in the car park.

'Anyone want to eat?' Denning asked.

'Yes, but not another hamburger,' Henrick said. 'I'd sooner get to this pad you've rented.'

'Follow me.'

When they reached the house Denning waved Henrick into the garage.

'The Dodge is clean, but we'd better get your stuff off the road.'

'You bet. We'll haul everything indoors after dark, just in case you've got nosey neighbours.'

Henrick was delighted with the basement.

'This is perfect, Earl. The glove box will fit in that corner . . . the rest here . . . yes, it's perfect.'

Gallagher hovered uncertainly behind the others. With Denning and Henrick together he had once again been relegated to the role of bystander. But he had no intention of remaining in the background for long. He recalled his tip about the rabbit's blood, which prompted Denning to get rid of the ferrets and dash off to Washington. That had certainly eliminated a serious danger of discovery. And the raid on Mike's Place couldn't have taken place without his help, though he had received none of the credit during the mutual back-slapping sessions since. But now he had an idea that could be a knockout.

'How far are we from the Capitol?'

Gallagher's question surprised the others. Denning decided to humour him.

'A few blocks. Five, maybe six hundred yards. Hey,

what's on your mind?'

'How much of a hurry are we in to explode the bomb?'

'No special hurry. Why?'

'I was listening to the radio in the van last night. If we could plant the bomb and wait till January . . . well, it's the State of the Union address. The president's big speech. No one's talked about where we'd plant the bomb, but how about right here? Everybody who's anybody would be just a few blocks away.'

'Jesus . . . bloody Christ.'

Denning's blood raced as he seized on Gallagher's suggestion.

'The bomb should be effective at that distance, shouldn't it?' Gallagher asked. 'Just think. The president, everyone in the line of succession to the presidency . . . '

'Christ, and the heads of all branches of the US government,' Denning added. 'We'd get all the Supreme Court justices, the entire cabinet, all the legislators, the Joint Chiefs of Staff. Sean, baby, you're a genius. A first-rate, five-star bloody genius.'

'Well, if it would work at this distance . . . '

'You bet it would,' Henrick said. 'Depending on how much stuff we get, there won't be very much of anything left within a quarter-mile of the blast.'

'And I was just thinking of wiping out the White House,' Denning said. He clapped Gallagher on the back. 'Baby, you're a genius.'

14

Sheehan submitted himself to inspection from Sheila before they left the hotel for the UN meeting. She smiled at his bulky tie knot, undid the tie and fastened a smaller, neater knot.

He smoothed back his recently trimmed hair. He felt like a middle-aged graduate.

'I'm sure it will go well, Ken. I know it will.'

'It had better. Keep your fingers crossed for me. It's not my scene . . . all that yak, yak, yak. I get turned off when all those devious bastards start fighting for position. They should have sent someone else.'

'Nonsense. You know more about the problems than anybody. You'll be fine.'

He mechanically accepted his briefcase from her and merely grunted when she told him how the papers inside were arranged.

Sheehan was among the first of the delegates to be seated. The tables were arranged in a square and he found himself facing the new director-general of the United Nations, a Swiss diplomat whose predecessor had died recently. The new chief was a pedantic observer of formal procedures. Sheehan could only hope that his statement to the assembly would not get strangled in a mass of amendments and counter-resolutions.

He flipped through the day's agenda as a group of other delegates arrived. The approval of the minutes of the previous

UN meeting was to be followed by a formal welcoming of the new director-general. Item three was listed as 'Nuclear security.' In smaller type on the agenda was added, 'Address from UK delegate.' The brevity of the words gave little hint of the verbal hurricane Sheehan hoped to stir up. He was grateful that the issue was high on the agenda. At least he would not have to survive a bombardment of other speeches before delivering his own.

He wondered idly if the frustrations of every job increased with responsibility. Was it as debilitating for a road digger to fail as for a president? Or was failure an ultimate, damaging all men equally? Had any actor suffered a greater intensity of stage fright than that which he now felt? Did a doctor, unable to save a dying patient, feel more futile than a farmer whose crop was killed by frost? His father, as a miner, would have known fear; was the uncertainty he now felt a similar fear? Sheehan's conclusion that all men probably shared similar extremes of experience helped him to feel less isolated.

Vorishilov averted his eyes from Sheehan on taking his seat. Sheehan had hoped for some sign of recognition – an indication, perhaps, of Vorishilov's likely reaction to the security issue.

Sheehan knew that his chances of securing immediate action from the United Nations were no more than fifty-fifty. He weighed the value of American support against the known apathy of other nations, and was not pleased with the calculation. Even apathetic delegates were likely to pontificate in the hope of gaining political prestige. Sheehan regarded the United Nations as being cursed with too much leadership and not enough fellowship. Everybody seemed to want to get in on the act. And there were a score of precedural pitfalls. The wheels of the UN grinded exceeding slow at the best of times, and there was always someone around to put a spanner in the works.

'How's your love life!'

Stoddart had walked unseen behind Sheehan and whispered in his ear. The Englishman, startled, looked around.

'Pete, you're insane. Hello.'

'Welcome to the club. This lot are all crazy.'

The American lifted the headphones from Sheehan's desk and flicked a switch on the microphone that connected Sheehan with Sheila, who sat with other secretaries around the perimeter of the conference room.

'Hello, beautiful. What are you doing for lunch?'

Stoddart had dated Sheila several times since they had first met over dinner at Sheehan's hotel. Sheehan was unhappy about the relationship. He admired both, but Stoddart's reputation as a womanizer threatened eventual hurt for Sheila.

'I'm going to accept the first invitation I get.'

'You've got it.'

'I accept.'

The two exchanged broad smiles. Sheehan waved casually to her as Stoddart replaced the headphones.

'Sock it to 'em, Ken.' Stoddart said. 'We're with you all the way.'

No sooner had Stoddart taken his seat than the meeting began. The minutes were approved without comment and a welcome to the director-general was delivered in a flat monotone.

Suddenly, Sheehan was aware that the director-general was looking directly at him. He was being introduced. This was it.

'. . . by Mr Ken Sheehan, delegate of the United Kingdom.'

Sheehan remembered just in time to flick back the switch of the microphone so that his speech wouldn't be heard by Sheila alone. He hurried through the traditional formal opening and launched into attack.

'Nuclear security, worldwide, is appalling. I have recently headed an investigation into the security of weapons-grade nuclear materials in most of our countries. The investigation was instigated by the International Atomic Energy Agency and followed the restructuring of the Atomic Energy Commission within the United States. I'm not critical of that restructuring. It's a step in the right direction. But we now need a similar restructuring in all member countries.'

He risked a pause. All eyes were on him. He was holding the attention of the assembly.

'The general situation is dangerous in the extreme. There is no longer any mystique about the manufacture of nuclear weapons. Not so long ago the Massachusetts Institute of Technology invited a teenaged student to design a nuclear weapon. His only aid was a host of technical publications which are unclassified. The result was a foolproof design. What a student can do, a terrorist can do.

'These materials are becoming available in increasing quantities. Weapons-grade nuclear material exists in approximately thirty countries. By 1985, more than fifty countries will have at least one power plant with the capacity to produce every year enough plutonium for several dozen nuclear bombs.

'We have to ask ourselves: are security measures adequate to deal with this increased productivity? We have to answer: no.

'Current projections by the International Atomic Energy Agency indicate that by the year two thousand the annual worldwide production of plutonium may exceed a million kilograms. That's enough to make a hundred thousand or more nuclear bombs. I doubt if a single delegate here would claim that projected security plans are good enough to deal with this increase.'

Sheehan sipped a glass of water. The meeting was still with him.

'Suitable authorities of your countries have been made aware of the specific findings of our investigation. It would not be appropriate to give details at a public meeting such as this. But I can say that the team I headed devised more than twenty separate plans for covertly obtaining weapons-grade nuclear material. In our opinion, which was shared by executives of the various target nuclear installations, each plan could have been successfully carried out by a team of no more than four armed men.

'It would be naïve to suppose that any of a hundred

terrorist forces throughout the world are less ingenious than the members of my investigative committee; it would be naive to suppose that we had uncovered all the danger spots.'

Sheehan caught a wink of encouragement from Stoddart, but one or two foreign delegates had removed their headphones. He decided to end rapidly while he still held the attention of the majority.

'The whole issue is not one of individual national prestige or pride. It is an issue of worldwide safety. I anticipate, therefore, that there will be little debate and propose that the budget of the International Atomic Agency be increased immediately by $5 000 000 to provide for the setting up of an international investigative force to advise member countries on nuclear security.'

Stoddart was the next to address the meeting.

'I imagine we're all in favour and I second the resolution. I call for a vote.'

The director-general seemed about to agree when Vorishilov interrupted.

'I protest. We should follow conventional procedures in this matter. Why so fast? Why so much of a hurry to spend $5 000 000? Why, I may ask, should the Soviet Union share this financial burden when its own nuclear security is adequate for all contingencies?

'The United Nations have the appropriate machinery for such matters, and I suggest that we use it. I propose an amendment that the matter be referred to the Political and Security Main Committee of the United Nations for further investigation. It is unacceptable that members of the International Atomic Energy Agency should determine their own expenditure. We all regard our little hobbyhorses with some affection . . .'

Mumblings of disapproval interrupted Vorishilov.

'. . . and while I'm not suggesting that the delegate for the United Kingdom, who is also that nation's delegate to the International Atomic Energy Agency, wishes to buy himself some status by hustling this proposal through . . .'

Louder shouts drowned Vorishilov.

'Nevertheless,' he went on doggedly, 'what possible reason can there be for not resolving this matter through normal channels?'

Vorishilov nodded to the director-general.

'If the amendment proposed by the Russian delegate is seconded,' he began, 'I . . . '

'It is. I second the amendment.'

The Hungarian delegate had joined the battle.

Sheehan groaned. An investigation by the Political and Security Main Committee would take months. A sub-committee would have to be formed and its members would have to familiarize themselves with all aspects of the nuclear power industry. Then members of the sub-committee would make enquiries about security in all member countries. Tons of paper work would be produced.

'We haven't got the bloody time,' Sheehan shouted.

'I cannot permit such outbursts,' the director-general said.

'I must protest and ask the Russian delegate to withdraw this amendment,' Sheehan persisted. 'There isn't time for such an investigation. This danger exists now. Today. This very hour, this minute. The problem is worsening. With the greatest respect, I must point out that the machinery of the United Nations isn't the most rapid in reaching conclusions. This is an issue over which conclusions are needed instantly. The International Atomic Energy Agency is a non-partisan body. Its members comprise virtually the same nations who are represented here today, and inevitably such an investigation can only produce conclusions similar to our own.'

'I'm really not sure this is proper,' the director-general said, 'but I'll put the question. Does the Soviet delegate wish to withdraw his amendment?'

'I do not.'

'In that case, unless the Soviet delegate wishes to reply to the protest . . . '

Vorishilov shook his head.

'. . . I shall take the vote on the amendment now. If it is carried, the proposal of the United Kingdom as amended will be approved. Those in favour?'

It was obvious immediately that Sheehan and his supporters were outnumbered. The law of precedent had won the day. He didn't bother to put up his hand when the votes against the amendment were called for. As the result was announced he stormed out of the conference room.

He was striding down Second Avenue when he became aware that Sheila was hurrying alongside him.

'Ken, slow down. Please.'

He stopped and turned to her. His shoulders sagged.

'Ken, we'll just have to be patient. I'm sorry you didn't get what you wanted.'

'Shit, Sheila,' he said in exasperation. 'That Russian bastard . . . Why is the world full of lunatics?'

He took her hand and pulled her toward a nearby bar. He snickered as he looked up at the sign. The bar was called The World Upside Down.

Two hours and eleven bottles of Budweiser later, Sheehan was perched precariously on a bar stool. Sheila sat alongside him. She was nursing his wounded pride and her second gin and tonic.

'Me and that guy Vorishilov were supposed to be . . . well, sort of mates,' he complained. 'He promised not to rock the boat, the bastard.'

'Yes, Ken.'

'I've known the bastard for years. He . . . what the hell? Let's me and you go and have lunch.'

He drained his glass.

'Well, I do have an arrangement . . . '

'Oh, yes. Stoddart. I forgot.'

'Of course, if it's business . . . I could cancel.'

'No, it's not business. It was going to be purely social.'

She gathered her purse and slid from the stool.

'So long, Ken.'

Sheehan seemed not to have heard. He was already competing with other customers for the bartender's attention.

15

Gallagher's suggestion that the bomb be set off during the State of the Union address had sent all five members of the group into a frenzy of drinking and pot smoking that had lasted until dawn. Henrick and Sarah Jane had zipped their sleeping bags together under the table and huddled inside. Wanda had fallen asleep in an armchair. Denning and Gallagher had collapsed into unconsciousness on the floor at opposite ends of the room.

Denning was the first to awake. It was almost one p.m. He was glad he had taken more marijuana than alcohol. At least he didn't have a hangover. He opened a window to clear the stale sweet smell from the room, swallowed several deep breaths of fresh air and vigorously touched his toes fifty times. His pulse rate increased only slightly with the exercise.

'Time to get up,' he yelled. 'It's a brand new day.'

Grunts and groans announced the return of the others from oblivion. Gallagher let out an anguished cry. As usual, he had drunk more than twice as much as anyone else.

The women reheated the remains of a pan of chilli they had prepared the previous evening and dished out five portions. A pot of instant coffee completed breakfast. Denning atc impatiently and refused Wanda's offer of a second cup.

'Let's get moving,' he urged. 'We're going to have to act fast.'

Gallagher and the women looked up expectantly. Henrick continued stirring his chilli with a fork.

'First of all,' Denning said, 'the plutonium. Like Wayne here, I've been doing homework on the nuclear power business. Here's the score. Plutonium is created in all power stations and is present in the discarded fuel elements, which are just long metal rods. So, do we hit a power station? No. The stuff is highly radioactive and too much trouble to handle, and the plutonium has to be separated from the other junk by complex chemical means. Right, Wayne?'

'That's right.'

'Those used fuel rods are sent to chemical reprocessing plants, where the plutonium is separated, usually in the form of a nitrate solution. Here's the big question: Wayne, can you use plutonium nitrate?'

Henrick shrugged.

'I'd sooner have the fully enriched metal, but . . . yes, I guess I could work with the nitrate. I'd have to separate the metal, but I could work something out.'

'Great. Then we're in business.'

'We're going to hit one of them reprocessing plants?' Gallagher asked. His voice was almost a squeak. 'Shit, we can't do that. They're guarded by armies. They . . . '

'Drop dead,' Denning drawled. 'Just hang in there. I got a lot of helpful stuff on this from the reading room at H Street. So just listen.

'The plutonium is placed in stainless steel cylinders, each one like a giant thermos, four feet long and five inches in diameter. Each flask is placed inside a fifty-five gallon drum and braced in the centre of it with welded struts. They call these drums birdcages, and they're necessary to prevent the stored material going critical.'

Denning smiled at Sarah Jane's vacant expression.

'Don't worry that beautiful brain box of yours, Sarah. All will become clear in time.

'Anyway, one of these drums weighs about four hundred pounds. Two men can handle one drum.'

This time it was Gallagher's turn to be the butt of his mild sarcasm.

'Even one man and Sean could lift one. But don't worry,

Sean. I'll be around to give you a hand.'

Gallagher bristled.

'OK, then,' Denning added. 'So far, no problem. When I got this far at H Street I got one hell of a fright. Some companies shipping plutonium have started packing these bird-cages with concrete – top, bottom and sides. That brings the weight of each one up to around a ton, even more. The concrete plug in the top weighs three hundred and fifty pounds. The practice has been urged by the Nuclear Regulatory Commission but, and it's a big but, it hasn't been put into effect by everyone. H Street gave us the names of a few companies who are resisting the idea. The drivers are complaining about extra work, and thc companies are complaining about extra cost. The one particular shipment I'm interested in comes from a company where there's more aggro than most. We're going to hit before the squabbling is settled.

'For storage, much of the plutonium is shipped to special depots. It seems crazy, but relatively little of the stuff is used. It just gets shipped to these depots, where it lies waiting for some bright boy to find an economical way of using it.

'It just so happens there's a storage plant a few miles north of here. That's the place me and Wanda have been staking out. And they're the folks who are going to give us all the plutonium we need. Plutonium is being shipped in and out of there in some form or other virtually every week.

'We're going for the nitrate because it's not as well guarded as the fully enriched plutonium. Each one of those cylinders contains ten litres of nitrate, out of which we should get two-and-a-half kilograms of plutonium metal. The pure stuff. Right, Wayne?'

'Sounds about right.'

'That's what H Street tells us. Now get this. Uncle Sam is going to give us nine of those birdcages. That's how many we can get on the truck – twenty-two-and-a-half lovely kilograms of fully enriched weapons-grade plutonium-239.'

Henrick laughed cynically at Denning's enthusiasm.

'That's far more than we need, Earl. If we can cut down the risks by cutting down the quantity, let's do that. I reckon we need about seven kilos of plutonium to make a fairly good bomb. Ten kilos at the most.'

Denning fixed Henrick with a stare.

'I know, Wayne. Like I said, I've been doing my homework. Seven kilos will make a bomb. But who says we're going to settle for a bomb, singular?'

Gallagher's arm knocked over a coffee cup. Even Sarah Jane, normally the slowest of the group to react in any situation, sat up sharply without, for once, mentally rehearsing the movement beforehand. Wanda was the first to speak.

'The boy's finally flipped. He wants to start World War Three.'

Denning snatched her wrist in a cruel grip.

'Listen,' he said. 'We make three bombs. Got it? One bomb goes off in an unpopulated area so they know we're not bluffing. OK? No one gets hurt. The second bomb . . .'

'You're hurting me . . .'

Tears stung Wanda's eyes. Denning released his hold on her wrist.

'The second bomb is planted somewhere in . . . I don't know . . . say, New York. But suppose they give in to all our demands. Suppose the United Nations goes through the motions of establishing a world food council, a world wages council, and so on. Like good little boys we tell them where the bomb is. Right? And they throw us in the slammer. But with a third bomb planted, they'd have to give way. They'd have to leave us alone. So three bombs it is. If all goes well, no one gets hurt. Not even us. If they try to trick us, boom. A hell of a lot of people get hurt, with either the second bomb or the third. I don't care which. Does everyone get the picture?'

The stunned silence that followed told Denning that the question had been unnecessary.

'How much time do you need, Wayne? Can we blast that first bomb . . . when? Two weeks?'

'That's pushing it. I've got to make some moulds, and

there's still a few things. I need a lot of steel, and that's a headache. I don't know if we've got enough plastic explosive, but we might have. There's plenty of detonators. To be sure everything's set up right I need two days. Then, if we don't hit any snags . . . we could be lucky. Two weeks? Maybe. I won't know for sure until I give it a try. When do we get the plutonium nitrate?'

'Four days. Friday. I've got a plan, but the fewer of us who know about it the better. I don't want to go into details. You're just going to have to believe that it will work.

'Now for the next phase. The watch on the fuel plant has to go on. Me and Wayne will hang on here to set up the bomb shop, and I've other things to fix. Wanda can keep us supplied with grub. I'll take Sean and Sarah to the camping ground and they can share the watch. If . . . '

'Correction.'

The tone of Henrick's interruption startled Denning. His facial muscles tensed. Since Denning had suggested that Sarah Jane should share her sexual favours more generously Henrick hadn't let her out of his sight.

'Correction,' he repeated. 'Sarah stays here with me.'

Sarah Jane, fearful of the outcome of the clash, looked from Denning to Henrick. She stood up from the table, sidled to Henrick, stepped behind him and ran a hand through his ginger curls.

Denning's first inclination was to crush immediately Henrick's challenge to his authority. He hesitated only for an instant, but the time was sufficient to allow mature judgement to prevail. There would be time enough later to show who was in charge. Meanwhile, Henrick and his goodwill were crucial to the success of the operation.

'Sarah stays, Wanda stays . . . What the hell? Who cares? So Sarah stays with us and cooks the grub. Fair enough. That's settled. No big deal, eh? Wanda knows the way, so that saves me a drive. And you know what we're after, honey. Same routine as before, but with Sean holding your hand. Keep to yourselves. Keep out of everyone's way and keep your eyes open.

'In particular, keep an eye on that guy who lives in the end house of Main Street. I've got big plans for that guy. I want to know every time he or his wife or anyone else enters or leaves the house. I want to know how many times a day he blows his nose.'

Secretly, Wanda was relieved at being able to escape from the flat and the incriminating materials in the basement. If anything went wrong . . . if the police somehow got on their trail . . . well, she and Gallagher would have a chance of convincing the cops that they were innocents abroad on a camping holiday.

Gallager grunted in acknowledgment of Denning's instructions but seethed inwardly at once again being relegated to what he regarded as a minor role in the operation.

'Right,' Denning continued. 'You might as well hit the road. Me and Wayne will keep the pickup truck here. You two take Wayne's van.'

Gallagher grabbed the keys, which Denning had held out to Wanda.

'Think you can trust me to drive?' Gallagher whined. 'Think you can trust me to do anything in this lousy outfit?'

'Come on, Sean,' Denning said soothingly. 'No hard feelings. Good hunting. We'll see you soon.'

Gallagher strode to the front door. Wanda shrugged, then followed.

As soon as Gallagher and Wanda had left Denning clapped his hands and flexed his biceps as though in preparation for action.

'How about I give you a hand to set the stuff in the basement?'

'Hold it,' Henrick answered sullenly.

Denning's eyes narrowed.

'Something bugging you, Wayne?'

'Maybe . . . maybe.'

Henrick looked from his empty plate to Sarah Jane and jerked a thumb toward the kitchen.

'Clear up and keep busy in the kitchen, honey. The big boys want to talk.'

She collected the dishes and closed the kitchen door behind her.

'Something is bugging me, Earl. You're dead right it is. If we're going through this thing together I want to get things straight. And I mean straight down the line. No bullshit.'

'Fair enough, man. Shoot.'

'It's this KGB crap.'

Henrick watched Denning closely for any reaction. Denning remained motionless, his eyes resting somewhere on the table's plastic top.

'I'm no dummy, Earl. I'm not buying it. Things just don't add up. I was all for wiping out the ambassador. Great. World food council . . . standard world currency and prices . . . all that's terrific. I'm with you all the way. But play it straight. There's no KGB behind us, is there?'

Denning sat bolt upright.

'Man, you're on dangerous ground. You'd better believe they're behind us.'

Intuition warned Denning against being honest. The direct contact he supposedly had with the KGB boosted his status. The implied threat of KGB discipline might well be a help in keeping everyone in line. Henrick had already shown he was capable of rebellion. If he knew the truth he might well share his knowledge with the others. He might try to break up the group – or take it over.

'Wayne, you've got to believe. If things go wrong you'll find out about the KGB, and fast. When those boys play, they play for real.'

Henrick drummed the top of the table with his fingers. He met Denning's icy stare.

'I'd like to believe, buddy. I really would. But I got to tell you, I think ACE is Earl Denning Incorporated. It's got to be. Things don't add up. We've no financial backing. Where's the bread? We had to hit a bar to get a few lousy thousand bucks. We have to go through all this hassle to design a bomb and get the stuff. Why didn't your KGB buddies slip us a plan? Why not at least a few kilos of plutonium? Even a few bucks? We've had to take all the risks with no help. If this is such a big KGB deal, where the hell are they? They don't even seem to care where we place the bloody bomb, or whether we make one, two or three. Balls, Earl. It just ain't the way those pros operate.'

Henrick had addressed his outburst to the tablecloth. Denning's stare had remained fixed on the top of his head.

'Maybe you can fool Gallagher,' Henrick added. 'Maybe Sarah – let's face it, anyone could. Maybe Wanda's sucked in. But I'm not.'

Denning leaned forward menacingly on the edge of his seat.

'Now hold it,' Henrick said hurriedly. 'Before you blast off, let me finish. The aims of ACE . . . they're fine. What you hope to achieve is humane, and worth any price. I'm all for it. And I've just got to make this bomb. I've got to. One, two or three bombs . . . I don't care. If I can do it, terrific. How many private citizens have ever made a nuclear bomb? None. Not one. I'm going to be the first. I'm with you all the way, Earl, but for Christ's sake play it straight. Is this an Earl Denning enterprise? If it is, I think it's a hell of a good one and you can count me in. Or are you really trying to tell me we've got international backing? Don't sucker me with bullshit.'

Denning permitted himself a relaxed smile.

'Hear this, Wayne, and hear me good. It really isn't such a big deal to me whether you believe me or not. I know where I'm going. I know what the rewards are likely to be. But for your own sake, I've got to tell you one final time. This entire job has been directed by the KGB. There's going to come a time when they'll contact you and the others. If you like, I'll give you a phone number. You can call our contact. But I don't recommend it. Not yet. I'd sooner sit on a hornets' nest than do that. They'll get in touch when it suits them. They'll work out what rewards we're going to get. But first, our operation has to work. If it works, we're big, buddy. So let's get on with the job without any power battles between us.

'I'm not leading ACE, Wayne. You're not going to lead ACE. There's somebody at the back of us who's leading ACE, and that's the KGB. Believe it, man. End message.'

'You just won't give, will you?'

'No, Wayne. I won't.'

'OK . . . OK . . . Let's say I believe. Just for now. But . . . aw, to hell. Let's set up the bomb shop.'

'Now you're talking.'

Henrick called Sarah Jane from the kitchen.

'Come and give us a hand in the basement.'

Denning remained thoughtfully at the table for several moments, then followed.

The basement was the largest room in the house. A wooden workbench about fifteen feet long was fitted against one wall. In the corner nearest to the workbench was a door opening into a shower room. The basement was lit by concealed overhead lighting.

'This really is fine,' Henrick said. 'Workbench, power points, water supply . . . the lot. That bench is more than sturdy enough to support the glove box and furnace. All I need is one more table. The one in the dining room is just the job. If you don't mind, Earl . . . this foot . . . '

'Sure. I'll get it.'

When Denning returned with the table Henrick pointed to a position adjacent to the workbench and alongside the shower room wall. The table fitted perfectly into the gap.

'Thanks. I'll set up the rest of the stuff.'

'What else are we going to need?'

'I've got to make moulds – ceramic crucibles, if you like – but I've got the gear. The big headache is steel. I need a hell of a lot. Each bomb is going to need a two-inch jacket of steel around the plutonium core. It has to be good stuff, too – ideally with a maximum of one percent carbon, so it won't be too brittle. We'll need a hell of a lot to make three bombs and it just isn't normally bought by the general public, especially in such quantities. I guess we'll have to go through the old routine of pretending we're from some university or other and buying it, but we're likely to raise a few eyebrows.'

'We could always raid some steel joint . . . '

'I think I've got an idea,' Sarah Jane said.

Both men looked at her in frank amazement. She had been ignored during the conversation and they had forgotten she was present. That she should interrupt was surprising enough; that she should offer an idea was all but mind-boggling.

'You want a lot of steel, yes?'

'Yes, Sarah. But . . . '

Henrick broke off and exchanged a glance with Denning. Detecting their scepticism, she blushed angrily.

'I suppose you'd like to stage another raid, then there could be more killing and you'd all be happier. I just happen to think there's another way. That's all.'

'Come on, honey, don't go bananas,' Henrick pleaded. 'Let's hear it. We're listening.'

She smoothed back a blonde curl which had fallen over her forehead.

'Earl said the plutonium-something-or-other was in big steel thermos flasks, didn't he? And they're inside big steel drums. Well, if you're going to steal these drums anyway, won't that mean you'll have a lot of steel?'

Denning whooped. He grasped Sarah Jane by the shoulders and kissed her on the tip of her nose.

'The girl's not just a pretty face, goddammit. She's a genius. A godforsaken genius.'

To Henrick he said, 'How about that? She's right, isn't she? Would there be enough steel for us in those birdcages?'

Henrick made a mental calculation.

'I guess there would, just about. It'd be good stuff, too. Those cylinders will be made of pure metal and they don't use junk to make those drums, either.' He grinned. 'I've got to agree. Sarah, you're a genius.'

She curtsied with mock politeness.

'And that's all you need?' Denning asked.

'Yes, apart from a truckload of plutonium nitrate. Oh. One thing. I'm low on ammo for the automatic. Winchester-Magnum .303 bullets. If you could get me a couple of boxes . . . '

'Sure. You've got them. You better give me the licence.'

'Help yourself. It's in the suitcase in the hallway.'

'If that's it, I'll be on my way. Don't waste too much time screwing, you two.'

He bounded up the basement stairs four at a time.

Henrick immediately began to assemble the glove box. Sarah Jane helped to strip off the packing, then handed the sides to him one at a time. Each side and the top and bottom were made of extra-strength glass reinforced with lead. One side had two openings, each the size of a large dinner plate, into which Henrick fitted the radiation-proof rubberized gloves. When assembled the glove box filled more than half the length of the workbench. The sides were detatchable and equipment could easily be moved in and out. When sealed it was absolutely airtight.

Next, Henrick fitted together the induction furnace, a device not unlike a pottery kiln. When plugged into the electric circuit it would produce a magnetic field. Anything placed inside that was resistant to electricity – such as plutonium – would be heated to high temperatures. He placed a variety of crucibles on the workbench and stood back to survey his bomb shop.

'That's it, honey. We're all set.'

'You mean . . . this is all there is to it? You can make an atomic bomb with this stuff here?'

She had felt as though she had been living through a fantasy since the night when Henrick had called at her home to tell her of the killing of the ambassador. Could that have been only . . . was it two or three weeks? Although each stage of the operation had been explained to her, the words had so often seemed to lack meaning. It was as though she were taking part in some bizarre play. As she surveyed the equipment in the basement the fantasy suddenly achieved a frightening reality.

'It's unbelievable. I don't get it, Wayne. How, if it took all those years for our top scientists to produce an atom bomb . . . how come you can throw one together in two weeks or so in a basement?'

Henrick laughed.

'I probably won't need two weeks. Times are different, honey. Genius is no longer needed for this job. I'm just hitching a ride on discoveries made by others. They had to start from scratch. I don't. They had to discover plutonium. It's the first man-made element that has ever been produced. All we have to do to get hold of some is steal it. And it's so goddam deadly that I don't even have to make a good bomb. If I do, terrific; if I don't, it's still going to be good enough to kill a hell of a lot of people.

'As for the design, that's no big problem. As the Russians caught up with each stage of the development of nuclear weapons, the information which they obviously had was declassified. We couldn't see any point in trying to keep secret what the Russians knew already. So, those books in the corner there contain the product of years of work by many of the top brains in the world. There's nothing we need to know that isn't declassified and in print somewhere. The making of the bomb is simply the last, and by no means most difficult, part of the job.'

Henrick slapped her on the rear.

'Say what you like, I think you're clever, Wayne. You must be to be able to do all this.'

She circled with an arm outstretched as if scattering corn.

'I suppose you're right. I'm terrific. Now pass that clay powder and two bowls of cold water. We've got work to do.'

She heaved a ten-pound cloth bag onto the table Denning had brought down from upstairs. Henrick slit the cloth with a penknife. Inside the bag was the pottery powder he had bought – a special feldspar brand normally used only in industry. When moulded and fired it would withstand temperatures of 2000°C – more than sufficient for Henrick's purpose. Sarah Jane returned from the shower room with the water and he mixed several pounds of powder into a sloshy grey mud. He strained the mud through a fine culinary sieve that collected undissolved lumps and impurities, then pummelled and kneaded the mixture until satisfied with its consistency.

'The plastic stuff, honey. In that box.'

Henrick rinsed and dried his hands in the shower room while Sarah Jane found the 1/16 inch sheet of plastic and put it on the table. Henrick took a pair of dividers from a pencil box on the workbench and scratched onto the plastic a semicircle roughly the diameter of a baseball. With scissors he cut out the semicircle and smoothed the edges with fine sandpaper.

He turned again to the clay and fashioned it into a rough cube. With the plastic semicircle he scooped out a quantity of clay from the centre of the cube. By twisting the plastic back and forth he hallowed out a hemisphere.

At a signal Sarah Jane would splash water on the clay so that it remained easily workable. When the task was completed, Henrick repeated the procedure and soon had two moulds which together formed a perfect sphere.

'We let that dry, heat it in the oven and that's one small problem over.'

He referred to the *Plutonium Handbook* and checked a series of calculations he had made at least a dozen times. Given the density of plutonium, to ensure the right criticality he would need . . . yes, as near as dammit a two-inch steel reflector.

'Plastic again, Sarah.'

This time Henrick cut out a semicircle four inches wider in diameter than the previous one. Eventually he produced another two moulds which formed a larger sphere.

'That's it until those four moulds dry out and we can bake them. We've got time to kill.'

Sarah Jane was unable to suppress her curiosity.

'What was that all about?'

'Simple, honey. The smaller moulds will shape the plutonium core of the bomb. The large moulds are for the steel jacket. Once the moulds are baked I'll smooth the insides with sandpaper.'

He judged from her expression that she had been enlightened only a little.

'Don't bust that brain box with overwork, honey. Let's go and eat before Earl gets back. I've still got a few bucks left out of the loot from Mike's Place.'

Later Henrick would make a heat-resistant felspar sphere with the smaller moulds and pierce it through its centre with a fine needle that would act as a spindle. Grooves for the spindle would be made on the edges of the larger moulds. By positioning the sphere in the centre of each of the larger moulds and pouring in molten steel, the two halves of the reflector could be made.

Denning was relieved to escape from the flat. His lightheartedness had concealed the anger he still felt at Henrick's rebelliousness. Soon there would come a day of reckoning, Denning vowed, on which the lines of authority would be clearly marked.

He took a detour away from the Washington ghettos. He would need to park the truck while making several purchases. A white man's truck in black man's Washington might prove too tempting a target for vandals. He drove through the tree-lined highways of Silver Springs, a well-manicured suburb of spacious homes inhabited by the upper echelons of Congress and the judiciary. After several miles the houses gave way to an open road.

During the drive he went over each facet of his plan for acquiring the plutonium nitrate. He had to acknowledge that the risks would be great. But with luck, and if everyone kept cool . . .

A sign announcing 'Sunshine Square Shopping Center' loomed ahead and he spotted a branch of the Army and Navy Stores. From the store's stock of surplus uniforms he selected three navy blue woollen safari jackets and matching trousers.

'These are different sizes, you know,' the shop assistant pointed out.

'That's right. So?'

'Keep your hair on, man. Just thought you mightn't have noticed.'

Denning's glare discouraged the assistant from asking why he should want three such outfits in different sizes. Each resembled the uniforms worn by Marines for night exercises – and security guards at the nearby nuclear fuel storage plant.

His next stop was at a garden supply centre beyond an area of scattered houses. He ignored the greenhouses and displays of exotic plants and headed for the section signposted 'Supplies and equipment'.

A jovial ruddy-faced man approached him.

'Fencing?' Denning inquired. 'Seven-foot mesh fencing?'

'Sure. We got it. Want to keep out the neighbours, eh?'

'I got an orchard to fence off. I need about forty yards, and posts. And a couple of gates I can get my truck through.'

'You've got the right place, mister. Follow me.'

The old man entered a large shed in which was stored mesh fencing from two to eight feet high, all neatly rolled.

'Here's fifty yards – two twenty-five yard lengths already cut out and rolled. More than you asked for but I can let you have it cheap. Say, ten per cent off?'

'It's a deal.'

At the rear of the shed was an assortment of wire mesh gates. The old man pointed to a pair.

'Sure, they'll do,' Denning said. 'I'll get my truck.'

Denning helped the old man load the fencing posts and double gates.

'Four hundred and ten, son. It's a good buy.'

'It better be.'

Denning peeled off the notes from his shrinking wad. The old man handed over an open-ended spanner and a polyethylene bag full of nuts and bolts.

'I can set it up for you for a few bucks.'

'That's all right, old-timer. Forget it.'

'Need a lock to keep them gates shut?'

'Nope. I got what I need.'

Denning's earlier irritation vanished as he drove back onto the highway. It was all so easy. What could be less suspicious than a pickup truck loaded with fencing and workmen's clothing? He wished that he still had his ferrets. It would be reassuring to be able to go over the plan during an afternoon's hunting. But Gallagher had been right. It would have been madness not to have got rid of them once the police had discovered the rabbit blood on the handkerchief.

A signpost pointed to a side road along which Denning saw a white-bricked building on the side of which were the letters 'SPCA' – a dog pound ran by the Society for the Prevention of Cruelty to Animals. On an impulse he turned down the road. Maybe. . .

As he stepped from the truck he was greeted by the yelping, whining and barking of an orchestra of stray dogs of all shapes and sizes. He entered a wooden lean-to over the door of which was written 'Reception'. On the solitary desk in the room was a bell push and a card which read 'Ring for attention'. He rang.

He idly scanned the posters which all but obliterated the walls of the reception office until an auburn-haired girl in her mid-twenties joined him. The country type, he noted scornfully. She wore riding breeches and boots and a long loose sweater. The kind who wore the smell of horses and dogs instead of perfume. He tried to imagine what she would look like with a hair-do and in a slim-fitting dress. It was impossible.

'Any strays?'

He waved to a poster advertising dogs for sale. Strays unclaimed after seven days would be offered for sale for a further seven days for fifty dollars, regardless of breed. Any dog unclaimed or unsold at the end of that time would be destroyed.

'Sure. Come and see.'

She opened a side door and the yelping chorus rose to a crescendo. Beyond was a roofed-in corridor with cages on either side.

'Anything special in mind?' she yelled.

'German shepherd.'

'We've got one, but man, he's mean. Real mean. He's in with this lot – the ones to be put down.'

She pointed to a group of cages further down the corridor. The German shepherd seemed to be the only dog not making as much noise as it could. It contented itself with a surly, deep-throated growl. A choker chain attached to its neck was looped around a handle on the door of its cage.

'We had to leave the choker on. Otherwise there'd be no handling him. He's mean, I tell you.'

The dog's lips quivered and revealed glimpses of its glistening white teeth.

'I love him. He's beautiful. Bring him out.

The girl gave a short laugh and looked at Denning with the expression she reserved for forms of life lower than strays and for human idiots in particular.

'You've got to be kidding. That mutt's a monster.'

'I love him, honey. He's prettier than some people I know.'

Denning returned to the reception office, counted out the fifty dollars and handed them to her.

'Thanks. Look, before I hand this critter over you'd better get that stick from by the doorway. Use it to keep the dog at arm's length.'

Denning took her advice. As he accepted the choker the German shepherd snarled and lunged at his knee. Denning rapped the tip of its nose with the stick. The animal's head shot backwards and it crouched, ready to leap at Denning the moment his eyes turned away.

While the girl filled out a receipt Denning automatically gave the false name and address he often used – the one he had used when sending the telegram to the ambassador.

'Mister, I should pay you for taking that mutt away. I

thought he was for the box for sure. Good luck.'

Denning dragged the dog behind him, holding the stick never more than six inches from its nose. He pulled down the tailgate of the truck and, prompted by a tap on its rear, the dog leapt aboard. Denning secured the choker to one of the fence posts.

As he returned to the main highway he remembered that Henrick needed ammunition for the automatic. He pulled up at a phone booth and checked the Yellow Pages for the nearest gunsmith. He found one which would require no more than a mile detour on his way back to the flat.

He cursed at failing to find a parking space within a hundred yards of the shop. The youth behind the counter showed no unusual interest in Denning's request.

'Winchester-Magnum. 303s? Yes, sir. We've got some.'

'Give me two boxes.'

'Yes, sir. Licence?'

Denning handed over Henrick's false registration papers and the youth made an entry in a ledger.

In less than a minute Denning was walking back to the pickup truck. The .303s rattled in the pockets of his denim jacket.

As the door closed behind Denning the youth shouted toward the rear of the store.

'Dad! Dad! Quick.'

A bespectacled overweight man scurried into the store.

'What is it, son?'

'Those bullets the cops were on about – weren't they Winchester-Magnum .303s?'

The youth's father checked some papers which were filed underneath the counter.

'Yeah, that's right. They're pretty rare. What gives?'

'A guy just bought some.'

'Give me that ledger.'

He checked the name and address which the youth had copied from the gun registration slip.

'A New Yorker. Could be. Did he have a car?'

The youth ran to the door and looked both ways along the road. He returned disconsolately.

'Sorry, dad. I never thought . . .'

'Forget it. But just in case, we'd better call the cops. Pass the phone.

16

Gallagher and Wanda piled their equipment inside the tent, then stationed themselves at the lookout spot from which Denning and Wanda had kept their vigil. Gallagher, still seething from the off-hand treatment he had received from Denning, took along a bottle of Chablis. The more he drank the more indignant he became.

'I'll show that bastard,' he threatened. 'Who the hell does he think he is? He's going to have to stop treating me like shit.'

Wanda scanned the fuel plant with the binoculars. There was no sign of activity.

'Where would this outfit be without me?' he asked. 'In the cooler, that's where.'

He swallowed several gulps of wine.

'Who warned the crazy bastard to get rid of those ferrets? If he'd stayed in Queens with those ferrets we'd all have been in the can by now. Who put the cops off the track after we hit Mike's Place?'

Wanda put down the binoculars, stretched full length on the grass and closed her eyes.

'Who suggested setting the bomb off during the State of the Union address? Me. That's who.'

'Big deal, Sean. Wrap it up, there's a good guy.'

Wanda checked the time – seven fifty-five. At eight o'clock the shifts changed over. Through the binoculars she picked out a brown Oldsmobile threading along the lane toward the plant. She knew from previous observation that in the car were the four members of the night shift. The car was searched at both checkpoints before being driven to a parking area in front of the main office. The occupants of the car vanished inside. Shortly afterwards three of the four men who had completed the day shift emerged from the building and drove off in a Pontiac station wagon. The car was also searched at both checkpoints.

The fourth member of the day shift, wearing a leather motorcycle suit, pulled on a crash helmet and rode away on a 125cc Honda. He chatted with the checkpoint guards and was soon on his way. As usual, he didn't ride directly to his home at the end of the town's Main Street. Instead he went into the bar.

Gallagher continued complaining until the Chablis ran out.

'I'm going to the tent for more wine. Need anything?'

'No, I'm fine. Have a break and you can take over here about eleven.'

'So I get the night shift. That's great. Always the best deal with Sean Gallagher, the guy who's used to being bossed around.'

Wanda continued to look through the glasses. She feigned consuming interest in some non-existent object to avoid having to respond to his grumbling. She sighed with relief as the sounds of his steps through the undergrowth faded into the distance.

It was nine-fifteen when the motorcyclist returned to his Honda. Wanda followed the wavering headlight as he rode home. He let himself in with a key. His wife had not left the house since a shopping trip that afternoon.

On taking over the watch Gallagher dozed fitfully. In the early hours he had the first of the nightmares. In his dream he heard the voice of a narrator repeating a phrase he had once heard while watching a television documentary programme on the testing of nuclear weapons. 'This is the valley where the giant mushrooms grow . . . This is the valley . . .' Gallagher was walking on the hot sand of the valley. About him tiny mushroom plants sprang up, swelled to grotesque sizes and exploded into huge fireballs. Each explosion vapourized his body, but somehow he was conscious of all that happened. Then he was walking along the valley again. Another tiny mushroom plant appeared in the hot sand ahead of him and started to swell. The voice spoke faster and faster . . . 'This is the valley where . . . '

Gallagher awoke in a sweat. He sat up and wiped his moist palms on his jeans.

'Hang in there, man,' he murmured to himself. 'Don't crack up on me now.'

Denning, Henrick and Sarah Jane arrived at the campsite soon after noon on Friday. Denning greeted Gallagher and Wanda effusively.

'Come and see what I've got.'

He took Wanda to the rear of the pickup truck, dropped the tailgate and lifted a canvas sheet. The German shepherd blinked in the sunlight.

'Earl, he looks dangerous.'

'He is, baby. That's the idea. So you'd better behave yourself.'

He laughed and secured the tailgate, then joined the others.

'The bomb shop's all set up, but for now this is where the action's going to be. We've a few hours to kill, then we move. At seven-fifty precisely.'

'I suppose the maestro will let us all in on the details when he sees fit,' Gallagher whined.

Denning tapped him lightly but threateningly on the cheek.

'You still smarting, Sean? Come on, man. Let's be buddies. I'm a real buddy of yours, Sean. Honest I am. And I'm going to show you I am. Now give me a hand to put up this other tent.'

When the second tent was erected Denning flung more wood on the smouldering camp fire and gathered the others around. He began to spell out his plan for the raid.

At four thirty-five the woman who lived in the first house on Main Street returned from a visit to a neighbour. Denning had strolled to the edge of the wood and studied her through the glasses until she vanished into the house.

'Don't wait up for the old man,' he muttered. 'You'll be wasting your time.'

He panned the glasses to the end of Main Street nearer to the fuel plant. A telephone van was parked near an excavation in the pavement. A workman's hut sheltered two engineers working in the excavation.

'I wonder . . . ' Denning said softly. He turned back toward the campsite.

Denning became increasingly anxious as evening approached. Even Gallagher was more composed than he was. Denning thought longingly of the ferrets. If he could only have spent the next hour or so hunting cottontails . . .

The German shepherd, its choker still tied to a rigging support on the back of the truck, howled plaintively. Denning picked up a short stick from the heap of firewood near the camp fire and approached the truck. He freed the dog chain, gave the dog a warning tap on the nose with the stick and allowed it to leap to the ground. The dog's black and tan fur bristled and its golden yellow eyes held Denning's stare for several seconds before turning away. He yanked on the chain and hauled the dog after him as he headed back to the wood.

For the next hour he walked the dog back and forth. It became more submissive and Denning found fewer opportunities to use the stick. He was tempted to release it from the chain to let it chase a few cottontails, but caution prevailed. Perhaps they might go hunting together after the raid.

At six p.m. Denning again had the glasses focused on Main Street. The telephone engineers downed tools, packed them into two metal boxes and placed them in the rear of the van. They manoeuvred the work hut until it covered the excavation. One man put a rope fence around the hut and the other placed portable warning lamps beneath the fence. The two men climbed into the van and headed for the main highway.

'Marvellous,' he said. 'Bloody marvellous . . . '

Gallagher clumped through the edge of the wood toward him.

'The girls have got a meal ready.'

'Fine. Here, you take the mutt. You're the dog handler for the evening.'

Denning tossed the stick to him. Gallagher caught it, pointed it at the dog and accepted the choker. The dog growled, but followed obediently.

'He'll behave well enough,' Denning said. 'But keep that stick handy.'

Over the meal Denning told the others about the work hut. All agreed that the discovery justified a small change of plan.

At seven twenty-eight the five campers silently watched the setting sun.

'Not long now,' Denning murmured. 'Let's put on the gear.'

The three men entered one of the tents. Inside, Denning distributed the navy blue jackets and trousers. After all three had changed Denning drew three hunting knives from underneath a sleeping bag.

'We use the automatic for show, but no shooting,' he said. 'It wouldn't take the cops five minutes to match up the bullets with those that killed the ambassador. And if I get in trouble there'll be no more garrotting. It's fast and efficient, but it would be another obvious link. We use the knives – you all know what to do.'

Each man slipped a knife into his waistband beneath his safari jacket. They remained under cover of the tent, with Denning checking his watch every few minutes.

By seven thirty-five Denning had begun to find the waiting intolerable.

'Let's move out now. This is driving me round the bend.'

Sarah Jane moved into the driving seat of the truck. Henrick, clutching the automatic, Wanda and Denning crowded into the cab with her. Gallagher climbed into the rear with the German shepherd.

Sarah Jane turned from the main highway down the side road leading to the fuel plant. She pulled up under the shelter of trees at the side of the road about a hundred yards before the junction with the town's Main Street. The truck would be unseen by anyone travelling between Main Street and the plant.

It was seven forty-two.

Denning leapt from the cab and was joined by Gallagher, who had left the dog secured in the rear of the truck. At that instant street lamps flickered on. Denning cursed. He had hoped for the shelter of the darkness for a while longer.

Between the truck and Main Street was a narrow spur of wooded land. Denning led the way through the trees until he was at the edge of the street, but still shielded by trees. He looked to left and right. All was clear. He tapped Gallagher on the shoulder and both men ran to the telephone engineers' work hut and scampered inside. Gallagher panted heavily. Denning, whose pulse rate was normal, would have much preferred to use the fitter Henrick for this phase of the operation but for the handicap of his artificial foot.

'I'm OK . . . it's OK,' Gallagher gasped. 'Ready when you are.'

They stepped cautiously outside. Gallagher tipped the work hut toward Denning. He caught the roof of the hut and, with Gallagher supporting the base, scurried backward across the road. Together they heaved the hut onto the truck.

It was seven forty-eight. They had not been seen.

Denning ran to the driver's door and Sarah Jane opened the window.

'It went like a dream,' he gloated. 'We've got our sentry box. Now for stage two.'

Henrick and Wanda hurried with Gallagher toward the fuel plant. Denning lingered to ensure that Sarah Jane understood precisely what she had to do. She was unable to control a slight trembling and the white of her knuckles showed as she gripped the steering wheel.

'What if there's another vehicle? What if . . . ?'

'Honey, it'll happen just like I told you. Believe me. But if anything unexpected happens just sit tight. We'll get to you somehow.'

He ran after the others and stopped as he reached the dip.

'Here.'

He turned toward the sound of Wanda's voice and slithered into the undergrowth beside her.

'Wayne . . . Sean . . . you two OK?'

Henrick answered from across the road in a stage whisper.

'We're fine. All set.'

'How's the foot?'

'Forget it. I'm fine.'

It was seven fifty-one.

At seven fifty-three the Oldsmobile carrying the four men of the night shift sped toward the plant.

At three minutes past eight the Pontiac carrying three members of the afternoon shift swung into the dip and accelerated up the hill toward Main Street. As the engine note faded into the distance Denning hauled Wanda to her feet.

'Now! You know the drill. Same as when we hit the mailman.'

She ran into the roadway and sprawled full length, her arms and legs askew.

Denning hissed approval from the roadside.

'That's great. Just play stone cold dead.'

At five past eight the Honda's headlight snaked around the bend, pointed down the dip and flickered on Wanda's stationery form. The bike slowed to about ten miles an hour. Denning had no intention of allowing the driver the luxury of deciding whether to stop. As the bike drew alongside Denning, he sprang from his hiding place, held out his arms in the path of the motorcyclist, lifted him high into the air and ran with him across the road toward Henrick. Gallagher ran into the road, grabbed the riderless bike as it spun around on a foot rest and wheeled it under the trees.

'Breathe and you're dead,' Denning snarled.

The pickup truck skidded to a halt behind him. Sarah Jane had acted on cue and started the engine as soon as she saw the Honda vanish into the dip. As she approached the dip she was waved down by Wanda, who was back on her feet.

'Sean, get the dog,' Denning ordered. 'Wayne, make this jerk an offer he can't refuse.'

Denning ran to the truck. Henrick stepped astride the prone motorcyclist and thrust the barrel of the automatic into his mouth.

'Listen, mister, and I just might let you live a while longer. We've got your wife. Just do as you're told and everything will be fine.'

Gallagher handed over the German shepherd to Wanda and helped Denning haul the fencing, gates and work hut from the rear of the truck.

When she heard the tailgate being fastened Sarah Jane swung the truck into a three-point turn and backed up the hill toward the fuel plant. She remained out of view from the plant and the dip in the roadway.

Denning rammed the pointed end of one of the gate support posts into the soft earth at the side of the roadway and helped Gallagher lift the first gate onto its hinges. The second gate was assembled in the same way and the gates fastened. After ramming more support posts into the ground Denning soon had the twenty-five yard sections of fencing erected on either side of the gates. With a sledgehammer

Gallagher pounded the support posts more firmly into the ground. Denning then placed the work hut on the side of the gates nearer the fuel plant.

Gallagher grabbed the dog's choker from Wanda and took up a position beside the work hut.

The motorcyclist stumbled from the bushes at the roadside, followed by Henrick. His automatic hung limply at his side.

'He's accepted our offer,' Henrick told Denning.

'Good. Well, let's go over it one more time.'

Denning pulled off the man's crash helmet and tugged a fistful of greying hair.

'When you agree with me I want you to nod your head like this, see.'

Denning violently shook the man's head back and forth.

'We've got your wife. Right?'

The man began to nod in agreement. Denning again shook his head roughly.

'We've got you, too. Now, there's a truck due at eight-twenty or thereabouts. Yes?'

'Yes.'

'Plutonium nitrate?'

'Yes, but how . . . ?'

Denning again shook the man's head.

'Just answer, mister. You're going to help. Right?'

The man nodded. Denning beamed and shook the man's head more violently than before. Tears began to trickle from the corners of his eyes.

'Yes . . . yes. I'll help . . . '

Denning released his hold on the man's hair.

It was eight-fourteen.

For the two men in the plutonium truck it had been another uneventful drive from the reactor plant at Apollo, Pennsylvania. Like most of the truckers employed in the nuclear power industry, they had been irritated by new security regulations which had been introduced. For years they had been hauling such cargoes vast distances without incident. And suddenly the authorities wanted them to be subjected to rigorous checks.

During the first half of the journey they had to make a check call to Apollo every fifteen minutes; during the second half they had to make a call every fifteen minutes to the Washington storage plant. Then, on arriving at the plant, it would be check, search . . . check, search . . . check, unload. And there would be more hassle before they would be allowed to leave.

In the event of an emergency either the driver or relief driver could press an alarm button, one of which was positioned under each seat in the cab. This would operate a siren and notify the official receiving check calls that there was a problem. The official would then notify the nearest highway patrol.

The truckers' union had protested that if such precautions were necessary the job of hauling nuclear materials should be undertaken by the military. The employers had cautioned that if private industry showed itself unable to do the job according to the requirements of the authorities, the military might indeed take over. That would mean a heavy loss of jobs. The truckers had yielded to the gradual introduction of safety checks, but many of the procedures were carried out half-heartedly.

At eight-fifteen the relief driver made his final scheduled call to the fuel plant.

'Delivery NS 348 on time. Over.'

'Hello again. No problems?'

'Well, yes. We got hit a while back by this flying saucer. Some little green men stormed into the cab, but we sorted them out. We've got them tied up in the back and the flying saucer's in tow. We'll hand the whole lot over to you guys for inspection when we get there. Over.'

The joke was rewarded with chuckles from the fuel plant.

'Maybe those guys could help you unload when you

get here. Over and out.'

It was eight-sixteen.

At eight twenty-one Denning raised a finger to his lips. The distant purr of a truck engine grew louder. The truck's headlights bobbed into view.

Henrick stood in the work hut, his automatic behind his back. Gallagher and the German shepherd patroled nearby. Denning and the motorcyclist stepped outside the gates to meet the truck.

'What the . . . ? What do you make of this?'

The truck driver wondered whether to smash through the fence. But if this was a legitimate check . . .

'It's OK. That guy's a regular guard. I know him.'

The driver looked sharply at the man his colleague had pointed out.

'Yes. So do I. There's one of the guard dogs, too.'

The truck halted directly in front of the gates.

'What's going on?' the driver asked. 'More bullshit?'

Denning followed the motorcyclist to the driver's window.

'You said it,' the motorcyclist answered. 'From now on there's another check. Papers please?'

He glanced at the driver's work sheet.

'All in order. Open up, please.'

The relief driver dropped from the cab and, followed by Denning, went to the rear of the truck. He fumbled with two combination locks and hauled open the heavy steel doors.

The blade of Denning's knife flashed in the moonlight. He slammed the point of the blade into the vertebrae at the top of the driver's spinal column. A soft hiss escaped from his throat and he crumpled to the floor like a large rag doll discarded by a petulant child.

Henrick limped from the work hut alongside the motorcyclist. On hearing the rear doors open Henrick noiselessly drew his own knife, pulled himself onto the truck's running board and thrust the knife upwards through the driver's adam's apple. The blade jarred on striking the driver's skull. His eyes widened in shock as blood gushed onto the steering wheel and the window. His head toppled forward.

The motorcyclist turned to the pavement and retched. Henrick pushed him toward the rear of the truck.

'Move it, or you get the same.'

Gallagher dragged the dog toward the fuel plant until he could make out the faint outline of the pickup truck. He waved frantically to Sarah Jane. By the time she had parked alongside the delivery truck Denning and Henrick had manhandled three of the birdcages onto the roadway.

Gallagher again handed the dog to Wanda and ran to help.

Denning and Henrick tried in vain to lift the first of the birdcages onto the pickup truck.

'It's no good, Earl. My foot can't take it.'

'No sweat. Take it easy.'

Denning worked furiously with Gallagher to help get all nine birdcages off the delivery truck. Gallagher panted heavily.

'You. Help.'

The motorcyclist ran forward at Denning's command. Henrick rested while the other three men heaved the nine birdcages onto the back of the pickup truck.

Denning covered the cargo with the canvas sheet that had covered the fencing.

He turned to the motorcyclist.

'Thanks for your help. Your bike's over there.'

'You mean . . . ?'

'Sure. You can go. Your wife's OK, by the way. We never went near your place.'

'Thank God . . . thanks.'

The motorcyclist leaned over his bike. Denning thrust his knife up to its hilt below the man's left shoulder blade, withdrew it and wiped it clean on the dead man's uniform.

Gallagher was scrambling onto the rear of the truck with

the German shepherd. Denning joined Henrick and the girls in the cab and Sarah Jane pressed hard on the accelerator. She turned on the headlights immediately before turning onto the main highway and merging with the Washington-bound traffic.

It was eight twenty-eight.

The senior guard at the storage plant had not been unduly anxious when the truck failed to arrive at precisely eight twenty-two. He decided to allow a further five minutes before considering extreme action. Meanwhile, he kept watch on the road leading to the plant. There was no sign of the truck's headlights. The five minutes passed, and still there was no sign of the truck. Another check call would be due at eight-thirty, fifteen minutes after the last one was received. Another minute or so. He would wait and see. If he set off the red alert and all was well . . .

'Try them on the radio,' he ordered an assistant.

The calls of the radio operator were the only sounds heard in the room.

'. . . NS 248 . . . Hello, NS 348 . . . Come in, please.'

Finally came the verdict.

'It's no good, sir. They're not answering.'

At eight thirty-one there had been no check call.

'Get the car,' the senior guard rapped.

He would drive to the main highway in the hope of meeting the truck. If it did not appear by the time he reached the highway, there would be no alternative: He would sound the alert.

The car, like all vehicles entering or leaving the plant, was delayed at both checkpoints. Finally it accelerated toward the dip in the access road.

As the pickup truck approached the Washington outskirts a convoy of screaming police cars, travelling in the opposite direction, wailed into view.

Denning checked the time – eight forty-four. The speedometer needle hovered at sixty. They had put nearly fifteen miles between themselves and the storage plant.

A ring of road blocks isolated the plant at eight-forty-seven. The distance of each road block from the plant was approximately ten miles.

Sarah Jane drove into the flat garage shortly before nine-thirty.

'Let's move the stuff fast,' Denning ordered. 'Get that dog indoors,' he told Gallagher. 'Then get here and help.'

The three men struggled with the birdcages into Henrick's basement bomb shop. Denning joined hands with the others and led them in an exuberant dance around the basement floor.

'OK, Wayne baby. You've got your stuff. Now put your bomb where your mouth is.'

'No sweat.'

Henrick beamed.

'A week . . . ten days, maybe, and we'll have three of the bastards,' he added.

'Perfect. Bloody perfect. Let's get back to the campsite.'

Denning had planned that he, Gallagher, Wanda and Sarah Jane should return with the dog to the campsite immediately the truck was unloaded. He didn't want to arouse suspicion by abandoning their camping equipment. In any event, the site provided good cover. Henrick would begin work on the plutonium nitrate, and the others would rejoin him the following day.

'What if there's a house-to-house?' Henrick asked.

'No way,' Denning said. 'What, all over Washington? They haven't got the manpower. Anyway, why here? There's no logic in it. Why not south, east or west of the fuel plant? You take my word for it, they'll be watching airports and shipping ports and the railroad stations. They'll never suspect that the stuff is right up their own asses.'

'I hope not.'

Henrick had left the automatic leaning against the work-bench. He thoughtfully placed the rifle in a drawer.

'Till tomorrow, then,' Denning said. 'Don't worry about Sarah. She'll be fine.'

'Sure.'

Henrick's eyes were on the birdcages. Already he was considering various ways of separating the steel cylinders from the drums.

The road blocks had slowed traffic to a crawl on Washington's inbound highways. A line of vehicles nearly seven miles long, growing every minute, shunted along bumper to bumper. Traffic on the outbound lanes was light. Clearly, police felt they had no reason to stop traffic driving toward the fuel plant. Repeatedly the Dodge truck was overtaken by police vehicles, lights flashing and sirens screaming. Once it was passsed by a CBS camera team.

'Ain't that nice!' Denning gloated. 'We're going to make the TV again.'

At the campsite Sarah Jane pulled alongside Henrick's van, which had been left parked by the two tents since the previous day when Denning had driven from the apartment.

Denning prepared a fire while Gallagher produced a bottle of Chablis and four plastic cups. Wanda lit two marijuana cigarettes and passed them around.

'Here's to us,' Gallagher toasted, handing round the drinks.

As usual, he had been pleased with his performance. The killings had been messy, but he had felt strangely immune from the horror. After the first, the rest had seemed more tolerable.

'You did well,' Denning told him. 'We all did well.'

Denning raised his cup to the others. He had been particularly surprised at the determination and efficiency of the girls. True, their duties had not been arduous, but they had carried them out well and uncomplainingly. He would never understand women, he reflected ruefully. Wanda . . . so cold and calculating. Yet she had made love so gently. Sarah Jane . . . when she wasn't putting on the style she seemed almost level-headed. And she was certainly lovely . . .

He sucked deeply on the cigarette handed him. A brain-wave hit him. Now would be the time to repay Henrick for his revolt.

The distant wailing of police sirens wafted through the night air and broke in on his thoughts.

'There's going to be a change in the sleeping arrangements,' he said.

Sarah Jane looked nervously at him. Denning had assured Henrick that the men and women would share separate tents.

'I want to get together with Wanda to work out the terms we put to the authorities. Our manifesto, and all that. Sarah, I think we all owe Sean a favour. He did well, didn't he?'

'Yes . . . but . . . ' she simpered.

'You swine,' Wanda snarled. 'You can't do it. You wouldn't.'

'Sean, when did you last have a woman?' Denning asked, unconcerned. 'Weeks ago, eh? Well, tonight's the night. We're all in this together, see. All for one and one for all. Sarah, get in the tent.'

'Never, I . . . '

'In the tent,' he repeated. 'Or I'll give you one as well.'

He reached out as though to grab her. She scrambled to her feet, stepped back out of his reach and dusted her skirt.

'OK, Mr Denning. I'll do it. I'll do it, but you're going to be sorry. My God, you're going to be sorry.'

She pushed aside the tent flap and stepped inside. Gallagher gazed at the fire.

'Go on,' Denning urged. 'Get in there. I told you I'd show you I was a good buddy, didn't I? Now get in there.'

He handed Gallagher the cigarette. Gallagher put down his cup, accepted the cigarette and joined Sarah Jane.

17

With a saw Henrick cut through the struts securing one of the cylinders to its fifty-five gallon drum. He heaved the cylinder onto the workbench, removed a side of thc glovc box and secured the cylinder horizontally with clamps. Beneath one end of the cylinder he placed a large crucible. He checked that all the equipment he would need was at hand alongside the cylinder . . . drill . . . tongs . . . scales . . . Geiger counter. Satisfied, he repositioned the fourth side of the glove box, enclosing the cylinder and equipment. He slid his hands into the rubberized gloves, grasped the power drill and flicked the starter button. Within seconds the drill plunged forward inside the cylinder. He was through. As he withdrew the drill the liquid surged into the bowl.

He gazed through the glove box at the fluid as though hypnotized. So this was it. Ten litres of plutonium nitrate. Just a bowl of yellow-green water . . . yet this was one of the most valuable mixtures on earth.

He noticed that his throat was parched and hobbled to the kitchen fridge for a beer. On passing the TV he moved as though to switch on the set, then changed his mind. He realized with surprise that he had no interest in watching news bulletins about the raid. So what? Reaction to the theft was of no concern to him. All that mattered was that he had the plutonium nitrate. He had the material he needed to complete a task no civilian had ever carried out in the history of mankind.

He returned to the basement and browsed through the *Plutonium Handbook* while finishing his beer. The calculations still checked out. The beer can was empty, he dropped it to the floor and limped back to the glove box.

With the tongs he poured a prepared amount of oxalic acid into the crucible containing the plutonium nitrate. The mixture seethed and bubbled. The crystals gradually took shape. Precisely as he had anticipated, the plutonium combined with the acid to produce crystals of plutonium oxalate. He placed the crucible in the furnace and evaporated the water in the crystals. The result was a cake of plutonium oxalate – a fluffy, yellow-green salt.

'Sarah, honey, you'd be proud of me,' he murmured.

He scooped a small amount of the salt onto the scales. When he was satisfied with the amount he tipped the salt into another crucible, which was attached by a tube to a quartz container. He closed the lid of the crucible, poured hydrofluoric acid into the quartz container and heated it in the furnace to 500°C.

Henrick sat on the edge of the workbench to await results. His eyes unblinkingly watched the Geiger counter. If he had got his calculations wrong the whole mixture would go critical. That would be the end of Wayne Henrick, the flat and a fair-sized chunk of the population of Washington DC.

The results were exactly as he had expected. Hydrogen fluoride gas belched out of the quartz container and baked the salt to produce plutonium fluoride. Constantly watching the Geiger counter, he repeated the procedure and built up a small stockpile of the fluoride. He weighed precisely five hundred grams of the fluoride, put it into a specially treated crucible and added a hundred and seventy grams of metallic calcium and fifty grams of crystalline iodine. He snipped the corner from a plastic bag to release a quantity of argon gas and allowed it to settle on the mixture. He closed the lid of the crucible, placed it in the furnace and turned the temperature gauge to 750°C.

This was the most dangerous moment so far. In one minute the mixture in the crucible would react and, without aid of the furnace, heat itself to 1600°C. The pressure would be considerable.

Henrick watched the second hand of his watch – the Bulova Accutron he intended to use as part of the bomb's explosive mechanism. The minute passed agonisingly by. Still all was well. Henrick found he was biting his tongue. The mixture would be cooling now. He turned the furnace's temperature gauge to 'off', waited a further ten minutes and slid his hands once more into the flexible gloves. He removed the crucible from the furnace. He could scarcely control the urge to open the crucible lid, but the reaction would not yet be complete. The text books said that his mixture should be allowed to stand until dropping to room temperature.

'Twenty minutes – that's all you're getting,' he announced gleefully to the crucible.

The second hand of his watch twitched forward with tantalizing slowness. He decided to try to drink a six-pack of beer before opening the crucible in the hope that the time would pass quickly. It didn't. He still had two minutes to wait when he had drained the sixth can.

At last the twenty minutes had gone.

His hand shook as he raised the lid. The mixture looked like some white-yellowish flaky salt. But there was a dull metallic glint. He washed away the flakes and salt with nitric acid and gaped at the substance that remained. It was a small dull yellow piece of metal.

It was fully enriched, weapons-grade plutonium-239.

18

Stoddart winked at Sheila, leaned across the table and lightly ran a finger across her full, wide lips.

They were oblivious to other guests in the dining room at the top of Manhattan's Pan Am building. The meal and cabaret had been superb. And when they had danced she had nestled closely against him, every movement of her body conveying a secret, tingling promise.

'Aren't I supposed to say something like "How would you like to see my etchings?" '

She tossed back her head and laughed.

'Have you got any?'

'No.'

His teeth glistened in the candlelight as he grinned at her.

'Pete, really. Is that the best pass I'm going to get?'

'Well, how about . . . "Will you come to bed with me?" '

She sipped her brandy.

'I think I'd like that,' she said.

A waiter suddenly appeared at his elbow and his smile faded to a frown.

'Mr Stoddart?'

'What is it?'

'Telephone, sir. Your office.'

Stoddart shrugged at Sheila in bewilderment. As a matter of routine he always left a number where he could be reached with the switchboard of the Nuclear Regulatory Commission offices. He wished that for once he hadn't done so. He crossed to the phone on the bar.

'This is Stoddart. What is it?'

'Pete. Thank God we got you. There's been a heist.'

'What? Where?'

'The Washington storage plant. Nine birdcages.'

'Uranium?'

'No. Plutonium nitrate.'

So it had happened. The very situation so many had feared for so long had actually happened. And on the day that the United Nations had turned a Nelsonian eye to the issue.

'Any calls?'

'The switchboard's jammed. I haven't been answering. I wanted to get hold of you first.'

'Hold them off, but stand by for a scramble call from the Old Man. Get a car here for me right away.'

Sheila's heart sank as she sensed Stoddart's concern while he hurried back to the table.

'You're going to have to take a raincheck on those etchings. There's a staff car on the way to pick us up.'

'Trouble?'

'You can say that again. And how.'

He brought her up to date on the drive to the UN building and ordered his driver to take her on to her hotel.

'Get your boss over here,' Stoddart told her. 'Fast.'

Sheila raced from the lift to her hotel suite and found Sheehan sprawled on her bed. At least she wouldn't have to search the bars. The sour smell of beer in the room warned her that he was likely to be utterly drunk. She rolled him onto his back and shook him by the lapels.

'Ken, for God's sake. There's been a raid.'

Slowly, his eyelids fluttered. Two bloodshot eyeballs rolled into view like the red cherries of a fruit machine.

'Hi, honey. Welcome home.'

His eyelids closed and he turned on his side.

'There's been a plutonium raid,' she shouted, pummelling his shoulders in despair. 'Terrorists have stolen nine bird-cages of plutonium. You're wanted at NRC headquarters.'

Sheehan stiffened as though he had been shot. He lurched off the bed, stood shakily and staggered to the bathroom. He lowered his head into the wash basin and turned on the cold water tap. His head felt like it had just been hit for a home run. He thrust two fingers down his throat, leaned over the toilet bowl and threw up the remains of a substantial dinner.

When he emerged from the bathroom, ashen faced and with his clothes crumpled and splashed, he would have won first prize at any tramps' ball.

'One more time,' he croaked. 'What happened?'

Sheila summarized what she knew.

'Pete wants you at the UN – NRC offices,' she added.

'Don't wait up.'

He walked fairly steadily to the bedroom door.

'Ken, you look bloody awful.'

Sheehan slumped into a chair in Stoddart's office. A sledgehammer blow to the base of his spine sent up a shock wave that threatened to lift his head clear of his shoulders.

'I feel great. Nothing a head transplant can't fix. What's new?'

'They've got nine birdcages of plutonium nitrate from the nuclear storage plant north of Washington. Ninety litres, capable of producing twenty-two-and-a-half kilograms of plutonium-239. Three killed – the two men on the delivery truck and an off-duty guard. All stabbed.'

'Escort car?'

'There wasn't one.'

'Bloody typical. Do we know who did it?'

'No. They've vanished into thin air.'

A red phone on Stoddart's desk buzzed. He pressed a button enabling him to take the call on an intercom so that Sheehan could overhear.

'Mr Stoddart?'

'Yes.'

'The president's office, sir. The president would like

you to come to Washington. A conference will be held in the Oval Office as soon as you get here.'

'I'm on my way.'

Stoddart ordered a staff car to take him to the airport. He decided to put Sheehan fully in the picture while waiting for the driver to arrive.

'You look like you need a reviver, Ken.'

'No thanks. One sniff of booze and I'll be singing God Save the Queen.'

Stoddart helped himself to a large bourbon.

'The Old Man wants me in Washington. Want to join me?'

'It depends. How's the investigation going to be handled?'

'That depends very much on the meeting at the White House. I guess it's going to be all-cards-on-the-table and who's-got-any-ideas? Where would you go from here?'

'The same way I expect you would. It's the sort of situation that needs an SAS, or a CIA with its chains cut. The cops . . . well, they're good, sort of. But this is war. We need a small corps of the best men, able to barge through all closed doors.'

'Exactly. How would you like to be in the corps? Just like in the old days. A comeback by the old S-S team? Sheehan and Stoddart.'

'You must be joking, Pete. The old physique ain't what it used to be.'

'But the brain box is. No one's given more thought than you have to problems like this; no one has greater knowledge of the nuclear industry, or how the terrorists might act. I'm going to ask the President to set up just such a corps, and I want you in.'

Sheehan walked to Stoddart's drinks cabinet.

'I think I will have that reviver.'

He poured a small whiskey, filled up the glass with water and took a cautious sip.

'If we're going to be working together again I'd better get in training. I don't want you drinking me under the table because I'm out of practice. Here's to the old S-S. Sheehan and Stoddart are back in action.'

'Great. Where do you want to start?'

'Here and now. I'd like to see all you've got on terrorist groups, particularly any new ones on the scene. This could be one of the established outfits, but I don't think so. Nearly two hours have passed and no one has claimed responsibility or issued any demands. An established force would have had that all set up. I think these people probably haven't made up their minds what to do next. Maybe by the morning we'll hear something from them. Another thing, I suspect a new outfit because of the method of killing. All the victims stabbed . . . that just isn't an efficient way of killing people. It's messy, and it doesn't always work. Why stabbing? I don't see it. Guns are far more reliable, quicker and they don't have to be noisy. I can't make things add up. It must be a bunch of amateurs on the rampage. If so, God help us. They're the hardest to anticipate.'

Stoddart pressed a button on the intercom.

'Bring in the files on currently active terrorist groups, and recent related unsolved crimes.'

'Yes, sir.'

Within five minutes an NRC official carried into the office an armful of folders and placed them on Stoddart's desk. Each folder was stamped, 'Most Secret. Classified.'

Stoddart signed a receipt for the files and dismissed the official.

'Help yourself.'

The phone rang. Stoddart's car had arrived.

'I'll follow on by a later plane,' Sheehan said. 'I want to browse through all this junk. There just might be something.'

The folders could not be removed from the building, and Sheehan wanted to study them all.

'Fine. Use the sofa if you want to flake out. You can get hold of me through the Washington NRC office.'

From coast to coast, America reeled from the shock of the plutonium theft and the killings. TV news flashes interrupted regular programmes as the major networks battled to bring the latest information to viewers. Rumours and counter-rumours were rife.

A local TV station in Idaho broadcast 'unconfirmed reports' that terrorists had ruptured the nuclear core of a power plant near Washington and that radioactive particles were billowing into the atmosphere.

Reporters frantically rang universities in the hope of contacting experts with specialized knowledge of the nuclear power industry who might help to clarify conflicts in the deluge of reports. Inevitably, more than one crackpot was given air time. One suggested that citizens should head for underground shelters where they were available – 'Go to your basements, the subway stations, anywhere below ground, and stay there'. Thousands acted on his advice before it was discredited.

Hundreds of families in the vicinity of the storage plant fled by car in all directions. Along the grapevine the story was that 'that place' was going to go up. Traffic got snarled up in the already massive jams caused by the police road blocks.

By the time the real extent of the raid had become known many fears were dispelled only to be replaced by others equally alarming.

One TV interviewer harried a senior technician who had been rushed from a power plant in upstate New York to a studio in Manhattan. He was the most senior authority the network could snatch in a hurry.

'What are they likely to do with the stuff?' the interviewer asked.

'God knows. We've just got to hope they can't isolate the plutonium metal, or any other substances potentially just as harmful.'

'Such as . . . ?'

'Such as . . . well, plutonium is deadly if you breathe it. A few isotopes of relatively impure stuff attached to the bumpers of taxi cabs could wipe out a city. A tiny amount in the ventilation system of a large building would kill everyone inside.'

'Could these terrorists make a nuclear bomb?'

'Hell, if they know what they're doing, yes. It isn't that tough. Nine birdcages were stolen, yes?'

'Yes.'

'That's enough . . . let's see . . . yes, they could make two or three bombs with that lot. Three nuclear bombs.'

For hours Sarah Jane's pleadings kept Gallagher at bay. She became convinced that he lacked the courage to touch her. She was dozing lightly when suddenly he clambered on top of her.

'No . . . no . . . '

He ignored her and brutally pinned her arms above her shoulders. She held every muscle in her body taut as he plunged into her.

'Let it soon be over,' she prayed silently. 'Please let it be over soon.'

Then her revulsion gave way to horror. Her muscles contracted with the first stirrings of desire.

'No . . . please don't let me,' she gasped.

She sobbed and began to heave upward in unison with Gallagher's plunging.

'Wayne . . . I'm sorry . . . '

Her tongue thrust its way into Gallagher's mouth as she clasped her legs around his waist. At that moment he became soft inside her.

'Don't stop now . . . '

But it was too late. She felt dirtied, degraded . . . and she wanted him. She gave way to tears.

'Don't stop . . . Do something . . . Touch me . . . '

She took his hand and crushed it between her thighs. 'Touch me . . . '

At last her senses exploded. She fell limp. Release surged through her loosening muscles. Sobs shook her body.

'Wayne, I'm sorry . . . '

'I'm sorry, Sarah. I didn't mean . . . Hell, it was Earl's idea. I wouldn't have . . . Honest.'

She pushed away the hand he placed on her breast.

'It was Earl,' he simpered. 'I'm sorry.'

'I know. Yes . . . it was Earl. I'll get him. I'll . . . by God, I'll get him.'

19

'We've turned up another phoney set of papers, lieutenant.'

The lieutenant greeted the sergeant's news with a battle-weary sigh. Attempts to trace two buyers of Winchester-Magnum .303 bullets who had produced false papers had already failed. The sergeant's matter-of-fact manner hinted that yet a third possible lead had reached a dead end.

'And?'

'No luck, lieutenant. This guy bought two gross near Washington. The papers are in the name of an ex-small-time hood from the Bronx.'

'Ex?'

'Right. The guy's dead. Car crash, two years ago. Good riddance.'

'But he'd taken out licence papers?'

'Correct. A .303 automatic. It could be the gun that killed the ambassador, but the licence was never switched over.'

'What about his associates?'

'No luck. He only worked with one other guy. He's been in San Quentin two years now on a ten-stretch. Won't talk. Doesn't know anything about a .303 automatic. So he says.'

The lieutenant crushed out a half-smoked cigarette in a plastic tea cup.

'Sergeant, how come a small-time hoodlum gets a gun licence? Are we crazy or something?'

'No convictions. We never got the chance to get the licence revoked. He'd only dropped out of Columbia a year before the crash. He did us a favour by wrapping up his Olds before we could nail him.'

The lieutenant lit another cigarette. The mention of Washington set him thinking about the plutonium raid. Surely, he thought, there couldn't be a link.

'That plutonium raid, sergeant . . . '

The sergeant sat up sharply on his chair.

'There was no suggestion of a gun being used, was there?'

'Er . . . no, lieutenant. All victims stabbed. You don't think . . . '

'I don't know what to think. You say the guy who owned the gun went to Columbia?'

'Right.'

'That barman . . . what's his name? Gallagher. He went to Columbia, too.'

'Could be just coincidence, lieutenant. Gallagher first went there a year after this other guy quit.'

'I suppose so. But let's keep it in mind. What about the description of the guy who bought the bullets?'

The sergeant placed a sheet of paper on the lieutenant's desk.

'Great,' the lieutenant said. 'This fits about fifty per cent of the adult male population of the United States.'

'It is a bit vague . . . '

'You bet your ass it is. Get onto Washington. I want a fuller description. Get them to give us a sketch. This is a homicide investigation, sergeant. Get those jerks to move it.'

Sheehan awoke with a start as his arm slipped off the edge of Stoddart's desk. He tried to stand but one leg was numb. The back of his thigh had been pressing against the edge of the chair and the circulation had been blocked. He twinged as the feeling in his leg returned.

He searched a directory and located the number of the Washington NRC office. Stoddart, having slept only briefly after the White House meeting, had recently arrived there.

The American brought Sheehan up to date. The president

had authorized the setting up of a special investigative committee, headed by Stoddart. He was to have full access to the resources of the CIA and FBI.

'I'd like your help in co-ordinating the operation,' Stoddart added.

'You've got it.'

'Meanwhile, we've got clues scattered like confetti. The sentry box these guys used has been identified. It was a work hut ripped off from the post office. Workmen had left it in a street near the plant.'

'Prints?'

'No such luck.'

Sheehan shuffled papers on the desk in search of notes he had made during the night. He found what he was looking for – a map of the area surrounding the plant.

'That bit about the sentry box. It could tie in.'

'With what?'

'Something I was figuring out . . . Look at this campsite. It's just over a mile from the plant. A great place to hide out for anyone keeping a watch on the plant.'

'Ken, you're a genius. I'll get the FBI to check it out. That'll keep them busy. They're also checking out joints that sell fencing. We've got a clue fifty yards wide. Something's got to turn up.'

'Anything else?'

'A few tyre tracks. The truck that was used was at some stage pulled off the road. We've a few good prints.'

Sheehan wedged the phone between his chin and shoulder, and again fumbled through papers on the desk.

'Tyre marks,' he mumbled. 'That rings a bell. Where the hell . . . ? Got it.'

He located a page of sprawled notes.

'Look Pete, this is a long shot, maybe . . . '

'Let's hear it.'

'Well, if these punks are planning to make a bomb they'd need explosive and detonators. In those folders I came across notes on a raid between here and New York. A huge load of detonators and explosive was taken. It would be more than enough. No one was nabbed, but tyre marks were left near the hut.'

'You could be right. I'll get that checked out, too. When are you going to get over here?'

'Right away. The next plane.'

Denning began to break camp after breakfast.

Gallagher avoided looking at any of the others as he rolled up the sleeping bags. Sarah Jane wore her mask of martyrdom. In silence, she and Wanda packed their belongings.

'Sarah, darling,' Denning said threateningly, 'I don't think we want to let Wayne into our secret of your little honeymoon last night, do we? It just wouldn't be healthy. Understood? He mightn't like it, so we won't tell if you won't. And if you do, well, that isn't going to be nice at all. For Wayne or for you.'

Sarah Jane, tight-lipped, continued to stuff clothing into an overnight bag.

'Leave her alone.'

Denning looked at Wanda in surprise at the low, angry tone of her voice.

'You've done enough,' she added.

He chuckled, seemingly unconcerned at her hostility. 'All I'm saying is, belt up. Three wise monkeys. Now let's hit the road. Me and Sean take the Dodge and you two follow in the van.'

Denning and Gallagher stowed the last of the camping equipment in the two vehicles. Gallagher suddenly paled.

'The uniforms,' he gasped. 'The knives . . . '

'Forget it. I hid them in the wood last night. You're not the only guy with brains in this outfit.'

Denning turned to the girls.

'Stay with us. We'll probably get stopped and searched, but just keep cool. There's nothing hot on board. We give our real names and say we're heading back for New York after a camping trip. We're all good buddies returning from vacation.'

The German shepherd, secured by its choker to the passenger door handle of the Dodge, growled as Gallagher approached. He unfastened the choker and hauled the dog into the cab after him.

On reaching the main highway Denning was confronted by a slowly moving line of traffic, backed up nose to tail as far as the eye could see. Obviously police were thoroughly checking all vehicles within the vicinity of the plutonium plant. Eventually a car held back to allow the truck and the van to join the line.

A quarter of a mile ahead traffic was funnelled by police into a single lane. As each vehicle reached the front of the lane a swarm of officers descended on it. Bonnets and boots were opened.

Denning and Gallagher exchanged an anxious glance.

'Just keep quiet, Sean. I'll do the talking.'

At last a policeman motioned Denning forward. An officer walked to each of the front doors.

'Papers.'

Denning handed over his licence and the truck's registration slip. To the second officer Gallagher handed his wallet, which contained a batch of credit cards.

'Step down, please.'

Denning sensed Gallagher stiffen. Only a few people ahead of them had been asked to leave their vehicles.

'Keep hold of that mutt, Sean.'

Denning had spoken lightly and swung down to the roadway. Gallagher, prompted by the remark, held the German shepherd on a short lead and followed suit.

'We're with those girls behind,' Denning explained.

The officer looked with a bored expression to the van, then checked Denning's registration slip.

'You've just bought this truck?'

'Yes.'

'It's time you had these plates switched.'

'Sure . . . I will. I'm going to do that when we get back to New York.'

'You do that.'

The second officer was inside the cab of the truck. He rummaged through the glove compartment and, apparently satisfied, rejoined his colleagues on the roadway. He lowered the tailgate and checked each item of camping equipment at the rear of the truck.

'I hope you get these bastards,' Denning said.

'We will, sonny. We will. On your way.'

Denning and Gallagher returned with the dog into the cab and the truck moved forward. Twenty yards up the highway Denning pulled on the shoulder and watched in his rear view mirror as the girls left the van. Wanda was grinning broadly.

'Good girl,' he muttered.

The search over, both girls returned to the van and a policeman waved them forward.

Denning patted the German shepherd on the head and slipped the truck into gear.

At the flat Sarah Jane ran to Henrick, threw her arms around him and laid her cheek on his chest. He tottered uncertainly on his one good leg and laughed at her demonstrative greeting.

'Hold it. You'll bowl me over.'

A curl of his ginger hair fell forward as he bent his head and kissed her.

Denning had moved behind Henrick into the room and turned to face Sarah Jane. He warningly waved a forefinger back and forth.

'Let's eat,' he said. 'Wanda, the grub.'

Wanda had picked up hamburgers from a nearby store and now handed them around. Denning winced at being offered one smeared with ketchup.

'Hey, mine's undressed. I like my hamburgers neat.'

She chose one of the remaining hamburgers and handed it to him. Denning noted with relief that the diversion had parted Henrick and Sarah Jane.

'Let's eat in the basement.' Henrick said. 'I've got something I want you to see.'

He went directly to the glove box and turned to face the others as they gathered behind him.

'There it is,' Henrick said.

The others followed his eyes to the dull piece of metal in a small crucible.

'That's plutonium-239. Weapons-grade. That little lot came out of three of the cylinders. There's just under seven-and-a-half kilograms.'

'You don't mean . . . '

'I do, Earl. The worst part's over. From here on in it's plain sailing. That's enough for one bomb, and there's enough for two more in the rest of the cylinders.'

'Is . . . Isn't it . . . ' Gallagher stammered. 'Isn't it dangerous?'

'Nope. Not as it is. You can hold that in your lap if you want to and I promise your balls won't drop off.'

'So why the glove box?' Gallagher asked.

'Because it's radioactive at various stages before the metal is produced, stupid. Also, one thing you can't do with plutonium is breathe it. It ain't healthy. One sniff and your lungs will rot in double-quick time. A thousandth of a kilogram in the system will kill anyone.'

Denning thoughtfully fondled the German shepherd. 'How long before you can extract the rest?'

'A day. Maybe two.'

'And the bombs?'

'We're ahead of schedule. Three days. Perhaps a bit more.'

Denning grasped Henrick around the waist and led him in a clumsy waltz around the basement. Laughing, Henrick awkwardly favoured his injured foot. Denning's good humour was infectious. He danced with the others in turn and even Sarah Jane smiled indulgently. The German shepherd, bewildered, yapped continually.

'Silence, hound,' Denning ordered.

He tickled the dog's ears and gently pushed it into a sitting position.

'See, Sean, he's harmless. You don't have to be scared of

this old mutt.'

Gallagher frowned at once again having his obvious fear of the dog broadcast.

'Now that the ball is over,' he said sarcastically, 'isn't it time the world heard what ACE is all about? The demands and all that.'

'As ever, old buddy, you're one breath ahead of me. Course it is.'

Denning straddled a chair and rested his arms on the chair back.

'Wanda will take over the communications bit,' Denning said. 'OK, honey?'

'Sure. But one question.'

'Shoot.'

'How much is that stuff worth?'

'I don't know, honey . . . '

Denning looked inquiringly at Henrick who had heaved himself onto the workbench. Sarah Jane stepped alongside him as Gallagher and Wanda each squatted on one of the birdcages.

'It's worth a lot,' Henrick said. 'At least ten dollars a gram. When I've extracted all the metal we'll have a bit more than twenty-two kilograms. At least $220 000 worth.'

'And I guess the authorities would pay a lot more than that to get it back,' Wanda said.

The others looked eagerly for Denning's reaction. Henrick whistled through clenched teeth. His freckles merged into a broad grin.

'Shee-it,' he said. 'We could be rich for life. I could still make the bombs, then we well them to Uncle Sam. How about that?'

'No way,' Denning answered. 'It's a great idea, but no way.'

Denning had wavered for only an instant in his resolve to achieve the original demands of ACE. To change the plan now would mean he would have to confess that the KGB were not involved.

'We'll be looked after,' he added. 'We stay with the

original plan. Wanda sends the demands to the director-general of the UN.'

'And how do I do that? Call at reception, say I've helped to steal the plutonium and ask for an interview?'

Denning withdrew some papers and a pencil from his pocket and handed them to her.

'Here, these are telegram forms. Print out the demands and give the form and a few bucks to some kid near a post office, then beat it. You can take the shuttle plane to Chicago to help take the heat off Washington. The more false trails we lay the better.'

Wanda shrugged in agreement. Denning began to count on his fingers.

'Priority number one. ACE demands that the UN sets up a world food council to control the distribution of food worldwide. The tonnage of all food commodities for any one nation will be determined by population, and not wealth.

'Number two. ACE demands that the UN institutes a standard world currency – the Russian rouble. All banks will be internationalized. All financial institutions will be dismembered. To hell with those goddamn leeches who manipulate paper values on the foreign exchange markets.'

Denning paused as Wanda scribbled on a pad.

'Three. A UN wages council will institute standard wages based on a worldwide evaluation of jobs. All workers will receive a share of profits remaining after reinvestment. The trucker gets the rate for the job wherever he lives, whatever his colour.

'Four. A UN prices council will institute standard prices worldwide. Food will cost the same in the US, Russia and Bangladesh.

'The UN is to meet in public within forty-eight hours of these demands being received. We'll judge how seriously they're taking us from press reports of the meeting.'

Wanda finished writing.

'What do we tell them about the bombs?' she asked.

'We tell them we've got enough plutonium to make

two of them. Don't mention the third. That's going to be our little surprise in case of emergency. Unless the UN declares its intention to follow our demands, bomb number one goes off at an unnamed destination seven days from now. Tell them the bomb will be placed so as to cause minimal loss of life, but if we have to use bomb number two we won't be so considerate.'

'And just where do we place the bombs?' Wanda asked.

'I'll look after that. The first one I'll drop off at some deserted spread south of here. Virginia or North Carolina. The second bomb . . . well, somewhere in New York. The third one will be right here, waiting for the State of the Union address. We might have to leave the apartment so we'll hide the bomb in the wall or somewhere. OK with you, Wayne?'

'Suppose so. We could hide it easily enough, but if anyone comes around with a Geiger counter or some other bomb detection device . . . '

'And why should anyone do that? They can't search the whole bloody United States. Still, it might be an idea to booby-trap the apartment. Could we do that?'

'I could work something out. Yes, sure I could.'

Gallagher shuffled and coughed.

'I don't like it . . . this "somewhere in Virginia bit". How do we know no one will get hurt? What about the fallout? Do we know just what damage one of these bombs is going to do?'

He looked anxiously at Henrick.

'A lot depends on how well the design works. It should be around twenty kilotons – that's the same as exploding twenty thousand tons of TNT. It's the same as the bombs that wiped out Hiroshima and Nagasaki. Beyond a range of one-and-a-half miles the dangers will be minimal, except for fallout. And there's no way of judging how much fallout there's going to be. No one has ever set off a bomb quite like this before.'

'Meaning what?' Denning asked.

'Our bomb is going to be set off on the ground. Tons of

rock and soil are going to be vapourized, sucked up into the atmosphere and belched out over a wide area. That stuff will all be radioactive. When the experts set off a bomb they explode it high in the atmosphere. That way the fireball bounces off the ground without sucking up too much debris. The result is what they call a clean bomb. We simply don't have the apparatus to achieve an air burst.'

Sarah Jane uttered a low groan.

'Oh, Wayne . . . no. We're not supposed to be killing people with the first bomb. If what you say is true, we can't help . . . '

'Honey, if you want to fry an egg you have to break the shell. But it needn't be too bad. A lot depends on the wind. The radioactivity soon decays. Within two days the danger will be slight; within two weeks it will be non-existent.'

'How many are going to die, Wayne?' she said. 'How many?'

'God knows, honey. Not many. With luck the winds will carry most of the radioactive stuff out to sea.'

'Virginia . . . ,' Sarah Jane said softly. 'I've got an aunt there.'

Henrick laughed at her concern.

'Honey, come here.'

He put his arms around her, laughed again and patted her back.

'You're priceless, Sarah. Look, your aunt will be OK. Radioactivity is a funny business. We know roughly when the danger will be over. What we can't do is predict the fate of each little atom. It might decay in a second or a hundred years. If it's got your aunt's name on it, sooner or later it will find her out.'

Sarah Jane freed herself roughly and stepped back from Henrick. Her face was contorted by anger.

'Damn you, Wayne. You're like he is.'

She pointed an accusing finger at Denning.

'My aunt's got kids, Wayne. I . . . '

'Honey, honey. Let me put it another way. Radioactivity treats people in the same way the life insurance people do.

We can read off from the statistics tables that so many people will die, but we don't know whether the preacher will survive and your aunt die, or vice-versa. Chances are she'll be fine. I'll make sure she's fine. We'll place the bomb well away from her place. OK?'

Sarah Jane groaned in frustration and fled from the room. Upstairs the mattress frame creaked as she flung herself on the double bed.

'What the hell's up with her?' Henrick said, bewildered.

'Aw, she'll get over it,' Denning said soothingly. 'We've got things to do, folks. Wanda, you knock out that telegram and get off to Chicago. Sean, you and me can paint the truck and the van while Wayne gets on with the real work.'

'Paint the . . . ?' Gallagher began to protest.

'Right. There's some white paint in the garage. No point in running the risk of those vehicles being too easy to identify. For all we know we just might have been seen around once too often as it is.'

Sheehan seethed with frustration during the car drive from Washington airport to the NRC offices near Germantown, Maryland. The old Atomic Energy Commission offices had been conveniently situated in downtown Washington. The powers that were had authorized a move to Germantown's more rural setting, and the NRC had inherited the new premises. Though the NRC reading room at Washington's H Street was still maintained for the convenience of the public, NRC officials repeatedly had to commute between Germantown and the capital. And visitors to the NRC found that on reaching Washington their journey was by no means over.

Stoddart looked up from a mountain of paper work as Sheehan entered his office. Already reports had begun to flood in from FBI and CIA agents in the field.

'Jackpot,' Stoddart announced.

He handed Sheehan an identikit drawing of a rugged, dark-haired youth. The eyes glared from beneath bushy eyebrows. The thin lips were tightly compressed. Beneath the sketch were the words, 'Male Caucasian. 5 ft 10 in, 180-190 lbs. Ruddy complexion. Speaks with faint New York accent. Muscular. Brusque in manner.'

'That's public enemy number one,' Stoddart explained. 'We found the guy who sold the fencing and he helped us put the picture together.'

'What now?'

'That mug shot is with all the papers and TV stations. He'll be on every telecast and the front page of every newspaper. Right now his pretty face is being beamed coast to coast. And the information that he was driving a pale blue Dodge pickup truck. He's going to be the most famous American since Richard Nixon. If he so much as peeps through a crack in a door we'll have him.'

'Name?'

Stoddart's golden tooth-filling glinted as he grinned. 'Hold on, buddy. Give me a chance, eh? Any minute now and we'll be getting reports of this guy being seen from Alaska to Alabama and we'll have all the names you've ever heard of. Still, it'll be a start. And we've got the resources to check out meticulously every one of those sightings.'

Sheehan plugged in Stoddart's coffee percolator. The American produced two cups from a drawer.

'Now the bad news. Your idea of checking the tyre marks drew a blank. The truck used for the plutonium raid wasn't the one used for the explosives snatch. Sorry.'

Stoddart suspiciously eyed the brew which Sheehan poured into the cups. The Englishman's idea of coffee was a soupy mixture in which a spoon could almost stand without touching the sides of the cup.

'Any luck at the campsite?' Sheehan asked.

'Not so far. They didn't keep proper records. So, no names and addresses of anyone who left on the day of the raid.'

'Anyone see a pale blue Dodge pickup truck?'

'We've only just heard about the truck. We'll have to

try again.'

Stoddart sipped the coffee cautiously.

'I'll check out the truck,' Sheehan volunteered. 'I'd also like to look over that campsite.'

'By all means. Just don't make any more coffee. OK?'

A secretary entered as Stoddart pushed the cup to one side of his desk.

'Urgent, sir. I thought you'd better see this straight away.'

She placed a sheet of paper on the desk and glided out of the room.

'Oh, boy . . . Ken, baby, this could be it.'

Sheehan grabbed the paper. A girl who ran a dog kennels had phoned the police after seeing the identikit picture on television. She thought it resembled a youth to whom she had sold a German shepherd.

'This name and address . . . '

Sheehan spoke as though to no one in particular.

'No, probably not,' he added. 'I'm probably imagining things.'

His attention was seized by the last line of the report.

'Pete. Did you see this? The guy was driving a pale blue Dodge.'

'That's right.'

The American chuckled.

'I thought you'd never notice.'

'I'd like to check this girl out, Pete. And the guy who sold the fencing. Want to come?'

'No. I'll keep things tied up here. But don't let me keep you.'

'I'm on my way. Got a spare of that picture?'

'Help yourself.'

As the door slammed behind Sheehan, Stoddart buzzed his secretary.

'Disinfect that percolator, honey. Then make some decent coffee. That guy's just tried to poison me.'

Sarah Jane watched in awe as Henrick slipped his hands into the gloves of the glove box and spooned a half of the metal into one of the homemade baseball-sized crucibles. He placed the crucible in the furnace and adjusted the temperature-control dial.

'Now we sit back, watch the Geiger counter and pray.'

He patted her arm reassuringly.

'It'll be OK, honey. But if that needle shoots through amber to the red band, don't bother to run. You'll be too late.'

'Don't tease, Wayne.'

She held his hand and clasped it to her arm.

'What's happening? I'm scared, Wayne.'

'Don't be, honey. The plutonium will melt and mould itself into the shape of the crucible. The metal cools, and we've got one half of the inside of the bomb. We do the same with the rest of the metal, put the two halves together and the inside of the bomb is complete.'

'It's so . . . so ordinary. It's so easy . . . '

He kissed her forehead.

'Don't you believe it. I'm brilliant. And there's a long way to go yet. We make one bomb, then extract more metal, make the second bomb, extract the last of the metal and make the third bomb. I can't risk extracting all the plutonium at once. With too much around it just might go critical. The more of that stuff you get in one lump, the more dangerous it is.'

Sarah Jane's eyes were fixed on the Geiger counter. The needle remained steady below the amber band.

The furnace temperature-control dial returned to 'off' with a loud click. Sarah Jane flinched.

'Wayne!'

Again he patted her arm.

'I told you, it's OK.'

He limped to the glove box, removed the crucible from the furnace and lowered it onto a small plastic square. He spooned the remainder of the metal into the second crucible of the same size, placed it in the furnace and readjusted the temperature dial.

'While the first lot solidifies, the rest will be getting ready. The needle hasn't budged, so I'm not going to blow us to bits just yet.'

When the first hemisphere of plutonium had cooled sufficiently, Henrick smoothed the flat surface with a file. Thin shavings of plutonium dropped onto the plastic. He removed the crucible from the plastic, folded over the ends and sealed the plutonium inside with sellotape.

The temperature dial again clicked to 'off'. Henrick repeated the procedures until he had two hemispheres of plutonium and two small polyethylene packets.

'We'll ditch those shavings later. They're deadly. Now for the steel jacket.'

He picked up a hacksaw and limped toward one of the empty birdcages.

The painting of the truck and the van was all but complete.

'You finish off, Sean. I'm going to have an early night.'

Gallagher sulkily continued painting. Throughout he had been the target of Denning's sarcasm. And Denning and Wanda hadn't even shown him the list of demands before she set off for Chicago.

A half-hour later Gallagher applied the last of the finishing touches. He all but stumbled over the sleeping German shepherd. His eyes fixed on a nearby coil of copper wire. His heartbeat raced as an idea took shape.

'That would show the bastard . . . ' he muttered.

His loose nostrils flared into a grotesque grin. He fashioned a lead out of the wire and looped it through the dog's collar.

'Come on, boy. We're going for a walk.'

It was nearly midnight when Sheehan booked into a hotel in downtown Washington. It had been an exhilarating evening. The roadwork had been good for his morale. And productive.

He phoned the NRC offices and learned that Stoddart was at a hotel in Germantown. The phone rang in Stoddart's room for almost a minute. Sheehan's good humour evaporated instantly when he recognized the voice that answered. It was Sheila.

'For Christ's sake, Sheila. You're supposed to be in New York.'

'I thought . . . well, everything's tied up there. I am supposed to be helping. I came here to join you. I couldn't get hold of you on the phone. Pete said . . . '

'Put him on.'

Stoddart abruptly cut Sheehan short.

'Back off, Ken. It was my idea. We need help.'

'I suppose so. Just . . . '

'She's a big girl, Ken. Or hadn't you noticed?'

'Forget it. I just don't like my secretary globe-trotting at the taxpayers' expense without letting me know.'

'Look, Ken. I'm sure you didn't phone up to discuss your secretary's sex life. What's new?'

'A bloody lot. That Dodge left tyre prints when the fencing was picked up. And I'm pretty sure this mob stayed at the campsite. People remember the Dodge. There are more tyre marks. They didn't leave the day of the raid – they left the bloody day after. Chances are they've slipped through the net.'

'I'll get the boys on to it. And we'll go over that campsite with a microscope. Where are you?'

Sheehan gave the name of his hotel.

'I'll join you there in the morning. Things can tick over here for a while and we'll compare notes. Did you get any description of these people?'

'I thought you'd ask that. No, dammit. The kid at the reception hut remembers the Dodge and a guy who gave him twenty bucks. The guy fits the identikit, but the kid can't remember anyone else. I suggest we flood the place now before anyone else bolts. I couldn't speak to everyone.'

'Sure thing. I'll see you about eight. And Ken.'

‘Yes.’

‘Don’t worry about Sheila. She’s in good hands.’

Sheehan sensed that Stoddart was flashing that swashbuckling grin.

‘That’s what worries me.’

Stoddart kissed Sheila as he hung up. She responded warmly, then pulled herself away.

‘That’s it for now, Mr Stoddart. Duty calls. Get me a cab, please.’

‘You’ve got to be joking.’

‘No, Pete. He’s right. I should be with him to help out. I’ll get a room in the same hotel. You’ll have to show me your etchings some other time.’

Gallagher writhed in his sleeping bag on the floor of the flat’s dining room. The voice echoed through his head. ‘This is the valley where the giant mushrooms grow . . . This . . . ’ His feet burned with the touch of the hot sand. The mushrooms sprouted to fantastic sizes, then exploded. His head spun crazily. At the instant he should have felt death, more tiny mushrooms appeared in the sand and started to swell.

He sat up, shaking. His sleeping bag was damp with perspiration. That bastard Denning . . . it was all his fault.

Gallagher remembered the walk he had taken earlier. He smiled, and settled down once more to sleep.

20

Sheehan, despite his irritation over Sheila's flight to Washington, was impressed by her efficiency. She had phoned the Minister of Trade and gained his sanction to remain in the United States for as long as Stoddart needed his services. She had phoned Sheehan's wife to tell her that her husband's return would be delayed. She had even arranged for a plumber to call at the Sheehan's home the following day to replace the faulty washer on the downstairs toilet. And she had reserved a table for three for breakfast.

'If there's anything else,' she said on finishing her update of events.

'You've done more than enough. Sorry about last night. It's just that . . . I know Pete a bit too well. I don't want you getting hurt.'

Stoddart's arrival at precisely eight a.m. prevented Sheehan from elaborating on the trail of broken hearts his old friend had left behind.

'You've done it again,' Stoddart said. 'Those tyre tracks. The blue Dodge was the vehicle used for the plutonium heist, all right. And we've got matching tracks at the campsite. Right now the FBI are swarming all over the place and interviewing everyone in sight.'

Sheehan swept toast crumbs from the lapels of his jacket.

'There's something else,' he said. 'But I can't get a handle on it. Something jives with all that stuff I read at your office in the UN. It'll come sooner or later.'

'Shows how much you need a secretary,' Stoddart teased. 'If you let her record all your info we might get somewhere.'

Sheehan gave a short laugh and grinned self-consciously at Sheila.

'Rebute taken.'

All three accepted the set breakfast of pancakes, orange juice and coffee.

'They're obviously amateurs,' Stoddart said. 'They've dropped so many clues we're up to our ears in them.'

'I just hope they're as dumb as they seem .The ball's very much in their court.'

Sheila poured the coffee.

'Do you really think they'll make a bomb, Ken?' she asked.

'If they're the same mob who stole the explosives and detonators, and my guess is that they are. It all adds up.'

A voice blurted out over a loudspeaker.

'Would Mr Pete Stoddart call at the information desk, please? Phone call for Mr Pete Stoddart at the information desk.'

Sheehan and Sheila ate in silence while Stoddart answered the call. He didn't bother to sit when he returned.

'Let's blow. FBI office.'

Sheehan and Sheila followed as he strode to the exit door. In the cab en route to the office Stoddart broke the news.

'They've shown their hand. Anonymous phone call to the UPI news agency in New York. A million dollars in used bills or a bomb goes off. Details to follow in another call.'

'Professor Ryan Fitzgerald, please.'

The salesman who had sold the glove box to Henrick had been disturbed by reports of the plutonium thefts. He also felt uneasy about the manner in which the glove box had been collected. According to the girl who had been on duty, the two men had been particularly anxious to collect the equipment rather than have it delivered. The salesman had decided to phone Columbia University in the hope of putting his mind at rest.

'Professor Fitzgerald's on vacation until next week.'

'Oh. I was calling about the glove box.'

'Glove box?'

'Yes. Equipment for the lab. Is it OK?'

'I'm afraid you'll have to speak to Professor Fitzgerald about that.'

'Exactly. That's what I was trying to do.'

'He's on vacation . . . '

The salesman hung up in exasperation and reached for the directory. He found a Professor Ryan Fitzgerald listed under a Long Island number and dialled. After a long wait there was still no reply. Again he hung up.

At least, he consoled himself, Professor Fitzgerald obviously existed.

Denning searched frantically for the dog.

'He must be somewhere . . . Got it. He was in the garage when we were painting.'

Sarah Jane, clearing the breakfast dishes, looked suspiciously at Gallagher as Denning hurried to the garage. Henrick was already at work in the basement.

'Where is it, Sean?' Sarah Jane asked. 'You didn't let it go . . . '

'I owed the bastard a favour, didn't I?'

Gallagher smirked.

'You fool, Sean. He'll . . . '

'He won't do anything if you keep quiet, will he?'

Gallagher looked anxiously toward the door. 'He seemed to think that bloody dog was more important than the rest of us.'

Denning burst into the room. Sarah Jane escaped to the kitchen.

'He's gone,' Denning snapped. 'Sean, he was in the garage last night. Now he's gone.'

Denning, his hands gripping his waist, stood beside Gallagher's chair.

'I never saw the bloody dog. He must have bolted when

you left.'

Sarah Jane flung open the kitchen door. In her hands she carried a transister radio.

'Listen,' she said breathlessly. 'This is more important than your stupid dog.'

' . . . the youth was seen driving a pale blue Dodge pickup truck,' a newscaster announced. 'He also had with him a German shepherd. Anyone who . . . '

Denning dropped his hands to the table and unsteadily eased himself into a chair.

'They're on to you,' Gallagher screeched. 'The identikit picture . . . the truck . . . that fucking dog . . . '

'Shut up,' Denning shouted. 'For Christ's sake let's hear the rest.'

The newscaster added that three denim safari jackets, trousers and hunting knives had been found hidden at the edge of the forest near a campsite a mile from the storage plant.

'Tests are expected to confirm that the knives were the murder weapons used during the raid . . . '

'You'll get us all nicked, Earl,' Gallagher said. 'For sure you will. They've got your picture, they've got . . . '

'Nothing,' Denning interrupted. 'They've got everything, and they've got nothing. They don't know who we are. That picture looks nothing like me.'

'It looks just like you, for God's sake.'

'To you, maybe. Because you know who it's supposed to be. You've only seen it flashed on TV. We'll get a paper and you can look again. I tell you, it could be anyone.'

'I'll get the paper. You're going to have to keep off the streets, Earl.'

Denning's eyes narrowed. The colour returned to his cheeks.

'Don't forget who's running this outfit,' he said softly. 'I got us this far, and we'll finish the job.'

'Sure, sure,' Gallagher taunted. 'You got us this far. The whole of America has your picture and is looking for you, the Dodge and the dog. You're . . . '

The slap resounded loudly. Gallagher didn't have time to move as Denning's open palm flashed across the table, hit him on the side of the head and knocked him from the chair.

'I told you, Sean. Cool it. We're OK if no one panics.'

Tears welled up in Gallagher's eyes as he scrambled to his feet. Already the cheek was beginning to swell.

'Now go and get a paper,' Denning said. 'We'll have a good look at this so-called picture. It'll look like a thousand people, I promise you.'

Stoddart and Sheehan found the FBI director-general pacing the floor of his office.

'Thank God you're here,' he said impatiently. 'We're wanted at the White House. I'll fill you in on the way.'

In the Oval Office Stoddart introduced Sheehan to the president and the chief of the CIA.

'Please sit down,' the president said wearily. 'I hope this won't take long. I want to make a decision fast and you're all involved – FBI, CIA and the NRC. It's a headache, I assure you.'

He picked up a tape cartridge from his desk.

'As some of you know, there's been a follow-up call to the UPI news agency. This is a tape of the conversation.'

The president slid the cartridge into a slot beneath his desk. A metallic-sounding voice, obviously disguised, spoke in flat monotone.

'I have the plutonium. Get this to the president . . . '

At that point the voice was interrupted by the UPI receptionist, who volunteered to transfer the call to the UPI newsdesk. The caller spoke more hurriedly, but still in the same monotone.

'No way. I'm not going to be on the line long enough for you to trace the call. Now get this. I want safe escort for the truck containing the plutonium to JFK airport.

I want a Boeing 747 and pilot on standby. A million dollars in used bills will be handed over and I board the plane with two colleagues. If anything goes wrong, I'll explode the plutonium by radio signal. When the plane's out of range, the police can move in. It will be announced on all TV networks at ten tonight that these terms are accepted, and I'll call again.'

A click announced the end of the message.

The president removed the tape and sighed.

'It had to happen. I've been dreading something like this. I'm sure we all have. Where the hell do we go from here? I suppose what this nut says is feasible.'

He looked inquiringly at Stoddart.

'It is, Mr President. It's no big deal to booby-trap a truck like that. If he's got his finger on the button of a radio transmitter it would be too risky to pick him off.'

'And if he blows up the truck?'

'It's hard to say. The danger's radioactivity, of course. We have to assume he knows how to cause maximum damage. That would mean pollution over a wide area. Miles, maybe. Deadly pollution.'

The FBI director-general, nearest to the president, accepted a box of cigarettes and handed them around.

'We could be lucky,' the FBI chief said. 'We've got supposed sightings flooding in from people who've seen the identikit picture. We're on the lookout for the Dodge and the German shepherd.'

'We can't count on luck,' the president said surlily. 'There are countless lives at stake. If we get a break, great. But we have to prepare for the worst that could possibly happen. And this guy's obviously alert to the danger of his calls being traced. What do the CIA have to suggest?'

The CIA chief fixed his eyes on the American flag behind the president's desk as though in search of inspiration.

'We could hide some men in the plane. In the washrooms. Wait till the plane's safely out of range and move in.'

'Please let's not do that,' Stoddart pleaded.

All eyes turned towards him.

'It's too risky. If we have to prepare for the worst that can possibly happen – and we do – we have to suppose he's not dumb. If he has that transmitter in his hand and insists on searching the plane before takeoff, boom. Forget it.'

All fell gloomily silent.

'I was hoping for a brainwave,' the president said, 'but I guess I was hoping for the moon.'

He crushed out his cigarette.

'I guess we have to play along. We'll have to pay. The stakes are too high, and we're not holding the cards.'

'We're assuming, of course,' Sheehan said, 'that this isn't a bluff.'

'We have to,' the FBI chief said. 'Naturally there've been other calls, but all obviously from cranks. Luckily, you can often spot the phonies. So many usually pretend it's a solo act, and we know this one isn't. But this call to UPI seems fairly convincing to me.'

'We have to assume . . . '

The president was interrupted by the ringing of a phone on his desk. He frowned and spoke into the receiver.

'I said no calls . . . I see . . . Very good. Send it in.'

He accepted a report from the secretary who entered and began to read. Again the Oval Office was silent.

'Jesus,' the president gasped. He passed the paper to the FBI chief.

'We've got another list of demands, gentlemen,' the president said. 'From another source, dammit. This lot was written on a telegram form and handed in at a post office in Chicago. It seems a woman gave it to a young boy to hand over. It seems he didn't notice what she looked like, only the twenty dollars she gave him.'

The report was passed in turn to the others at the meeting. Sheehan was the last to be shown the contents.

'ACE,' the president said contemptuously. 'A Chance to Eat. Stupid idiots. What the hell do we do now?'

'It sounds just daft enough to be genuine,' Stoddart said. 'Surely we can't assemble a meeting of the UN in forty-eight hours. And this sort of programme would never be agreed. It's crazy.'

The president chortled.

'It's certainly impracticable. I almost wish it wasn't. At least we won't have to wait long to find out if this message is genuine. Seven days. Then the first bomb goes off.'

Sheehan wrestled for some elusive clue he felt sure lurked somewhere in his mind. Involuntarily his attention was held by the mention of the telegram. That struck a cord somewhere, he thought desperately. But where?

'We still have to assume the first call is genuine and wait for events,' the president said. 'As for the second message, I don't know. Christ, we can't call a meeting of the UN. Let's hope things are clearer within twenty-four hours. We'd better pray we don't make any mistake.'

With a large clamp, Henrick secured the first of the two larger crucibles that were to mould the bomb's steel jacket.

'Don't you need to do this inside the glove box?' Sarah Jane asked nervously.

He grinned as he picked up the feldspar sphere he had made. It exactly matched the dimensions of the now completed plutonium sphere. The spindle that ran through the centre of the feldspar sphere rested on two grooves in the clamped crucible.

'No, darling, I don't. Plain old steel isn't going to hurt you. Come and hold this small sphere steady for me . . . That's right. Straighten your fingers and keep them out of the way. I'm going to pour in the molten steel.'

Sarah Jane cringed as he emptied the white-hot metal into the mould.

'OK, now let go. Fine. When that solidifies we have one half of the steel jacket with a section cut away that will exactly fit the plutonium sphere. Aren't I a genius?'

She put her hands to his freckled cheeks and kissed him warmly.

'Yes, you are. A modest one.'

'Not now, honey. Let's melt the second batch of steel.'

Intent on the task, he worked silently. He had cut the steel into squares no more than two or three inches on each side. He heaped the last of the steel into the large container he had just emptied, then lifted it into the furnace, which he had removed from the glove box and placed on the smaller table alongside. He turned the temperature-control dial.

'I'm worried, Wayne,' Sarah said suddenly. 'About Earl . . . about all the information the police have. There's a sketch, the Dodge, the dog.'

'I know, I know. So the hell am I.'

He breathed in deeply through his teeth.

'I keep trying not to think about it, Sarah. I've got to finish this job. It's important to me. If that bastard blows it . . . '

'He's dangerous, Wayne. Believe me, he's a freak.'

Henrick looked at her sharply, suspicious at the hint of some unspoken knowledge.

'Why do you say that?' he rapped.

'I know, Wayne. That's all. He's a freak.'

She sat on one of the birdcages and lowered her eyelids to the floor. Henrick studied the steel liquid as it crept up the sides of the container to swallow the last of the solid steel squares.

'Here we go again,' he said, his thoughts returning to the immediate problem.

He touched the first half of the steel jacket with a moistened finger to make sure it was sufficiently solid for the feldspar sphere to be removed. He unscrewed the clamp and used it to grip the second mould. Gently, he lifted the sphere, repositioned it in the grooves of the second mould and gestured to Sarah with a finger.

'Same again, honey.'

She held the sphere while he poured in the second batch of molten steel, then returned to sit on the birdcage.

'We'll soon know,' he muttered under his breath. 'It won't be long. This has got to be just right.'

He referred to the *Plutonium Handbook* and checked a list of figures.

'You're worried, Wayne, aren't you?'

'You bet. No civilian's ever done this before. On the other hand, as far as we know everyone who's tried to make a bomb since Hiroshima has succeeded at the first try. Let's hope we join the club.'

He sat beside Sarah Jane on the birdcage and his eyes strayed to the plutonium sphere, which rested inside the glove box. One side of the glove box was detached.

'Think of it . . . the same power as twenty tons of TNT. That much would fill several railroad cars. And we've got the same explosive force in a sphere the size of a baseball.'

'It's frightening. We really won't kill anyone, will we?'

She gripped his hand. Henrick continued speaking as though he hadn't heard the question.

'Inside that plutonium the atoms are whizzing around like crazy. Imagine a swarm of hornets zooming around inside a balloon, every one on its own orbit as if held by a piece of string. The outer surface of the sphere is the balloon; inside, the atoms are just like those hornets. You've got to have just the right amount of metal. Exactly right. A bigger balloon . . . more hornets, and they go berserk. The strings break, the hornets knock the hell out of each other and the balloon bursts.'

His voice faded to a whisper. Sarah Jane, alarmed at the passionate intensity of his concentration, pulled away her hand.

'Then imagine that you squeeze that same balloon with your hands. Tightly.'

He clasped his palms together and squeezed.

'The balloon bursts. The hornets splatter outwards. That's just what the steel jacket and the stuff we're going to put around the outside is going to do. It will squeeze the plutonium. The atoms will crash into each other. For an instant all that energy is crushed unbelievably, then it rips loose. Kaboom.'

'Wayne . . . Wayne, you're frightening me.'

She shook his wrist. He had seemed to be in a trance, but at last his eyes softened and looked down at her.

'Sorry, honey. I thought you'd like to know.'

Henrick removed the feldspar sphere from the second half of the steel jacket.

'Get some water, Sarah. A jugful.'

He poured the water over both halves of the jacket to accelerate the cooling. Rubbing the back of a hand across his brow he was surprised to feel perspiration.

'For this bit we do need the glove box,' he said.

He removed the steel hemispheres from their crucibles and smoothed the flat edges with the file. They fitted perfectly together. He put both halves inside the glove box and replaced the detached side. He slipped his hands into the rubberized gloves and lifted the plutonium sphere into one half of the steel jacket. The Geiger counter needle leaped forward a fraction of an inch.

Sarah Jane stifled a cry of alarm.

'What was that?'

'It's OK. We're just squeezing that balloon a little. The hornets don't like it.'

He withdrew his hands and wiped his moist palms on his jeans. He breathed deeply, returned his hands and lowered the second half of the steel jacket onto the first. The Geiger counter needle surged forward.

Henrick whistled.

'It's OK. We've got it right.'

The needle was still comfortably below the amber band.

'When we wrap the explosive around we should be just inside the yellow band. That means the bomb is almost critical – almost ready to explode. We need the steel jacket so those hornets can't get out too quickly. We want them to get real angry first. The explosive will give them a real good squeeze to make sure that happens. Lover, we're almost through.'

Henrick unwrapped several of the eight-ounce packages of plastic explosive. His nostrils twitched at the putty-like smell.

'I'm going to slap this on the steel jacket. Keep an eye on that Geiger counter. If it gets near amber and I don't notice, yell.'

With a final check of the *Plutonium Handbook*, he measured out the precise quantity of explosive he had calculated was necessary and placed it inside the glove box.

'I'm dry, honey. Get me a beer.'

When she returned with the beer, Denning followed her. The beginnings of a beard and moustache made him appear even more menacing than usual. He hadn't shaved since seeing the identikit picture.

'How goes it, Wayne buddy?'

'Pretty good. Take a stand seat. We're at a crucial stage.'

Henrick impatiently swallowed the beer, placed his hands inside the rubberized gloves and slapped a handful of the explosive on the surface of the steel jacket.

For more than an hour he worked painstakingly. As he built up the outer coat of the bomb he repeatedly used a thin steel rule to measure the thickness and symmetry of the explosive. Sarah Jane stared constantly at the Geiger counter. It budged only slightly. Finally he was satisfied.

'That sphere's as perfect as it's going to be. It'll have to do.'

'Does it matter?' Denning asked.

'Sort of. I hope not too much. If I had more sophisticated equipment I could ensure it was absolutely round, but I think it's near enough. I'm going to use twenty-five detonators, each one spaced meticulously the same distance apart. The explosive has to go off with more or less perfect symmetry all round, or the implosion won't be adequate. Two-thirds of the force is going to go outward anyway. We don't want the squeeze inward to be much less than the other third. If it sets off an implosion on one side of the bomb we'll lose a lot of the force.'

With a sharp knife and steel tape measure, Henrick drew lines on the explosive which roughly corresponded to the latitudes and longitudes of the globe. At certain intersections he pressed a detonator into the surface of the explosive. Soon all twenty-five were in place.

He stood back and looked at the Geiger counter. He grunted with satisfaction. The reading was precisely what he had expected.

'Now we ensure that each wire to each detonator is exactly the same length, and we're all set. Sean's already tuned his radio. I'll have to attach the receiver, but we're more or less there.'

Denning walked to Henrick and put a hand on his shoulder.

'Is that really it? The . . . the first bomb?'

'Yep. Sure is.'

Henrick's face broke into a wide grin. Denning whooped and ran to the basement doorway.

'Sean, come here. Come and see this.'

Gallagher appeared at the top of the stairway and began to descend.

'I told you things were going great. Know what this is, dummy? The bomb. All complete.'

Gallagher looked at Henrick for confirmation. He nodded.

'It's big, isn't it?' Gallagher said. 'I thought . . . well, it would be smaller.'

The steel jacket and explosive had enlarged the bomb to the diameter of a dustbin.

'Miracles I can do,' Henrick said. 'The impossible takes longer. Would you like one you can put up your ass?'

'No offence,' Gallagher said. 'Congratulations.'

'You can say that again,' Denning said. 'And how. Sarah, we're going to celebrate. Go fetch hamburgers all round, and I'm going to pay. Mine's neat.'

She slipped the five-dollar bill he gave her into a back pocket of her jeans. Inside the pocket her fingers touched a small plastic packet.

Wanda returned late in the evening to find the others well saturated with drink.

'Honey, we've got the first bomb,' Denning announced.

She writhed out of his way as he moved to kiss her.

'Great.'

'Come and see,' Henrick invited.

She accepted a beer while inspecting the bomb.

Suddenly Gallagher shouted from upstairs.

'The news. Quick.'

All crowded near the TV set. The president had agreed to the demands of the terrorists who had stolen the plutonium, the newscaster reported. A million dollars and a getaway plane would be provided.

Denning's jaw dropped. His beer can fell on the floor.

'What the . . . ? What . . . Jesus fucking Christ.'

21

A third ransom call was received by the UPI news agency in New York at 9.30 a.m. the following day. The same metallic-sounding voice greeted the receptionist.

'There will be no time to trace this call. So don't waste time, and stay silent. A Boeing 747, fully fuelled, will taxi to the westernmost runway at John F. Kennedy International Airport at 1145 hours. Only a pilot will be on board. He will remain in the cockpit with engines running.

'At 1150 hours the money will be driven to the plane. A million dollars in used bills. No tricks. The money will be placed on the first passenger seat on the right-hand side of the entrance door.

'The truck containing the plutonium will be driven along-side the plane at 1200 hours. I board the plane with my two colleagues and check the money and the fuel levels. If all is well, I signal for the stairway to be removed and we take off. Any tricks, and you know what will happen. Under no circumstances will anyone attempt to board the truck until after take-off.

'We are now in transit in a pale blue Dodge truck travelling north along the Garden Street Parkway from Atlantic City, New Jersey. We await your escort. No sirens will be used.

'We are in contact with an observer at the airport. This is a final warning. If these instructions are not followed to the letter, explosives in the truck will be detonated. A considerable quantity of plutonium will be released.'

Stoddart and Sheehan were at the FBI office in

Washington's Pennsylvania Avenue when news of the call was phoned to the director-general. All three exchanged despairing glances as they listened to a replay of the call.

'The bastard seems to have all the angles covered,' Stoddart said. 'I don't like it. He seems pretty desperate to make sure we don't get too near that truck until he's airborne.'

The FBI chief and Sheehan looked sympathetically at Stoddart. Neither envied him his responsibilities as the man in overall charge of the operation to recover the plutonium.

Abruptly Stoddart grabbed the phone.

'Military jet for New York. Two passengers. Now.'

To the FBI chief he added, 'Perhaps you could run things from here while Ken and I get to New York.'

'Sure thing.'

'Let's blanket the Garden City Parkway with every patrol cop we can find. And grab a radioactivity detection vehicle. There's one already at Kennedy Airport. I want to make sure as soon as possible that the plutonium's on board this truck. If it isn't, we send our boys in.'

'Right.'

'And call the president. Bring him up to date.'

Stoddart kept in touch with developments by radio during the flight to New York.

Two FBI officials collected the million dollars in used notes from the Federal Reserve Bank of New York in Manhattan. The transaction was handled personally by the bank president after a call from the FBI director-general. The money was taken to the airport under armed guard.

The radioactivity detection vehicle located at Kennedy Airport was despatched to lie in wait for the truck at a point on the parkway near Seaside Heights. The crew were instructed to get as near to the truck as necessary to take the appropriate readings and report directly to FBI headquarters in Washington. The director-general would remain constantly at the other end of an open line.

Every one of a hundred patrol cars sent to meet the truck

was also in direct radio contact with the radioactivity detection vehicle and escort motorcycles.

The first crisis came when all commercial pilots refused en masse to co-operate with the authorities. Not one was prepared to fly the getaway plane.

'I don't blame them,' Stoddart conceded. 'Try the military. Try the CIA. Try anybody, but get a goddamned pilot.'

As Stoddart's jet banked over Kennedy Airport came the message that the pilot problem had been solved. The CIA had persuaded one of its agents, a former commercial airline pilot, to undertake the job for a fat fee.

Stoddart sighed with relief.

He and Sheehan were greeted on the tarmac by a senior FBI official.

'All set?' Stoddart asked.

'Not quite.'

Stoddard stopped in mid-stride.

'What the hell does that mean?'

'We haven't found the truck.'

Stoddart's jaw dropped and his shoulders sagged.

'You haven't found . . . You've got to be kidding.'

'I'm afraid not.'

'A hundred bloody cop cars, God knows how many motorcycles and we can't find the bloody truck.'

An airport technician approached the group on the tarmac.

'Mr Stoddart?'

'That's me.'

'The plane's all set for fuelling, sir.'

'Good. Carry on.'

'Sir . . . Just a thought.'

'What is it?'

'Do you want us to fuel the plane, sir? I mean, we could rig up the fuel gauges. Won't the danger be over once the plane's airborne? If it doesn't have enough fuel to get very far . . .'

'Probably thc pilot gets a bullet in the back.'

The technician looked chastened.

'Sorry, sir. I just thought . . . '

'Nice try, and thanks. But get that plane fuelled. Full up to the brim.'

At eleven-forty-five a.m. a Pan American Airways Boeing-747 taxied to the west side of the airport.

'Still no sign of the truck,' the FBI official reported to Stoddart. 'Do we load up the money?'

Stoddart stared across the runways to the getaway plane.

'We have to, dammit. We can't take chances.'

At eleven-forty a black Cadillac swept alongside the plane and a plain-suited policeman clambered up the stairway. He vanished through the doorway, then returned without the small black suitcase he had been carrying.

'What do you make of this, Ken?' Stoddart asked. 'I'm worried as hell.'

'Me too. I hope those cops haven't been sent on a wild goose chase.'

At that instant a pale blue Dodge pickup truck swept in front of the airport terminal buildings and swung west. Through the windscreen Stoddart and Sheehan glimpsed three faces each covered with a black hood. On the rear of the truck were nine steel drums.

The FBI official ran to his car and yelled into a microphone.

'What the hell is this? Where did that truck come from?'

Stoddart and Sheehan overhead the reply.

'We've been set up, chief. The truck just shot in from the Van Wyck Expressway. The bastards have been nowhere near Atlantic City.'

The FBI man flung down the microphone.

'The radioactivity detection vehicle,' Stoddart gasped. 'Where the hell . . . ?'

The FBI man clapped his palms to his forehead.

'Oh, Christ. I sent it down the Garden Street Parkway. I . . . '

'You mother-fucking son of a . . . You . . . '

Stoddart ended his tirade as the truck pulled up alongside the plane. The three hooded men ran from the truck to the stairway. Through binoculars he saw that each man was holding what could well be a radio transmitter. He flung the binoculars on the floor.

'Ken, buddy, we've been ripped off. We've lost a cool million bucks.'

Two of the hooded men had vanished inside the plane. The third waved from the top of the stairway. Workmen rolled away the stairway and the passenger door slammed shut. The nose of the Boeing raised slightly as it shuddered along the runway. Stoddart and Sheehan watched helplessly as it soared into the sky and headed south.

At a signal from Stoddart a fleet of police cars swarmed around the pickup truck.

Stoddart and Sheehan remained disconsolately on the tarmac and waited for the verdict.

The FBI man was ashen-faced when he returned.

'Don't tell me,' Stoddart said. 'Those oil drums on the pickup truck are empty.'

'Well, no . . . they're full of oil.'

In Rio de Janeiro the million dollars was shared between the three men and two prominent government officials. Details of the transaction had been agreed twenty-four hours before.

It was four days before the Brazilian authorities allowed the Boeing-747 to leave for New York. The plane was piloted by a relief crew and the CIA's pilot travelled as a passenger.

The Brazilian authorities refused repeated requests to have the three men extradited.

22

Henrick, engrossed in fitting a make-and-break points device through the face of the Bulova Accutron watch, had not noticed Sarah Jane return.

'Wayne . . . '

The small screwdriver slipped from his grip. He cursed.

'Sorry,' she said. 'I thought you'd like to know I'm back.'

'Course. Got the watches?'

'Yes. They were surprised I wanted two of them. I said I had two boyfriends and I always treated them both the same.'

'Did you get the light meter?'

'Yes. The same shop also sold photographic equipment.'

'And another walkie-talkie?'

'Yes. It's all here. I told them it was for my kid brother.'

Sarah Jane deposited the watches, light meter and walkie-talkie on the workbench.

'Good girl.'

She sat on the solitary wooden chair in the basement as he again grasped the screwdriver. He worked on the watch for several minutes, then picked up one of the receiver-transmitters of Gallagher's retuned walkie-talkie and wired it to the terminals of a 6-volt battery. With the soldering iron he attached each of the wires leading from the detonators to the receiver antenna. He completed the circuit by wiring a switch which would be activated when the appropriate radio signal was transmitted.

'That's it, baby.' He winked at her. 'Don't touch that transmitter, for Christ's sake. Now for the next bomb.'

In the living room above the basement Denning lay full-length on the floor and fumed as he searched through a newspaper.

'Not a mention. Not a bloody word. There isn't a mention of a UN meeting being called anywhere in this goddamned newspaper.'

Gallagher replenished three plastic cups with white wine. He handed one each to Denning and Wanda and sat beside her on the sofa.

'It looks like we should have gone for the money, doesn't it?'

There was more than a hint of a sneer in Wanda's voice.

'Bullshit,' Denning answered. 'We'll see which was the right idea. Just you wait and see.'

He tugged at the ends of his young beard. The unaccustomed growth constantly irritated his chin and upper lip.

'You could have fooled me,' Wanda persisted. 'Three guys clear off with a million dollars and we're down to our last hundred bucks. I could sure use a share of that million.'

Gallagher's plastic cup toppled from the arm of the sofa. Wine splashed on Denning's newspaper.

'For Christ's sake, Sean. Watch it, you clumsy bastard.'

Tensions had all but reached breaking point during the days the group had lain low in the flat. Gallagher suddenly stood and uncoiled his tall, gangling frame. His loose mouth twitched as he struggled to find the courage to hit out.

'You're not such a smart ass, Denning', he spluttered. 'Ask anyone. Ask Wayne. We don't think you're doing such a great job of organizing this outfit. Ask Wanda. And you've got Sarah Jane hating your goddamned guts. Me too.'

Denning's thin lips widened into a cruel grin. He sat on his haunches, clasped his hands behind his head and sneered as he flexed his biceps.

'Feeling your balls, are you? Watch it, tough guy. I want to tell you, if I find you let that dog loose . . . Another thing, suppose I tell Wayne about your little escapade with Sarah. Think you could handle him?'

Gallagher sat slowly, his courage evaporating.

'You bastard.'

'Back off, you two,' Wanda interrupted. 'Anyway, from where I sit, Sean's got something. This whole project's looking shaky, Earl. And you know it.'

Anger flared from Denning's cold hazel eyes as he fixed her with a stare.

'Wanda, if . . . '

'If what, big boy? If you threaten to hurt Sarah again . . . ' She struggled to keep her voice low to avoid being overheard in the basement. 'What if I put it around about your love life? I hear tell you're no great shakes under the sheets. I hear there's a little something a bit not quite all there with Earl Denning, muscle man.'

Images of their lovemaking near the forest and in the tent afterwards flashed through Denning's mind. God, he'd been determined to keep sex out of this whole deal. The awareness of his failure swept over him like a wave of nausea.

'That's enough,' he growled. 'I . . . '

Henrick, disturbed by the angry voices, hobbled into the room.

'Hey, what is all this, you guys? If anyone's interested I've got two bombs set up down here.'

He sucked in a deep breath, clearly baffled by the lack of response.

'Well, I wasn't expecting a nomination for the Nobel Prize, but at least you all might come and have a look. We're nearly through, I tell you. Doesn't anyone want to know?'

Denning stood slowly.

'Sure, Wayne. Sure we do. Lead on.'

The two bombs, each sprouting wires like a globe in a string basket, rested in opposite corners of the room. The third bomb, still unwired, was in the glove box, half way between the two.

'I've disconnected the batteries for safety,' Henrick said. 'But those two are all set to go. We have to keep them apart just to be on the safe side. We can't risk the whole lot going crit.'

'Crit?' Gallagher asked, puzzled by the term.

'Yeah, crit. Critical. The more of this stuff there is around, the bigger the danger that the whole lot will fission spontaneously. The sooner we get the bombs planted the better.'

All eyes glanced at the Geiger counter. The needle was half way along the amber band.

'What happens with the third bomb?' Denning asked.

Henrick's face creased into a boyish grin. He was obviously pleased at being given the opportunity to explain.

'I'm glad you asked. We set it up just like the others, but with one difference. I've bought a photographer's light meter. I'm going to add that to the circuit. We leave the bomb in the basement here. It can be set off in the same way as the others. But the mechanism will also be sensitive to light. If anyone turns on the lights in the basement before the wiring is disconnected, that's it. The light or a radio signal activates the whole thing. The bomb goes off.'

Denning clapped Henrick on the back.

'Wayne, that's terrific. Isn't it tricky?'

'A bit. But I can handle it. Obviously this bomb will have to be live twenty-four hours a day. Otherwise the booby trap would only work between twelve and one. There'll be more drain on the six-volt battery, but it should be good for quite a while. Long enough.'

'How long's that?'

'Hard to say. Weeks, for sure.'

'How long will it take to fix up that last bomb?'

'Not long. It'll be finished tonight.'

'Oh, boy,' Denning said softly. 'Are we in business.'

Stoddart had foregone his usual garish tie for the meeting with the president. For once his dress was entirely sombre. Even the unruly black hair had been swept more thoroughly than usual.

'This isn't a happy confrontation, Pete.'

'No, sir.'

'There'll have to be changes in the FBI. Right at the top.

And you don't entirely escape blame for this airport fiasco.'

'No, sir.'

Stoddart accepted a cigarette from the silver box.

'But you could square the account,' the president added. 'Just get these bastards. Where the hell are they?'

Stoddart ran a hand through his hair.

'That's about the one thing we don't know. We've got a lot, but we still can't nail them. So far all reports by people who claim to recognize the identikit have been discounted. We've stopped thousands of Dodge pickups. No luck.'

'What about intelligence sources?'

'Not a whisper. Whoever these people are, they must be acting alone.'

'What now?'

'We have to rely on regular policing procedures, sir. We're sifting reports of all recent crimes with which there could be the remotest link. Every cop in the United States has this picture. Every Dodge truck is being stopped on sight. We've got to get a break, sir. Soon they'll have to come into the open.'

The president swivelled his chair round to face the window.

'What's your feeling about this UN business, Pete?'

'I think those demands are probably genuine. It all ties in with the overall picture of crackpot amateurs. I think somehow we should humour them, sir.'

The president turned to face Stoddart.

'Are you seriously suggesting that I summon a full-scale meeting of the United Nations General Assembly to consider the ravings of a bunch of lunatics?'

'No, sir. But a statement, maybe. Let them know it's just not on. We could offer to set up a channel of communication. We've got to smoke them out somehow, sir. We've used up five of the seven days they gave us.'

'I know it. Don't remind me.'

The president repeatedly prodded an ashtray with his cigarette butt.

'You really think they'll set off this bomb, don't you?'

'I think they might. Let's hope they mean what they say and choose a safe area.'

'We're patrolling likely sites, of course.'

'Well, yes. But there are so many. And the bomb could be relatively small. We could be lucky, but we can't search every inch of the United States. It might be planted already.'

'I seem to have said this before, but we can't afford to take any more chances than we have to. I'll put out a statement stalling for time. I hope they buy it.'

He again swivelled his chair and gazed across the White House lawns.

Denning congratulated himself that the photograph on his driving licence was such a bad one. The Avis assistant had given it only the merest glance. Neither the photograph, nor his new appearance, bore more than the slightest resemblance to the identikit picture.

One bomb, covered by a raincoat, rested on the back seat of the Impala. The second was in the boot. Henrick had checked the car with the Geiger counter before Denning drove off. The needle had been perilously high up the amber band.

'Get rid of one bomb as soon as you can,' Henrick had warned. 'Then you should be OK.'

Denning was delighted to be alone, and even more pleased to be out of the flat. If he got stopped, well, that would be just too bad. At least Henrick's automatic lay comfortingly close under the front seat.

He crossed the North Carolina border as the first rays of dawn pierced the sky. Four or five times he had driven through what seemed to be a likely spot, only to come suddenly across a group of houses. He thoughtfully rubbed his fingers over his beard and moustache. The next place would have to do, he decided. To hell with nearby houses.

His headlights flickered on a sign. Dismal Swamp. He laughed at the name. It sounded promising. This would have to be it.

Denning drove a further ten miles. Not a house in sight. Flat scrubland was bathed in the morning's golden rays as far as the eye could see.

He coasted to a halt.

'Here we go,' he said softly.

He removed the bomb from the boot, concealed it between two low hummocks, extended the antenna to its fullest extent, covered the entire assembly with undergrowth and ran back to the car.

He measured the distance back to the first sign he had seen. Ten point eight miles. The signal would have to be sent from eight point eight miles beyond the sign.

'Eight point eight,' he mumbled, committing the number to memory. 'Eight point eight . . . eight point goddamned eight.'

On reaching New York Denning drove toward the United Nations headquarters in search of a site to plant the second bomb. Near the UN building he found an Avis agent.

He laughed under his breath. This was perfect. The garage was only several hundred yards from the UN. If Henrick had calculated correctly, every building within a quarter of a mile of the blast would be flattened.

'Goodbye, United Nations,' he said softly and parked at the end of a line of rental cars.

He stepped into the office and produced his papers. 'I want to hang on to the car but I'd like to park here,' he explained to the assistant.

'Come off it, man. Sorry, but this ain't no parking lot.'

Denning produced a wad of dollar bills.

'I know, but screw these goddamned parking charges. My plans are open-ended and I just might have to leave the car here for a day or so. I might not. I just don't know.'

He had counted out ten dollars.

'Sure you can't help?' he added.

The assistant reached out a hand and slid the notes into his wallet.

'Like the sign says, man, when it comes to pleasing the customers, "We try harder". Leave the car here as long as you like.'

Denning travelled by train to Queens. His eyelids hung heavily because of lack of sleep as he slipped the key in the lock of the townhouse rented by Sarah Jane and Wanda. He made straight for the nearest bedroom and collapsed on the bed without undressing.

Instead of the elation he had anticipated, gloom clouded his thoughts. Everything was all set . . . almost. But the animosity of Wanda and Gallagher had fouled the taste of triumph.

'You bastard, Gallagher,' he muttered. 'You started it, you bastard.'

He slammed a fist deep into the pillow.

Darkness hung heavily in the room when he awoke. For an instant he was bewildered by the strange surroundings. He crossed to the window and flung it open. Of course. He was at Sarah's place. He checked his watch. It was a few minutes before one a.m.

'Jesus . . . '

He had slept throughout the entire day. This was Sunday. The seven days were up.

Denning ran downstairs and dialled the number of the Washington flat. He groaned in frustration at the long wait. Finally Henrick answered.

'Wayne?'

'What the hell time is it?'

'One o'clock, buddy. Did I spoil your beauty sleep?' Henrick answered with a yawn.

'It's OK, Earl. Forget it. I was out for the count.'

'Listen. We're all set. Today's the day.'

'The president's statement, Earl . . . Did you hear the newscasts?'

'No. There was no radio in the car. What statement?'

'There's not going to be any UN meeting. No can do, he says. He wants us to get in touch again.'

'Does he now? Stupid bastard. Well, we will. Wayne buddy, we will.'

'What's next?'

'The sooner you and the girls get here the better. I've planted both bombs. You rig up the third, then blow. Use the van. We'll have to leave the Dodge. It's too risky.'

'OK, I'll wake the girls and we'll be on our way. I suppose the first bomb goes off . . . '

'Yes, but no sweat. I found a place that's ideal. Nothing for more than ten miles in any direction. No one's going to get hurt. This time.'

'You're sure it's deserted?'

'Certain, Wayne. It's ideal. I promise you.'

'That's great. I wouldn't want . . . '

'Neither would I, buddy. Not yet, anyway. Now put Sean on, will you?'

Gallagher croaked a sleepy hello.

'Sean, listen. I'm sorry about yesterday. I really am. It's being cooped up like that. I'm sorry.'

The silence betrayed Gallagher's surprise at the apology. Denning sensed that his approach had softened the other's resentment.

'Hell, Earl. It's OK.'

'We've all been under pressure, Sean. But the people who matter know how important you've been in all this. They really do. Without you we'd never have got this far.'

Denning grinned at his mental picture of Gallagher blushing with pride.

'Look, forget everything, Earl. It's OK. Really.'

'Still want the big break?'

Denning had quizzed Gallagher the previous evening about setting off the first bomb. His fear had been obvious. So had his need to impress the others. That poor creep really needed to be somebody, Denning had thought contemptuously. He was confident that at the crunch Gallagher would do what was needed.

'I do,' Gallagher answered. 'You're sure no one will get hurt?'

'I am. The bomb's in the middle of a swamp. There's no one for miles around. I've spoken to Wayne about it and he agrees it's perfectly safe. You just press the tit and get the hell out of there. There'll be so much confusion you'll have nothing to worry about. And don't look at the blast. Just turn tail and beat it.'

'Don't worry. I will.'

'Fine. First, then, hire the car. You're clean so you've nothing to worry about there. Don't use the Dodge. We leave it where it is.'

'Suits me.'

'Right. After you've got the car, here's what you do . . . '

23

Denning and Henrick lounged in front of the TV and tried to concentrate on the first game of the NFL double-header. O.J. Simpson clocked up more than 250 yards rushing without the information registering with either of them. The first quarter came and went, and still there had been no newsflash.

'Wanda honey, fetch a couple of beers,' Denning said.

'Touchdown,' yelled the TV commentator.

Denning and Henrick showed only mild interest.

'He must be there by now,' Denning said. 'He must be. Christ, it's only North Carolina.'

'He'll make it, Earl,' Henrick said.

'He'd better. If that chicken-livered . . . Thanks.'

The two accepted the beers from Wanda.

For the umpteenth time that day Denning asked Henrick to spell out the events of the night before.

'I told you, Earl. He got back with the car about two. I'd just finished rigging up the bomb. We all set off together just after that.'

'Twelve hours ago. He must be there. The bastard's gone chicken.'

'Are you sure that place was deserted? If there were houses nearby he just might cry off.'

'Of course it was. They don't call it Dismal Swamp for nothing, I can tell you. It's deader than the moon.'

'He might have had an accident,' Wanda suggested.

'He'll have an accident if he doesn't press that tit.'

Suddenly Denning seemed to be amused. He roared

with laughter.

'What's the joke?' Henrick asked.

'Nothing.' He suppressed a milder burst of laughter. 'Must have been something I said. Forget it.'

Henrick shrugged and finished his beer.

'Hey, where's Sarah?' he asked.

'She must be in the bedroom,' Wanda answered. 'I'll go and get her.'

'Do that,' Henrick pleaded. 'Make sure she's OK. She's been acting up all day.'

Wanda found Sarah Jane lying face down across the bed. She had removed her sweater, as if preparing to change. A half-choked sob shook her softly rounded shoulders.

'Hey, what is this?'

Wanda sat beside Sarah Jane and stroked her silken blonde hair.

'I'm late,' she said, still looking at the floor. 'It should have been yesterday. Or today at the latest.'

She rolled onto her back and sat up against the head-board. Her cheeks were blotched and puffy.

Wanda was bewildered at what seemed to be a trivial problem.

'Good God, girl. You must know that doesn't mean a thing. A day or two. What the hell?'

'It does,' Sarah Jane insisted. 'I know it does. I've been sick. Three times today I've been sick, Wanda.'

She looked desperately at Wanda as though somehow she might be able to help.

'You can't possibly be so sure so soon, Sarah.'

'I can, I tell you. I was pregnant once before, when I was married. I lost it, but I know the signs. I'm always right on the button, Wanda. Apart from the last time I was pregnant I've never been late in my life.'

She dabbed at her eyes with a handkerchief. Wanda patted her comfortingly on the knee.

'Sarah, how does a big girl like you get in a stupid mess like this?'

'I wanted to, sort of. Well, with Wayne . . . '

Wanda's eyes widened in shock at the significance of Sarah Jane's reference to Henrick.

'Oh, no, Sarah . . . You don't mean it's not Wayne.'

Sarah Jane's lips trembled. She blinked her eyes, fighting back more tears.

'Yes,' she said softly. 'I think it's . . . Sean. It must be. That night at the campsite . . . '

'Oh, Christ.'

Sarah Jane avoided Wanda's stare and lowered her eyes to her lap.

'He'll be . . . like him, Wanda. He'll be bony, gangly. I know it's going to be a boy and he'll be . . . ugly.' She had paused, reluctant to utter the last word. 'He'll be ugly. Wayne will know.'

She collapsed onto the pillow and abandoned herself to a flood of tears.

Gallagher was amazed at his self-control. He had pulled off the main highway shortly before dawn and had even been able to sleep soundly for several hours. For once he hadn't been tormented by that nerve-wracking dream. Not for a moment during the drive had his determination to explode the bomb weakened. This day he would prove to himself once and for all that he had courage. For the rest of his life he would be sustained by the knowledge that Sean Gallagher had a secure place in history. He would be the first civilian to explode a nuclear bomb. Never again need he feel in awe of the intellect of Wayne Henrick, the physique and strength of Earl Denning. Sean Gallagher would forever be something special.

He was conscious of the bulk of the radio transmitter in his jacket pocket as the North Carolina border sign loomed into view on Route 17. Within minutes he reached the sign to Dismal Swamp. He stopped exactly alongside the sign and turned the knob that returned the lower set of figures on the speedometer dial to zero. He almost seemed to be able to hear the pounding of his heart. With a deep breath, he drove forward.

The place was certainly deserted, he noted. Swampland stretched for miles on either side of the narrow tarmac road. Salty air from the Atlantic Ocean wafted through the car's open windows.

He checked the milometer. A little further to go.

Gallagher weighed his chances of escaping from the scene. They had to be good, he decided. He hadn't seen another vehicle for miles. On seeing the blast all traffic would flee from the area in all directions. He would be just another panic-stricken citizen fleeing for his life.

He checked the milometer. Another four-tenths of a mile to go.

If by some chance he was stopped . . .

He dismissed the thought as, his eyes fixed on the milometer, the car mounted a grassy roadside bank. He pulled at the wheel to return the car to the road.

A little further now . . . This was it.

Gallagher turned the car around on the road to face north. He left the engine running and stepped onto the roadway. Not a house or another vehicle was in sight. He turned to face the ocean and breathed deeply. A flock of waterfowl startled him as it soared, screeching, from two nearby hummocks.

He withdrew the transmitter from his pocket and placed his thumb on the switch that would transmit the radio signal. This was it. A sudden doubt nagged him. He ran to the car and again checked the milometer. Yes, he had got it right. From the Dismal Swamp sign he had driven precisely ten point eight miles.

He pressed the switch.

The detonators exploded the outer surface of the bomb with virtually absolute symmetry. The steel tamper and plutonium sphere were compressed with sudden and phenomenal force. The plutonium, for an instant, was crushed to three-quarters of it's previous size. In one-millionth of a second, the temperature of the plutonium soared beyond a hundred million degrees Centigrade. It was now a miniature ball of fire many times hotter and brighter than the sun. The plutonium began to expand again at a speed Henrick had rightly calculated would be in the region of five million miles per hour – faster than any body in the galaxy. The atoms in the core were torn asunder with a release of energy equivalent to the force of fifteen kilotons – marginally less than Henrick had hoped for.

Tons of rock and soil over more than a quarter of a mile, the rental car and Sean Gallagher were instantaneously vapourized.

The fireball expanded to three hundred feet in diameter. It swelled into a dome-shaped furnace of searing golds, yellows, greens and reds, then erupted into a giant mushroom cloud. At the speed of light searing waves of heat scorched through the countryside. Then followed the shock waves, a fraction faster than the speed of sound. Finally came a tremendous rumbling, louder than the noise of the most violent electric storm. The fireball began to lose some of its brilliance as it swirled beyond thirty thousand feet into the air.

The heavier particles of radioactive debris began to spatter down on Dismal Swamp.

A wild shriek from Denning greeted the first newsflash. Wanda's grip on Sarah Jane's wrist tightened.

'He's done it, goddamn it,' Denning shouted. 'He's done it.'

Sarah Jane slipped her sweater over her head and followed Wanda from the bedroom. Denning sat on the floor, his arms held tightly around his knees as he rocked back and forth as though in rhythm with the voice of the news announcer. Henrick sat bolt upright in a chair, his artificial foot resting on a stool.

' . . . We will bring more details of the explosion as soon as it is available,' the newscaster said.

Denning grinned at the girls as the football game resumed. 'What's up with you two? Smile, goddamn you. We've done it. Didn't I tell you we'd do it?'

'Done what?' said Wanda. 'All we've done is set off a bomb. We've still had no hint that the authorities are going to do anything about those demands.'

'They will now, sweetheart. Believe me, they will.'

The screen went blank, then again showed the face of the news announcer.

'We are interrupting regular programmes for news of a momentous disaster in the United States,' he said. 'Some minutes ago a nuclear device was exploded in the Dismal Swamp region of North Carolina. The device was in the twenty-kiloton range. There is no news of casualties for the moment. The massive mushroom cloud is reported to be drifting toward the Atlantic Ocean.'

Denning laughed above the voice of the announcer. Within ten minutes the first pictures of the mushroom cloud were shown, filmed from five miles beyond the centre of the blast.

'Will you look at that,' Denning said in awe. 'Go baby, go!'

He stood and grasped Henrick by the arms and playfully shook him in his chair.

'Wayne, baby, didn't I tell you that you were a genius?'

'It's certainly worked,' Henrick said. 'I thought it would.'

'You knew it would, you genius. Man, you're terrific.'

Henrick listened intently to later broadcasts speculating on the effects of radioactive fallout. Sarah Jane was clearly disturbed.

'You said no one would be killed, Wayne,' she said accusingly. 'They're talking about thousands in danger. You said . . .'

'Honey, they haven't got it worked out right. They're in a panic. The winds are westerly and most of the junk will get blown out to sea. I suppose there's bound to be some danger. There's just got to be.'

'It's not our fault the bomb went off,' Denning interrupted. 'They could have done what we asked. It's their own, stupid, damned fault.'

Wanda had shown no reaction. Suddenly, she grabbed a coat from the arm of a chair.

'What's with you?' Denning asked.

'You all seemed to have overlooked the point, but we have to eat. No? I'll get some hamburgers.'

'Women,' Denning said despairingly. 'I'll never understand them. OK, go get the grub. Me, I'm going to write to the goddamned president of the good old USA.'

He added, 'What's left of it.'

Wanda closed the front door on the sound of his raucous laughter.

24

The president gloomily surveyed the assembled officials seated around the Oval office. Stoddart sat between the chiefs of the FBI and the CIA. They had been joined by the director-general of the United Nations. Each man had a copy of the latest demands issued by ACE.

'Same routine, I understand,' the president said. 'A telegram handed to a passerby near a post office.'

'Yes, sir,' Stoddart replied. 'This time in New York. Again, a woman handed over a telegram. Unfortunately, we don't have a description that's worth anything.'

Stoddart scanned the words of the telegram.

'ACE demands that a meeting of the United Nations general assembly be held within twenty-four hours. The agenda will be as outlined in the previous telegram.

'A second bomb has already been planted at a site where maximum damage would be caused in the event of detonation. Unless the United Nations declares its intention to meet these demands forthwith, this bomb will be detonated at 1230 hours on Wednesday.'

Stoddart closed the folder with a slap.

'I suppose,' the president began, 'there was sufficient material for a second bomb?'

'Yes, sir,' Stoddart said. 'We've had countless scientists trying to gauge how much plutonium would have been used in the bomb already detonated. Unfortunately, we've no way of knowing. The evidence went up with the blast. So much would depend on the design of the bomb. We don't know how sophisticated this bomb was. That effect could have been achieved with all the plutonium stolen, half of it or even less. If these people say they've made a second bomb, I guess we have to buy it.'

'What's the latest on the radioactivity?' the president asked.

Stoddart again flipped open his folder.

'Not as bad as it might have been. The bulk of the radioactivity has been swept out to the ocean. Tests this morning on the perimeter of the blast area indicate that more than half of the radioactivity has dissipated. We should be able to lift the blockade of the area within two weeks.

'Two families on the east coast are showing signs of severe radiation sickness. Nine people. Their chances aren't good. Others will no doubt be affected. A small plane known to have been in the area has vanished – probably blasted away like a piece of paper. Six people on board. If we're lucky casualties will be in the hundreds rather than the thousands.'

'And what damage would be caused if a similar bomb were exploded in a city?'

Stoddart ran a hand through his hair as if reluctant to speculate.

'The first bomb has left a crater nearly three-quarters of a mile in diameter. In a city, buildings would cushion the blast, but we'd still get a hell of a big hole. The fire damage would extend to, oh, maybe a mile. Radiation would be intense within two miles and a severe hazard to health up to within two or three hundred miles, depending on the wind direction.'

'Casualties,' the president snapped. 'Give me a likely figure.'

'Depending on where the bomb is detonated, not fewer than a hundred thousand.'

The president left his desk and turned to the window behind the American flag. The others in the room remained silent. Slowly, he returned to his desk and slumped in the wide leather chair.

'There's no way out I can see,' he said. 'We'll have to play along.'

The UN director-general leaned forward to get the president's attention.

'I don't know that we can, sir. Not all delegates are in the United States. They're scattered all over the globe. Twenty-four hours . . . I don't know how many people we can round up in that time.'

'Get as many as you can. I don't care if only half a dozen turn up for the meeting, a meeting there's got to be.'

'Another thing, sir. I wouldn't want to anticipate the outcome of such a meeting. These demands are ludicrous. The whole deal is insane. A considerable body of opinion will resist subjugating the United Nations to the blackmail of terrorists. Even if these demands were not so ridiculous, the UN, I fear, might well insist on retaining its freedom of action and integrity. Whatever the cost.'

The president flung a pencil on to his desk in exasperation.

'I know . . . I know.'

'Frankly, sir,' the UN chief added, 'I would have to support such a body of opinion.'

'And let a hundred thousand people die. Maybe more. Many more. God, Stoddart, why can't you get these bastards?'

Stoddart did not answer the president's outburst. The question allowed no suitable answer.

'The UN meeting goes ahead,' the president insisted. 'It's got to. All you have to do is stall. A resolution saying that the whole deal will be looked into. Invite an observer from this ACE outfit along, if you like. Safe conduct and all that.'

The FBI director-general caught the president's eye.

'I'm not sure we should do that, sir. There'd be an outcry if we fraternize with these terrorists. We'll get them, sir. Sooner or later.'

'Before a hundred thousand people die, or after?' the president said bitterly. 'All right, then. No deals with the terrorists. At least for now. But that meeting of the UN goes ahead. And they'd better come up with some time-saving formula.

'And Pete. I suggest you use these goddamn special powers and resources you've got available. Let's have some action.'

Sheehan was not dismayed at being excluded from the White House meeting. It threatened to be a dismal affair. He had remained with Sheila in his hotel room to sift the mass of notes he had accumulated during the investigation of the plutonium theft and possibly related crimes.

'I know the answer's somewhere here,' he said. 'I can feel it. It's in my bones. I can't escape the feeling that we know all we need to know. If only we can get the pieces to fit.'

Sheila was mentally testing various subject groupings that would enable her to file Sheehan's papers in some logical order. It was difficult. So many of the papers bore no obvious relation to others.

'All the information relating to the plutonium raid goes in one drawer,' she said. 'That bit's easy. But the rest is a deluge of reports on what must be every violent crime in the United States over the last twelve months. It's a nightmare.'

Sheehan grinned at her untypical loss of composure. 'Don't I know it? Just group the lot incident by incident. Ideally, I'd like some sort of cross-reference system so I can refer from one type of crime to another. You can do it. And when we get back I'll tell all the boys of Whitehall how great you were.'

Sheila looked up from her desk.

'I've been meaning to talk about that, Ken. Going back, I mean. I'm not sure I will. At least, not to stay.'

His eyebrows lifted in surprise. His wide-eyed look gave him a suddenly youthful look.

'I see I've shocked you,' she said, smiling. 'I've been thinking it over for some time now.'

'How will Whitehall get on without you?' he teased. 'This isn't because of Pete?'

'Correct in one.'

Sheehan tutted and shook his head slowly from side to side.

'Sheila, you're out of your mind. He's a great pal of mine and I hate to say it, but Pete's no marriage prospect.

He likes to be fancy free. You'll get hurt, Sheila.'

'I don't think so.' Her eyes were thoughtful. 'I'm not sure. I'll have to think it out.'

She neatly stacked a file of papers. Sheehan took the hint that she didn't wish to pursue the conversation.

Perspiration saturated Denning's body, but he was unable to control the violent shivering. Henrick covered him with an extra blanket.

'My throat hurts,' Denning complained. 'I feel cold. What the hell is it?'

'Maybe tonsilitis. You'll be OK. I'll sent one of the girls to get something.'

Henrick noticed what seemed to be a blood spot under the skin of Denning's already mottled complexion.

'I'm never ill,' Denning said angrily. 'Christ, look out.'

He swung from the bed and, the blanket held tightly around him, hurried to the bathroom. He was still shaking uncontrollably when he returned. Wearily, he flopped on the bed.

'Christ, I've got the runs.'

Henrick ignored the complaint.

'I'm going to take over, Earl.'

Henrick had spoken softly, but with determination.

'What do you mean?'

'I'm in charge of ACE. I'll make the decisions. I'm not sure I like the way things have been going.'

'You bastard.'

Denning made as if to heave himself from the bed, but slumped back on the pillow.

'What about Sean, Earl? Why isn't he back?'

'How the hell should I know?'

'I think you do. Let me put it another way. If Sean isn't coming back, neither is his transmitter. The new walkie-talkie was only enough to assemble the other two bombs. Earl, do I have to buy another transmitter and retune it?'

Denning's quivering lips widened into a smirk.

'You think of everything, don't you? Yes, you'd better get another transmitter.'

'I knew it. You sent him in too close, didn't you?'

'What if I did? So what? The damned fool was a menace.'

He forced a laugh.

'That bomb went off right up his ass,' Denning went on. 'He asked for it. Before long he'd have led the cops to us. He had more hang-ups than a coat-rack. He was a walking bleeding heart. Fuck him.'

'You too, Earl. I just might let you lie and rot. You're ill, you know.'

Something sinister in Henrick's manner alarmed Denning. For a moment the trembling stopped.

'Hey, what do you mean, ill?'

He paled.

'Wayne, what do you mean? Those bombs . . . I was right next to them for hours, wasn't I? I've got something, haven't I? I've got . . . '

The sentence died with a gasp.

'I think so. I could be wrong, but those symptoms. Well, I reckon it could be radiation sickness. You're in trouble, buddy.'

Henrick paused to watch Denning's agonised expression before slowly leaving the room.

In the living room he looked wearily at the girls in turn.

'How is he?' Sarah Jane asked.

He searched her face. It showed what could only be interpreted as genuine concern.

'Ill. Very ill. Fever. Plumbing problems. There's one or two tiny blood spots under the skin. Radiation sickness, I think. If so, he's probably had it. Curtains.'

Sarah Jane raised a hand to her mouth and stifled a cry. Henrick studied Wanda. Her face showed no emotion.

'How . . . how could it have happened?' Sarah Jane said.

'He thought it might have been being next to the bombs all that time in the car.'

Neither girl showed any sign of doubting the theory.

'What about Sean?' Wanda asked. 'Did Earl . . . '

'I'm afraid so. He sent the poor bastard in too close. Sean went up with the bomb.'

'Murderer,' she snarled. 'He's just a two-bit pathological killer. "A Chance to Eat" my ass. I hope the bastard rots.'

'My bet,' Henrick said evenly, 'is that you'll get your wish.'

Sarah Jane had drifted unnoticed to her bedroom. She rummaged in a drawer for the plastic package she had hidden. It was still there. She squeezed the package between her fingers.

She couldn't be certain, she decided, but it seemed that there were fewer plutonium shavings than there had been.

25

Only fifteen delegates attended the hastily convened United Nations meeting. Stoddart noted with disgust that they were outnumbered by the press by more than eleven to one.

'Who's first to dip in the bank vaults when another country is in trouble?' he remarked to Sheehan. 'The USA. And who runs to help when we're in trouble? Just fifteen lousy delegates. And all the world's press rush to the funeral to cry in their bloody Marys. We even pick up the bar tab.'

The director-general called the meeting to order and Stoddart returned to his seat.

Formalities were cut short and the director-general motioned to Stoddart to address the meeting. He held the wording of a formal resolution which had been dictated by the president.

'We are all aware of the grave threat issued by the terrorist group identifying themselves as ACE,' he said. 'The deadline for the detonation of the nuclear bomb is twelve-thirty p.m. tomorrow. Accordingly, I propose the following resolution forthwith:

' "That this extraordinary meeting of the United Nations refers immediately the demands of ACE to the Political and Security Main Committee of the United Nations. The committee is urgently requested to investigate means of meeting these demands".'

The director-general looked around the scattered gathering.

'Is the resolution seconded?'

Vorishilov raised a hand a fraction ahead of Sheehan.

The director-general nodded to the Russian.

'It is,' Vorishilov said.

Sheehan chuckled under his breath. So his old Russian colleague was trying to show there were no hard feelings despite his earlier lack of co-operation.

The resolution was carried unanimously on a show of hands.

'I wish to make a personal appeal which I hope will be extensively reported to ensure that it reaches the appropriate quarters,' the director-general added. 'I beg the members of ACE to act with restraint. The United Nations has met these demands in the only way possible at such short notice. I urge these people, who obviously have a deep and genuine concern for world welfare, to accept the steps we have taken today in good faith.'

Henrick sneered at the TV news report at the meeting.

'The brush-off. This whole deal could be bogged down in committee for centuries. They've no intention of giving in.'

He hobbled to Denning's bedroom. His face and pillow were soaked with perspiration. More blood spots had appeared beneath the skin. Still the body trembled, but less violently. He appeared to be asleep.

Henrick roughly shook his shoulder.

'Your brilliant scheme is a flop, maestro.'

Denning seemed barely awake.

'Wake up, Earl. The UN have told you to piss off.'

Denning's eyes opened slowly. A trickle of blood seeped from one nostril.

'Now we're going to do things my way,' Henrick said.

Denning's eyes closed as an uneasy sleep overwhelmed him.

A special batch of new police reports arrived at Sheehan's hotel late in the evening. He and Stoddart had decided to remain overnight in New York and return to Washington the following morning. Despairingly, Sheehan set to work. He flipped through reports of a rape, an aggravated assault, a bank raid.

'Can I help?' Sheila volunteered.

'No. Get some sleep. I'll . . .'

He caught his breath as his eyes fell on a single-page report. A German shepherd had been found buried on waste ground on Washington's north side. It had been strangled with wire.

'I've got it!'

Sheila turned sharply as she reached the door to her suite. Sheehan snatched at the phone and cursed as it clattered to the side of the desk. He dialled and pummelled the desk with his free hand as he waited for Stoddart to answer.

'I'm on to something, Pete. That German shepherd. Have you seen the report? . . . OK, well get this. A German shepherd has been found in Washington. Its throat had been cut with wire. Get it? Those guys who rubbed out the ambassador garrotted the mailman and his wife, didn't they? And they pulled that stunt with a telegram. A telegram, Pete. And this mob keep listing their demands on telegram forms. They also murdered that bartender. It's the same mob, Pete. Has to be.'

'Christ, man, you're right, goddamn it.'

'Something else. It's been at the back of my mind. When I was last in Vorishilov's office he tried to hide some newspaper clippings about the ambassador's murder. That bastard knows something, Pete. I'm sure he does. I'm going to see Mister Vorishilov.'

'Good hunting.'

'Thanks. I'm on my way.'

He grabbed Sheila's wrist.

'Come on. Just as you are.'

Vorishilov was not in his hotel suite.

Sheehan cursed his luck. One a.m.

'He's probably with a goddamned woman,' he said to Sheila. 'What a night for a screw.'

Sheehan booked two rooms at the hotel and ordered a seven o'clock alarm call.

'There's nothing else for it,' he told Sheila. 'We might as well get some sleep.'

Stoddart and Sheila arrived at the offices of the USSR Commission at eight, only minutes before Vorishilov.

'And to what do I owe this honour?' he inquired sociably.

'Cut the small talk, Karl. Let's get in your office.'

The Russian led the way and gestured to two chairs.

'There's no time,' Sheehan said. 'Last time I was here you were reading newspaper reports of the ambassador's murder. I want it straight, Karl. Have you ever seen this man before?'

He handed Vorishilov a copy of the identikit picture of Denning.

'Of course not,' the Russian said.

Sheehan dropped into a chair.

'I might have known it wouldn't be easy.'

'What's the problem?'

'I think this guy was behind the killing of the ambassador as well as this bombs business. I'd hoped . . . oh, forget it.'

The Russian reached below his desk for a file. He withdrew a photograph and compared it with the identikit picture.

'They're not very alike,' he said. 'I don't know. Identikit aren't always reliable, of course.'

'What is it, Karl? You're killing me.'

'Perhaps I might be able to help you. We were approached after the ambassador had been murdered. I never saw the man and the, er, company official who did has returned to Moscow. But here is the man's name and address.'

'I want a car. Can I have one.'

'Certainly.'

Vorishilov spoke briefly into his intercom.

Sheehan spoke hurriedly to Sheila.

'Call Pete. Tell him what's happened. Get him to catch me up at the FBI office. Then we'll go and call on this Denning guy.' He studied again the name and address Vorishilov had handed to him.

'This is the bastard we're after, Karl. Sure as shit.'

'Lieutenant, this is hot.'

The sergeant thrust forward a wire picture and the identikit picture of Denning. The two were almost the same.

'What is this?' the lieutenant asked impatiently.

'That's the guy who bought the .303s.'

The sergeant pointed to one of the pictures.

'The other mug shot you know about. Boss, the guy who nicked the plutonium just might be the guy who killed the ambassador.'

'Sergeant, you're brilliant,' the lieutenant said sarcastically. 'Why the hell didn't we get this before?'

'Washington, lieutenant. They've been tied up with the plutonium business. You know . . . '

'Crap, sergeant. Crap. Get the commissioner on the line. Fast. And the FBI. Then we hit that Gallagher bastard.'

'Professor Ryan Fitzgerald?'

'That's me.'

'Great. I've been trying to contact you. I just wanted to make sure the glove box is OK?'

'Who is this?'

'Fisher Scientific, Manhattan, professor. Is the glove box satisfactory?'

'Are you crazy? What glove box?'

'You mean, you didn't collect a glove box from us? For the physics lab.'

'We sure didn't. I don't know what you're talking about.'

'Oh, shit.'

The salesman hung up on a bewildered Professor Fitzgerald

and dialled the police.

Stoddart and Sheehan approached the driveway to Denning's home. From hidden vantage points more than twenty police sharpshooters lined up telescopic sights on the doors and windows.

An elderly man answered the door. He blinked in consternation as the two men brushed him aside, ran up the staircase and stormed into the top room. It was empty.

The old man, protesting loudly, scrambled after them.

'Earl Denning,' Stoddart said bluntly.

'Earl . . . oh, him. We haven't seen him for weeks.'

'But he lived here.'

'Yes. Him and those crazy ferrets.'

'Ferrets?'

'Polecats. You know. Used to go hunting cottontails with them. He's a weird kid. What's he done?'

'Cottontails.' Stoddart repeated the word, then looked knowingly at Sheehan. So that accounted for the blood-stained handkerchief.

'Mister, haven't you seen this picture in the papers?'

The old man gazed at the identikit.

'That, why sure. But that's not him, is it? He don't look . . . well, yes, he does a bit.'

The old man gasped at finally noticing the similarity between Denning and the picture.

'Who else came here to see him?'

'To see that guy? No one. People don't come to see guys like that. Once or twice, maybe, but I never saw them.'

Sheehan flicked through several Columbia University textbooks. A search of the room was fruitless.

'Let's hit the university,' Sheehan said. 'Find out who he knocked around with. I'm taking bets that a few of his buddies haven't been attending classes lately.'

The police convoy cruised to a halt two blocks from

Gallagher's home. Out of view from the house sharpshooters again took up positions covering the front and back of the building. Stoddart and Sheehan had raced to join the convoy on hearing of the latest lead over the police radio.

Stoddart checked his watch. Eleven a.m.

'An hour and a half to zero. Let's hope Mr Gallagher's at home.'

The ringing doorbell went unanswered. Sheehan pulled aside his lapel to display his gun holster and looked inquiringly. Stoddart nodded. The Englishman drew the gun and raised it in line with the door lock.

'Hold it!'

The shout came from a uniformed captain running toward them. Unmarked police cars had been checking with neighbours of more than twenty students who hadn't turned up at that semester for classes at Columbia. The captain had been maintaining radio contact with the crews.

'We've got them,' he said breathlessly. 'One's a guy called Henrick . . . They're holed out in his girlfriend's home. At least one guy and two broads. They've been seen from one of the prowl cars. It's just a few blocks . . . '

Sheehan struggled to keep up with Stoddart as he dashed back to his car.

During the drive the captain gave Stoddart the missing details over the radio. A prowl car crew, checking the third address on their list, had passed Henrick's home just as his mother was leaving. When she was out of sight of the house a detective had approached her. No, she hadn't seen her son for weeks. He was never at home much since he'd met that girl. Yes, he'd been going around with that Earl Denning. She didn't approve, but young folks didn't take much notice, these days. Yes, she knew where the girlfriend lived and she wouldn't mind taking them there. Through the window a red-haired man could be seen limping across the room.

'That's Wayne,' the old woman had said.

The officer had recalled the recently circulated descriptions of the men who had collected the glove box. One had limped heavily.

Henrick was revolted by the stench from Denning. Vomit covered the pillow. Blood spots disfigured the entire face and arms. He groaned continually through his quivering lips.

'Can you hear, Earl?'

'Y-y-yes. Wayne, was . . . was it the bombs in the car?'

'No, it wasn't buddy. The bombs couldn't have done this. You made just one enemy too many, Earl.'

He returned to the living room and shook his head in answer to Sarah Jane's anxious look.

'He's had it.'

Sarah Jane looked from Henrick to Wanda.

'I know how, Wayne,' Sarah Jane said. 'I know how it happened. Oh, why, Wayne? You didn't have to.'

She ran to him and flung her arms around his waist.

'I wanted to do it, Wayne. That's why I took those shavings. I wanted to, but I just couldn't.'

Henrick had stood stiffly, his arms loose at his sides.

'What the hell, Sarah? You don't think . . . I thought it must have been Sean.'

'I did it.'

Henrick and Sarah Jane turned slowly to face Wanda. She smiled.

'I did it,' she repeated. 'No one gets the credit for teaching that bastard a lesson but me. I saw that plastic packet in the drawer, Sarah. I guessed what was in it. I didn't want you to do it.'

Sarah Jane released her hold on Henrick and gaped in astonishment.

'Wanda . . . you shouldn't have, Wanda.'

'Why not? I'm glad. He deserved it. He gave me the idea with all those hamburgers. "No dressing . . . I like mine neat." Well, the last one I gave him wasn't neat. It was nicely dressed with a few specks of those shavings.'

'You . . . you did it for me, didn't you?' Sarah Jane muttered.

'I did it for the human race, honey. That guy was psycho. Now, let's cut the crap. It's time I was on my way.'

From the table she picked up the transmitter Henrick had recently purchased and re-tuned.

'Are you sure you want to go ahead with this?' Henrick said. 'We can still go for money instead. The UN are never going to do what we've asked.'

'We've been over all that. We have to go through with it. If the bomb doesn't go off they'll know we've gone soft. If we set off this bomb we'll get some sort of food programme and money. I'm sure of it. As soon as we let them know there's a third bomb.'

'Don't let her, Wayne,' Sarah Jane pleaded. 'Please, Wanda. Don't.'

'I don't know, Sarah,' he said. 'I guess I'm chicken. She might be right. Earl might have . . . '

The slamming of the front door made further discussion meaningless.

'That's the Pniewski broad.'

Stoddart and Sheehan had been considering the next move while police sharpshooters surrounded the house. Wanda had been identified with the aid of binoculars from the building opposite by Henrick's mother. The old woman kept bursting into tears, but had agreed to help the police in return for a vague hint that her son might be given favourable treatment.

'So it is,' Sheehan agreed.

'You take her, Ken. She just might lead to the bomb. I'll wait here for the radioactivity detection vehicle. We'll have time to check out the house before we move in.'

Stoddart stepped from the car as Wanda reached the end of the block. The driver pulled slowly forward. Sheehan waved at Stoddart from the rear seat.

Wanda hailed the first cab and was driven toward Manhattan. Sheehan had become increasingly tense as the cab reached Second Avenue.

'The UN,' he said suddenly to the driver. 'She's making for the UN.'

Wanda left the cab some fifteen blocks short of the UN building and headed toward a basement bar.

'She's going underground while the . . . '

Wanda glanced around furtively as she drew a small black box from her coat pocket. Simultaneously Sheehan's gun flashed from his holster. Three bullets crashed into Wanda's rib cage before she hit the ground.

Sheehan's driver ran to the body and pulled the black box from the tightly clenched fingers. He recoiled in shock, held the box at arm's length and turned to the car.

'It's a transmitter. Christ . . . another fraction of a second . . . '

Sheehan leaned forward out of the car window and spilled the contents of a hurried breakfast in the gutter.

Henrick stared at the telephone as though mesmerized.

'Do it, Wayne,' Sarah Jane begged. 'Call the police. There's still time. We never meant to kill all these people, Wayne.'

'Stop gibbering, woman. I'm thinking.'

Sarah Jane pouted at the rebuke.

'Just what did you mean before?' he said suddenly, suspicion clouding his eyes. 'When you said Wanda did it for you? Did what for you, Sarah?'

She clasped her hands in her lap.

'I've been wanting to tell you, Wayne. It's why we can't let Wanda do it. I'm going to have a baby.'

'But that's . . . '

The beginning of a smile had softened the corners of his mouth for only an instant.

'You wanted a baby, Sarah.' He struggled to control the rising tone of his voice. 'So why the dramatics? You'd have made a lousy actress, Sarah. Why did Wanda do it for you, Sarah?'

The chair fell as his hands leaped to her shoulders.

'What's Earl got to do with all this, Sarah? Why did you want to poison him?'

His voice had risen almost to a scream. Sarah Jane threw back her head. A long screeching wail escaped from her throat. Her sobs were all the confirmation Henrick needed of his most tormenting suspicions.

'The bastard . . . '

Henrick hobbled quickly upstairs. She heard the suitcase scrape along her bedroom floor, then the crash of the door as he burst into the room where Denning lay.

'No!'

Her scream was cut short by the zap-zap-zap of the gunfire as bullets sliced back and forth across Denning's prone body.

Stoddart had just received the all-clear from the crew of the radioactivity detection vehicle when the gunfire echoed across the street. A second fusillade crackled through the air as sharpshooters at the rear of the building opened fire in the belief that colleagues at the front were under attack. Soon every police gun was ablaze.

In fury Henrick ran to Denning's bedroom window and aimed his automatic into the street. Sarah Jane, screaming, ran toward him.

'No, Wayne . . . We're going to have a baby, Wa . . . '

Blood spurted on her face from what was left of Henrick's skull. More bullets plummeted into her chest as she fell forward on to the corpse.

26

Stoddart returned from the bar in the VIP lounge at Kennedy airport with three highballs.

'One of the great things America has to offer,' he said. 'The best drinks in the world.'

'I'm with you there,' Sheehan agreed. He raised his glass to Sheila.

'Good luck. So he's going to make an honest woman of you.'

'It's the only way I'll ever get to see the etchings he keeps promising to show me.'

All three clinked glasses.

'You did great, Ken,' Stoddart said. 'But just so your head doesn't burst, you let one small point slip by.'

'Surprise me.'

'The address Denning gave that girl when he bought the German shepherd. It was the same as the address he gave when he dictated the telegram to the ambassador.'

'So who's perfect? Anyway, those famous New York cops of yours were slow off the starting grid when they found that barman had a walkie-talkie. That stuck out a mile.'

'Only to a genius, Ken. Like you.'

'Let's not be too premature with the congratulations,' he cautioned. 'If the first bomb had the same amount of plutonium in it as the one we found in the rental car, there's still seven-and-a-half kilograms of plutonium somewhere.'

'Maybe, but not necessarily. But don't worry about it. Their trail's still pretty hot. Every Geiger counter in the

States is being used. We're sweeping every inch of ground those punks might have covered.'

Sheehan gulped the remainder of his drink as an airport announcer summoned passengers to board the London plane.

'Must get back to the little woman. Good luck, both of you.'

'And you, Ken,' Stoddart said.

Sheila hugged Sheehan and kissed him warmly on the cheek. He was sure he detected more than a trace of sadness at the parting.

Stoddart and Sheila caught the next plane to Washington.

As they entered the hotel foyer he put an arm around her shoulder.

'About those etchings,' he began.

She snuggled teasingly against him.

The numbers in the lift flickered from one . . . two . . . three. The lift stopped at the third floor. Stoddard looked in puzzlement at Sheila as the doors failed to open. Suddenly the lift lurched violently and dropped ten feet or so in an instant before shuddering to a halt.

Stoddart laughingly scrambled to his feet and held out a hand to Sheila.

He forced apart the lift doors, only to find that the second floor was at head height. He allowed the doors to slam shut.

'I guess this isn't my lucky day.'

Sheila laughed girlishly.

He lifted a flap marked 'Alarm' and spoke into the phone.

'What the hell's going on?'

'No problem, sir. We'll soon have you out of there. How many of you are there?'

'Two. Listen. Who's "we"?'

'The elevator operator, sir.'

'Well, you're not operating too well, are you?'

Sheila's arms snaked around him. She crushed her breasts

against his back and slid a hand inside his shirt. She stroked the wiry hairs of his chest.

'This is a Westinghouse elevator, right?' Stoddart said into the phone.

'Yes.'

'Well get this. My name's Stoddart. You can check out my credentials with reception. And I don't want any bungling so-called elevator operator sending me crashing down to the basement. Get the Westinghouse people over here, and don't do a damn thing till they arrive. We'll just sweat it out.'

'That'll take an hour or more, sir.'

'I don't give a damn. We stay put till they get here. OK?'

'If you say so.'

Stoddart fiercely yanked the phone and snapped the cord. He squirmed around in Sheila's grasp, placed both hands on her breasts and kissed her warmly. She pulled him back against the rear of the lift and slithered to the floor.

Finally the lift jerked into motion. It descended slowly. The doors opened and Stoddart and Sheila stepped onto the ground floor.

The man who was clearly the operator sulked behind a workman in a Westinghouse uniform.

Henrick handed each ten dollars.

'Sorry about the phone,' he said. 'It had an accident.'

He took Sheila's hand and stepped into a lift directly opposite the one they had just left.

'Let's see if we can do that again,' he said.

'Phone, Pete. It's for you.'

Stoddart stepped from the bath, wrapped a towel around his waist and strode into the bedroom. He kissed Sheila as he answered the phone. She sat on the bed and filed a fingernail while he listened to the voice at the other end.

'You bet I want to be in on it,' he said. 'Hold everything.'

Sheila smiled expectantly as he hung up.

'They've found the other bomb. They're at the apartment they used. About ten blocks from FBI headquarters. Cheeky bastards. And the Geiger counters are going crazy.'

He dressed hurriedly and kissed her once more before leaving.

'Hurry back,' she said seductively.

'It seems to be in the bathroom at the far end of the basement,' the FBI chief told Stoddart. 'We'd better go easy in case of any clever stuff.'

'You bet.'

Stoddart opened the basement door and fingered around the frame. All clear. He peered into the darkness.

'Bring up the bomb squad. When we reach the bathroom some other hero can go in first.'

His fingers wandered over the wall inside the basement and he flicked on the light switch.

Other Arrow Books of interest:

A FINE NIGHT FOR DYING

Jack Higgins

The body was dragged out of the English Channel in the nets of a local fishing boat. After six weeks weighted down with seventy pounds of chain, there wasn't a lot left of Harvey Preston – and what there was made Paul Chavasse's stomach lurch.

Special Branch had handed the case over to 'The Bureau': the little-known branch of British Intelligence that deals with only the most delicate and hazardous operations. And soon bureau agent Chavasse finds himself involved in one of the toughest cases of his career as he uncovers a trail that seems to lead straight to millionaire Enrico Montefiore – a recluse who hides from the public gaze in a stronghold on the wind-swept marshes of the Camargue . . .

65p

HELL IS ALWAYS TODAY

Jack Higgins

'We're pretty hot on parking tickets, but not so good on maniacs who walk the streets on wet nights murdering women.'

Police morale is low. A callous, motiveless killer has the city in a stranglehold of fear as he casually selects his fifth victim. Even the whores are staying at home, and as public anxiety increases, Mallory and Miller, the hard-pressed officers assigned to the case, realize their troubles are only just beginning . . .

Not only a new corpse found in the driving rain, but, just to complicate matters, news of a dangerous criminal on the run.

70p

TOLL FOR THE BRAVE

Jack Higgins

Ellis Jackson had woken up hugging a twelve-bore shotgun. In the next room, his mistress and his best friend lay naked on the bed, their heads blown to pulp.

Active combat, a Viet Cong prison camp and the callous treachery of his interrogator and lover, Madame Ny, had all taken their toll. Back in England, Ellis had finally cracked.

Or had he? Maybe things weren't as simple as that – in any case, Ellis wanted some answers. Making use of his highly developed talent for survival, he found them: and they proved he wasn't mad.

It might have been easier to take if he'd *really* been out of his mind . . .

70p

THE D'ARTAGNAN SIGNATURE

Robert Rostand

A dying man whispers a name to his torturers and the hunt begins for the D'Artagnan Signature – the power of attorney that will authorize the release of a fortune held in a Swiss bank account.

It is money tainted by violence, money extorted by the O.A.S. to fund its reign of terror in Algeria; and now the scent of death is strong once more as old hatreds flare and blood feuds are revived.

75p

NARROW EXIT

Paul Henissart

Tunis. Shortly after a shaky government welcomes Arab terrorist Salah Al Houaranni, Israeli counter-intelligence pulls off one of its most spectacular coups: the guerilla leader is kidnapped from under the noses of his own guards.

Then Alex Gauthier, head of the Israeli espionage network in Tunisia, misses a vital radio transmission. Within hours Operation Flood is in ruins as three commandoes and their prisoner wait on a lonely beach for a submarine that will never appear . . .

80p

HOW TO ORDER

If you would like to order any of the books advertised in these pages, send purchase price plus 8p postage per book to Arrow Books, Book Service by Post, P.O. Box 29, Douglas, Isle of Man. Customers outside the UK should send purchase price plus 10p postage per book.

Whilst every effort is made to keep prices down and to keep popular books in print, Arrow Books cannot guarantee that prices will be the same as those advertised here or that the books will be available.